THE QUIET VOICES

Anthony Balkwill

ISBN: 9798398588156

Copyright © Anthony Balkwill, 2023

For

Dorothy Watts, nee Moody

"If we stay here long," he said, "you are going to go mad, Tenar. The anger of the Nameless Ones is heavy on your mind. And on mine. It's better now that you're here, much better. But it was a long time before you came, and I've used up most of my strength. No one can withstand the Dark Ones long alone. They are very strong."

                        Ursula Le Guin, *The Tombs of Atuan*

THE QUIET VOICES

This is a story about Cat, and it's a story about Joan, and the Eddies, who aren't really called Eddie, and a bunch of other people who play roles in Cat's story and in Joan's story. And, of course, there's Harry, and the story wouldn't be the same without Harry.

But, I should warn you, not much really happens in the story. You won't be on the edge of your seat with excitement, and you couldn't point to any one thing, and say, that was it, that was the most important thing. Or perhaps you could. And in that way, this story is very much like most people's stories. Not much really happens, though it can seem like it's been going on for a long time.

And it is a story about time. About going back in time. Not in a time machine, or anything like that. Stories like that are daft, Joan would say. No, the only time machine in this story is the time machine that everyone has got inside their head, which can take you back to any time you like, sometimes whether you like it or not.

And it's also a story about voices, which is why it's called *The Quiet Voices*, obviously. You'll hear my voice again towards the end of the story, telling you everything about everybody in a very know-it-all kind of way, but I'll try to stay out of things till then. If you listen very carefully, though, you might catch echoes of my voice earlier on in the story, and maybe also the voice of Alicia, my editor. She's the one who tries to keep me on track, saying things like 'That episode doesn't earn its keep' or 'Those sections are the most perplexing for the reader'. I've learned that it's best to listen to her voice, since, in the end, the story is the better for her interventions.

But the main voices are Cat's and Joan's, since this is their story, or, rather, these are their stories. Nothing much happens to them, except that everything happens to them – at one time or another.

ONE

Never go back, they say. And for a time I didn't have the intention, nor the desire, nor, till I turned eighteen this year, the ability to return. But ghosts speak with compelling voices and, though they might only be whisperers, below the threshold of the human ear, their messages make themselves heard. I know this. I've known this since long before the dreadful thing happened.

101, 131, 151, 181, 191, 313, 353, 383, 727, 757, 787, 797, 919, 929,10301

The sound of the wind threshing the long grasses at the edge of the rough path silences thoughts, while the wide expanses of gun-metal sky and grey-brown water deaden reflections, literally as well as metaphorically, since the mast and hull of the single yacht braving the tide make no impression on the solidity of the slow-moving river. This is a good place to have chosen, below the level of the path, so that, when I crouch to lay out the tent and the fly-sheet, the coils of guy-lines, the poles and pegs, the river cannot be seen, although the sky spreads overhead, broad and grey and low in all directions. And the wind, carrying with it the thick odour of the river, a base note of decaying muddy clay beneath the freshness of grass and cold, clean air, is kept at bay by the height of the path. Here, shielded from the wind, out of view, I have pitched my place of return.

First, I lay out the inner tent with its built-in groundsheet, and peg it down with a slender metal spike at each corner. The spikes go easily into the ground, which feels slightly damp beneath hands and knees. The fabric gives off its musty fragrance as I pin it out, well-used canvas and the perfume of dry pine needles, mingled with the dusty herbal scents of Mediterranean hillsides. The chill of a Yorkshire riverbank in October is a world away from where I've passed the last two years since the dreadful thing.

10501, 10601, 11311, 11411, 12421, 12721, 12821

Next, construct the A frame, inserting aluminium poles into plastic connecting hubs, and raise the tent, securing it to the horizontal pole, and pegging out the guy-ropes. As I stand and affix the ties which hold the tent in place, the wind whips across the path, and with stung eyes I look down at two dark patches on the knees of my jeans where the damp has stained them. Dipping down again to push the pegs for the guys into the ground, the wind disappears as though a sudden calm has descended over the East Yorkshire landscape. Finally, the fly-sheet, billowing briefly but secured with six guy-ropes, provides a rain-proof roof, and I'm ready to crawl inside, pushing before me rucksack and guitar case.

Passing through the opening from the outside to the inside requires no special negotiating, unlike other thresholds which can cause problems. A tent's opening is not a door, and even though the carrier bag with my recent purchases from the supermarket in the village has been forgotten outside, it is a simple matter to crawl outside and then go back without performing the customary threshold rituals. I sit in the tent, and feel peaceful, thinking of the tent's symbolism, its connectivity, its independence, its legacy. Thinking is something I do a lot of.

The light which permeates the interior is different from what I have got used to over the past two years. Two years out of eighteen. One ninth. Zero point one one one one one one one one one one one one recurring. It doesn't do to dwell on recurring decimals, since they go on and on, and when do you stop? So, I think about the light. It's a flat light, gentle and blurred, unlike the sharp vividness of the Mediterranean sun and its deep shadows, which even in winter lit the inside of the tent with a fervid glow. Outside, I can feel the Yorkshire sky like a low ceiling, dissipating into far distances. The other sky was taller, soaring to a blue zenith above the surrounding mountains and the far-off sea. This sky, this light, is calm but cold, and I'm wondering about the nights as the year draws on. For now, a four season sleeping bag will be more than sufficient, even here on the windswept riverbank.

I roll out the bag, which looks like a dull green cocoon, trimmed with orange piping along the seams. Or like the ancient sarcophagus of a particularly unimaginative pharaoh. It's comfortable to sit on the slightly slippery fabric, and feel the padding slide softly beneath me. Cross-legged, I reach for the guitar-case, and unclasp the latches in the necessary order: neck latch, body latch, hinge side and handle. The plush interior glows like crushed velvet with a purple voluptuousness. It still looks as new as when I bought it from the cool guy at Music Workshop back in 1987, together with the guitar, a second-hand Yamaha, which might not be the flashiest piece of kit in the world, but it plays with a soft, clear tone, and the action is low and gentle. It's the guitar I taught myself to play on, and I have no reason to want to replace it. But I will go back to Music Workshop, even though they say never go back.

The Yamaha feels good, resting its curves on my thigh. I play through the arpeggios of one of the first songs I learned, and again I feel peaceful.

Am C D F Am C E E7 Am C D F Am E Am E

The gentle light, the chords, the distant sounds of the outside, this is the right time, the right year. Not prime, admittedly, but palindromic, and it factorises to two palindromic primes, 181 and 11. So it must be right to be here, to be now, to have come back, despite what they say. Part of me knows that there is no logic to this, but the clever voice in my head, my own voice, my dark and nameless me-not-me voice, tells me that it is perfectly logical, reasonable and compelling to disable threat and dread and distress by reciting the primes or by playing the sequences. Or by observing all the semi-secret rituals which have dominated my life for as long as I can remember. And especially since the dreadful thing.

101, 131, 151, 181, 191, 313, 353, 383, 727, 757, 787, 797, 919, 929, 10301

I stop playing, and there are voices outside, vague and blown on the wind. I put aside the guitar, safe in the case, and peer out and up through the tent's opening. Two figures in padded jackets, green and brown against the metal sky, are passing along the path above me. A dog pulls ahead of them, straining its lead, making one of the figures stretch forwards and walk with a juddering stutter, almost out of control. I'm wondering what they must be thinking as they pass, seeing a tent pitched on the riverbank, a little orange shelter like a piece of Toblerone, a boy's head protruding. Well, not a boy, a young man, someone in that liminal space between boy- and manhood. It's not a usual sight, but the dog walkers pass, heads turned to one another, their voices indistinct, their dog pulling ahead. They don't seem to have registered the tent, or me; or if they have, the tent and the boy-man hold no interest for them. They are caught up in their own concerns, embroiled in each other as the dog pulls strongly on the lead. Immersed in their conversation, they progress onward, and the dog pulls harder. And harder.

Then, I cannot stop the sky from darkening around them, as the dog forges forward, stretching its lead and the arm holding on, threatening to dislocate it from its socket. The two figures will be pulled headlong from the path under the glowering sky, and into the sucking mud where the reeds give way to the river's tide. They will be consumed in the grey thickness, pulled down by irresistible suction and unyielding gravity, their dog barking madly as it scrabbles at the wet clay, and their throats filling with the suffocating sludge. They will choke, speechless and thrashing, and their dog will die a horrible, gurgling death. Unless.

101, 131, 151, 181, 191, 313, 353, 383, 727, 757, 787, 797, 919, 929, 10301, 10501, 10601, 11311, 11411, 12421, 12721, 12821

The dog walkers recede into the distance, the dog still pulling ahead, but the sky has lost its darkness and the light has regained its flat greyness. The dangers of the river are real. People should be more careful as they walk along this path. The mud, when the tide of the estuary is out, is treacherous, although, at the right time of year, those who know the shifting sandbanks and the currents can walk safely from Yorkshire to the flatlands of Lincolnshire, a long low line on the horizon, across the mud. I remember being told stories of the crossings when I was a little boy, along with all the other village mythologies: the Romans and their ferry; Dick Turpin and his epic fateful ride and his escapes through local inn windows; the single bomb which fell during world war two and did no damage. I know I will probably have to rescue people from the river over and over if I stay here. In the same way, I know that it is really me who is driving them off the path.

The tent is an uncomplicated sanctuary, easy to negotiate when entering or leaving, and I like the self-sufficiency of erecting it myself, the ease of moving from place to place, the impermanence of it, although it embodies its own irreducible essence. It is both fluid and solid, moving and fixed. When it is pitched, its fabric thrumming against the breeze, it's like a point on a curve, or a moment on a journey, or a single note in a sequence of arpeggios. And I can enter and leave, enter and leave with the same automaticity with which I can pick out the patterns on the Yamaha's strings.

Am C D F Am C E E7

But it's more than just a fixed point, more like a point on a curve or a chord in the calculus, since it tends towards movement. The thrum of the fabric in the wind and the tension in the guy-lines imply the desire to be in motion, just as the tent came to me, passing through various hands. When the time came to leave the hot, dry hillsides and return to this chill expanse of water and wind-blown reeds, the fabric folded and the ropes coiled and the poles were disconnected with unresisting ease. The only difficulty was navigating through the airports and boarding the plane, but the clomipramine and the Prozac were a help. And now I am back, although they say you should never go back.

The flight from Larnaca to Manchester was long, but I slept most of the five hours, a side effect of the anti-depressants, along with a dry mouth and a certain amount of dizziness. That's partly why I've never liked medications, though Dr Angela was always keen on them. People can be very kind when you seem disoriented. Not always, of course, and not everywhere. There have been times of unkindness and difficulty, but in the airports and on the train coming here, people were kind if I asked for directions for where to go and what to do. And signs are helpful so that you don't always have to ask. I like the self-sufficiency of finding my way myself, reading the dense print of a railway schedule behind its perspex, purchasing tickets, and locating platforms. Then, checking and re-checking and checking again, before taking a seat in a carriage and watching the long miles of landscape unroll past the windows: first, the yards of iron lines with their carriages and engines, stretches of close and blackened brickwork as the train leaves the station; then the flashing glass of the windows at the crowded backs of houses, obscured by straggling unkempt hedgerows; then windscreens at crossings, giving way to the green blur of woodland and the brown expanse of bare fields, until, eventually, we came to the long grey-brown openness of the river, and, stopping at a tiny, unaccountably important station with an iron footbridge spanning the tracks, I disembarked carrying rucksack and guitar-case, gave up my ticket, and found myself back here, where it all began before I had to go away.

The details of the return journey are still vague, even though it was so recent. I'm sure it will all come back to me if I try to remember, but the important thing is, now, that I am here, and I can start to think about why it is that I have come back, and what I need to do. I fasten up the rucksack and close the latches on the case: far side, neck latch, body latch, handle. I peer out of the tent's opening, and see that the path is deserted. Two disconnected seagulls, which have strayed this far inland along the estuary, wheel slowly overhead, white against the iron sky, as though an exhausted mathematician were plotting two painful curves on a huge sheet of grey graph paper. As I consider their excruciating progress in relation to each other, I decide to hide the rucksack and guitar-case in one of the impenetrable bushes at the side of the path, and walk back into the village before it gets dark. So I crawl out of the tent, check again for passers-by, secrete the bags, and turn my thoughts to closing up the tent, which is the only real problem. The seagulls catch a current of the wind and are blown across the sky, recover themselves, and start once again their painful arcs. I crouch before the tent's opening and prepare to close the zipper, which fills me with dread.

If you don't mesh the teeth 3 times, one third of the zipper's length, 2 times, half the zipper's length, and once the full length of the zipper, your bags will be stolen while you are away. My nameless voice speaks plausibly in my head, my me-not-me voice, and I must obey because the consequence would be disastrous. To lose my rucksack and guitar, almost all I possess, except for the money. So I perform the ritual, 3, 2, 1, and the zipper is closed and I can tear myself away to walk away from the tent, up onto the path, and back towards the village, half a mile away.

When I got off the train, a few hours ago, with my rucksack on my back and my guitar-case in my hand, I walked the familiar lanes from the station to the village where a central crossroads hosts an arcade of shops, opposite a war memorial. The village streets, the towering trees which overhang the footpaths, and all the buildings were exactly as I remember them. After all, it's only two years since I have been gone, though it feels longer, one ninth, zero point one one one recurring; it would be unreasonable to think dramatic changes could have taken place, even though in my mind there is a definite line marking off the time before and the time after the dreadful thing 101, 131, 151, 181, 191, 313, 353, 383, 727, 757, 787, 797, 919, 929, 10301 when everything changed.

The buildings are all here and unchanged. I walk from the riverbank, passing two white painted pubs, both of which have their own mythologies in the village's memory: one where a future king threw pennies to children from an upstairs window; the other, like many inns in the area, where Dick Turpin the highwayman leaped from a window to escape the law. I turn a slow, arcing corner, and there is the bank, a squat, brick building where the money has been sent, fourteen thousand, seven hundred and forty-one pounds left over after the sale of the house. The rest of it I have in cash in the money belt around my waist, just over two thousand, and in my pockets for living expenses. The bank is closed at this time, but I have no need to pay a visit. The money is safe, a comfortably palindromic prime amount, and I have no intention of touching it. What would I spend it on? The arcade of shops is up ahead, but obscured by trees. The pitched roof of the village church, an ugly rectangular box without tower or steeple, rises above high hedges. If I walk past the church and turn right down a gravel path, passing beneath the overhanging branches of tall horse chestnut trees, I will be there.

I walk past the church. A noticeboard announces the times of weekly services and invites young women to join the Mothers' Union. I turn right, and the gravel crunches beneath my tread. The horse chestnuts are beginning to lose their leaves and there are brown-green globes, spiked like medieval weapons, on the ground at the foot of the trunks. Some of the globes have split open, revealing rich brown conkers within, which shimmer like the glossy coats of thoroughbreds. And then, with a sudden jerk of recognition which happens in my chest and head simultaneously, there is the house.

If you push the garden gate, which opens onto a straight path leading up to the front door of the house, it will make a low squeal and swing closed once you have walked through. It takes eleven paces to reach the door, but you will pause at steps three, five and seven, a brief, uncomfortable stutter of hesitation as your foot comes down onto the concrete each time. The door is painted a midnight blue which looks black in most lights, but when the summer sun shines through the foliage of the big trees in front of the house and strikes the paintwork directly, the full, deep blueness of it emerges with a dark glow. Late on an October afternoon, though, the door is black.

The new owners have not repainted the woodwork of the house's frontage, although alien curtains now hang in the windows. The rooms are in darkness. It seems as though no-one is home, since the double gates which lead to the garage stand open and the drive is empty of vehicles. The vacant, lightless windows, deserted drive and open gates signal that the occupants are out, but there is a sense of expectancy in the air around the building. Something taut about the house's appearance makes it feel as though the new owners will be arriving home at any minute.

If you walk between the garage and the side of the house, passing a recessed doorway which opens into the kitchen, you will find yourself in a long garden, enclosed by privet on one side, tall fencing on the other, and a line of trees at the far end. Beyond the trees there is open land before a development of newer houses, and, eventually, the riverbank. If you climb high enough in one of the trees at the end of the garden, you will be able to glimpse the river in the distance.

I know everything about this house, the layout of its rooms, which floorboards creak when you step on them, the sound the wind makes in the bedroom fireplaces. I know that when it rains heavily, water will pool on the tiled floor just inside the kitchen door. I know that on a warm summer afternoon if you come into the house, hot from lying in the sun-filled garden, the rooms will feel cold and you will shiver. I know that I both want and do not want to go back into the house and uncover the lost things.

I turn away and walk back towards the church, as a car crunches over the gravel, heading for the open gates behind me. Two, unrecognised faces look out from the windscreen, as the driver raises fingers from the steering wheel in a laconic greeting. I catch sight of the tops of two children's heads in the back seat as the car passes.

No-one in the car is wearing a seat belt.

101, 131, 151, 181, 191, 313, 353, 383, 727, 757, 787, 797, 919, 929, 10301

It doesn't get dark for another hour or two at this time of year, but the afternoon is grey and the light is flat as I walk away from the house, my initial reconnoitre complete. The roads here are never filled with traffic, although there is an intermittent flow of cars along the main street past the row of shops. And there are pedestrians walking with a purpose on both sides of the road. A woman with a push-chair and a small child holding onto her arm are approaching on my side of the street. Two cars come into view in the distance, rounding the gentle curve of the main road. I begin to recite the primes under my breath as they approach, willing the cars to pass before I reach the woman and her charges. She is about ten yards away. I switch to the sequence of palindromic primes, racing to get to 929, and the cars are still some distance off. The woman is almost level.

"It's Cat, isn't it? Christopher?" Her voice is familiar, with hard consonants and flat vowels like my own. She stops in the middle of the pavement, the child at her side looking up at me with uninterested eyes. The two cars pass just as I reach 929, and the child is safe. There's another child in the push-chair, bundled in a quilted bodysuit, only its face showing from within its cocoon. I hesitate and stumble through an acknowledgement.

"We haven't seen you for some time," she continues. "Are you back here visiting?" I am at a loss how to respond. "You and my little brother were in the same class at primary school years ago. I'll tell him you're back. We thought you'd gone away forever, after ..." She stops herself.

"I've got to go," I say. "Tell your brother hi from me." I smile at the two children who stare back. They both have red noses and pale eyes like their mother. The face of a sandy-haired boy wearing a black and amber soccer kit surfaces in my head. Stuart? Graham? Steven Harris?

"I've got to go," I repeat, and hurry away from the woman, her children, their push-chair. The need to return to the riverbank and crawl into my tent feels almost irresistible, so I half walk, half run along the pavement, back past the Bank, past the two white pubs and onto the riverside path, where the wind has freshened further. The reeds and grasses bend towards the horizontal and the water's surface is agitated into furrows. As I hasten in the direction of the tent, heading towards the west where the sky has taken on a lighter glow with the lowering of the sun behind the banks of cloud, the left side of my head aches with cold. Up ahead, level with the tent, stands a group of figures, hands thrust into jacket pockets, black against the metal sky like a stand of slender, stunted tree trunks, shorn of their branches.

The wind, which is making the left side of my skull feel as though it is being held in a vice, is buffeting the jackets of the four teenage boys. They are gazing down at the tent. Its walls are unmoving, protected by the raised path which forms a natural windbreak. As I approach, one of the boys turns to face me. His dark hair, long with razored layers in the style of Eddie van Halen, whips across his eyes as he speaks. His words are whisked away by the wind.

"What?" I ask, and he shouts his question again.

"This your tent?" His friends have turned to look at me also. Each of them wears his hair in the same style, differing only in colour. One is blond; the other two are mousy brown. All of them are having difficulty maintaining a heavy metal image of unflustered, glowering cool in the East Yorkshire wind.

"Yes," I answer. They are maybe three or four years younger than me. I think I recognise the little boys they had once been under the hairstyles and in the coarsening features of their adolescent faces.

"D'you have to get permission to have a tent here?"

"I don't know," I say. "I haven't asked anyone."

The five of us stare down at the tent, and the wind flicks a few icy drops of water from the surface of the river.

"You going to sleep in it tonight?" The blond Eddie van Halen's voice is gruff, but marred by a mid-teen squeak. He pronounces his final word with a slurred, local vowel: ternaht. "You'll freeze your bollocks off if you do."

We laugh a little together.

"It won't be too bad," I tell them. "It's below the level of the path so the wind won't be a problem."

"Why do you want to stay out here anyway?" the dark-haired boy asks. "Haven't you got a house to live in?"

I wonder how I could explain, supposing that I wanted to, how it happened that the house where I had once lived in the village had had to be sold; how the house I could now live in was with my grandparents in a tiny mountain village on a Mediterranean island out on the farthest edge of Europe; how living in a house, anyway, has become increasingly difficult for me. One of the other Eddie van Halens joins in.

"I wish I could live in a tent down here, and not have to put up with all that shite at home." He pulls out a black and gold cigarette packet from one of the zippered pockets of his jacket, and offers it round our little group. His three friends each take a cigarette while I give a shake of my head and thrust my hands into the pockets of my jeans. All four of them take out their own lighters and set about trying to light up, cupping hands in front of faces and repeatedly clicking sparks into life.

"It must be great not having your mum and dad always telling you to do stuff."

"Yeah," agrees the blond, exhaling a cloud of bluish smoke which disappears immediately on the breeze. "And you can play your music as loud as you want, and nobody'll complain."

"Don't be a dickhead," says another. "He hasn't got any electricity. How's he going to play any music?"

"Maybe he's got a battery tape player."

The dark-haired one looks at me, raising his eyebrows as he takes a pull on his cigarette. "How do you get electricity? You know, lights and stuff. Music? Cooking?"

"I manage," I say. "You don't need much when you live in a tent." They seem to be very interested in my arrangements, but it's getting cold standing in the wind and I want to get into the tent.

"Look, lads," I say. "It's really cold out here. I'm going in."

"I think it's cool living in a tent."

I drop down from the path, and immediately feel the difference in temperature when cut off from the wind. The boys are still looking down at me. I wish they would go away so that I can retrieve my rucksack and guitar case.

"See you, lads," I call up at them. I crouch to unzip the tent's entrance, first blowing on my hands to warm numb fingers. I manipulate the zip: half-way, close, half-way, close. Looking up, I see that the boys are drifting away in the direction of the village, their figures hunched over, the wind tousling their billowing hair. I scurry over to the bush and reach deep inside its branches, pushing aside the leafy coverage which hides my bags. My fingers find the textured surfaces of the guitar case, and I drag it out onto the grass. Then I retrieve the rucksack, hauling it out through the resisting foliage.

Back in the tent, surrounded by my belongings and with the sleeping bag unrolled beneath me, it's time to eat something from the provisions I bought when I first arrived in the village. The food is simple, a pre-packaged sandwich, ready salted crisps and a Mars bar, washed down with a pint carton of milk, and afterwards, I lie cocooned in the sleeping bag. The fading light outside is felt rather than seen, and I know it is growing dark with an autumnal swiftness. In the rucksack there are bottles with childproof plastic lids, containing clomipramine and Prozac, but I leave them untouched, thinking of chord sequences as I stare through the thickening air at the roof of the tent. The orange darkens into brown, and eventually becomes black.

Am C D F Am C E E7 Am C D F Am E Am E

Everything is still black when I come suddenly awake. If I have dreamt, I cannot remember anything of my dreams. The air on my cheeks feels cold, but I'm comfortably warm in the sleeping bag, and the sounds which filter through the fabric of the tent are reassuring and soothing. The gathering roar of a train approaching and then its slow, departing cadence rise and fall over the background ghost-whispering of the wind. In the aftermath, there is the musical jangle of the stays against the masts of the yachts in the boatyard further down the riverbank. With the blackness pressing on my eyes, I drift in and out of sleep until the edges of the tent begin to clarify into a brocade of dull light.

And then it is dawn of my second day back in the place where I grew up.

My plans for the day ahead are malleable and ill-defined in my head, as the events of a dream might be. There is no logical sequence of what I will do; I imagine blocks of activity, revisiting various locations in the village, catching a train into the town, going back to places I used to go: streets of shops, Music Workshop where I bought the guitar, a public park opposite long residential avenues of elegant Victorian terraces. I consider my schools, the primary school in the village, and the large boys' school in town which I attended from the age of eleven. I could go and look at the buildings without danger of running into people, since it is the October half-term break this week, and the schools are closed.

Through the unzipped entrance, today's sky is identical to yesterday's: leaden grey. I briefly stand outside to scan slow moving expanses of mud and water. The same wind thrashes the reeds which bang their heads insanely against nothing in time with some unheard metal anthem. Inside the tent, I let the hours pass over me as the air outside continues to brighten and solidify into the autumnal light of day. People pass on the path, unseen, their voices drifting and the sounds of their movements vague but identifiable. Then there is a shout I recognise.

"Hey!" It's the voice of one of the teenage Eddie van Halens from yesterday. "Hey!" he repeats, "you in there?"

I look out of the tent's mouth, peering up at three figures looming above me. The blond boy is not with them. The wind blows off the river behind them, making their hair stream forwards around their faces. They stare down like three male Gorgons. The sky is a hard, metallic grey above them.

"We remember you," the dark-haired boy shouts down to me. "You were in my brother's class at primary school. Then you went to another school."

"Chris Thomas," says one of the others. "They used to call you Cat."

The dark-haired boy jumps down from the path and the other two follow. Their interest is perplexing and disconcerting as they come towards the entrance of the tent.

"Why'd they call you Cat?" dark hair asks. Now that they are closer they are trying to peer past me into the sheltered interior.

"If your name is Chris, why'd they call you Cat?"

"It's a nickname," I say. "My initials. C.A.T. And people used to say I was nervy. Like a cat on hot bricks." I regret saying this as soon as the words are out.

"What are you nervy about?" I can feel that the questions are beginning to gather momentum. "Is that why you went to that other school? 'Cos you were nervy? Was it a special school?" The questions are flustering, and I'm not sure why I feel constrained to answer. The three pairs of eyes exert a powerful interrogatory gaze.

"It was just another school," I say. "Nothing special about it. Just different from the one the others went to."

"No one else went, my brother said. Just you from his class, like you were some kind of special kid."

"I'm not a special kid."

"And then you went away completely, they said. Had to leave, after –"

"Hey," I say, reciting the palindromic primes silently to myself. "Why all the questions? What does it matter to you?" I stand and the sky is like steel, a low ceiling of sheet metal over our heads.

21

"We're just interested," says the dark haired Eddie. "People were talking about you last night. We wanted to find out why you've come back."

"Why did they make you leave?" one of the others asks. I try to think of a sequence which will make them go away, but nothing follows, just disconnected individual chords which will not hang together. I gulp down deep breaths of the cold air. It is like breathing iron filings. I can feel the sky pressing down heavily on us.

"Is it true?" says a voice, as the sky's pressure becomes overwhelming. "You had to leave when your mum and dad were killed?"

One ninth. Point one. One one one.

101, 131, 151, 181, 191, 313, 353, 383, 727, 757, 787, 797, 919, 929, 10301

I yell something at someone, and there's a feeling of a confrontation, a taut stand-off. There is laughter, and shouting, and then the sky's pressure intensifies, and solidifies, full of dark threat. And then they are gone, a hateful refrain

fuckynutterfuckynutterfuckynutter

drifting back on the air and continuing to reverberate in my head, and I am somehow inside the tent, reciting the palindromic primes, which do not displace or interrupt the repetition.

fuckynutterfuckynutterfuckynutter

Outside the tent the sky is still pressing down, making the fabric bow inwards claustrophobically. But the thought of going outside just now is unbearable.

I rest the index finger of my left hand softly on one of the strings of the guitar, directly above the fifth fret on the Yamaha's neck. The softest of touches, not pressing down, just resting gently. As I pluck the string with a fingernail of my picking hand and simultaneously lift the finger from the fret, a high pitched, harmonic note rings out, two octaves above the open string. I repeat the action on other strings, and then move up to the seventh fret. The note which sounds is an octave and a fifth above. The ringing, clear sound is soothing in the charged air of the tent, so I repeat and repeat the gentle process, hearing the perfection of the natural harmonics gradually dispelling the sense of threat which had hung in the air above and around me like a dark carrion crow.

After a while, I can think more calmly about the Eddie van Halens who are after all just kids, and I should have told them to mind their own business and leave me alone. It's an uncomfortable feeling when people question you about who you are and what you are like. I never even felt comfortable talking to old Tad, the Headmaster at school, and he had a way of listening which made talking easier when I had to explain things that happened. And I especially never liked talking to Dr Angela in her sun-faded office, although she meant well. Right now, part of me regrets losing it with the Eddies and giving them a scare. The threats aren't real. I would never actually harm anyone. I don't want to hurt anyone. That's what the sequences and the rituals are about. Keeping everyone safe.

The harmonics ring. Fifth fret on the bottom E string and seventh on the A in perfect accord. Fifth on the A and seventh on the D. Perfect. I adjust the tuning of the G slightly with a tweak on the slick metal of the machinehead, and the two notes slide into alliance. You can't tune the G string and the B string like this, so I trust my ears to hear the harmony between the two strings – a third. Then, fifth fret on the B and seventh on the top E, another little tweak on a machinehead, and the Yamaha is perfectly tuned. I strum a chord, a G, and the notes ring, gentle and true. I settle the guitar into the plush interior of the case and close the lid. Hinge latch, neck latch, body latch, handle.

On the railway timetable in my rucksack the times of the morning trains into the town are tabulated in tiny print, greyish black figures, some in bold, some with asterisked or daggered footnotes about Bank Holiday services. There are trains throughout the morning, and no matter what time I turn up at the station there won't be too long to wait for the twenty minute train ride into town. In my mind I walk through the journey from the big Victorian terminus facing Hammonds' department store, along a wide, featureless thoroughfare and up a long, perfectly straight road which leads out into the residential areas to the north of the city. On this road, almost at the very end in a scruffy row of shops is Music Workshop where Tony keeps his stock of guitars and equipment.

The case on the groundsheet next to me is a little more worn than when I first bought it with the money from my fourteenth birthday. A few scuffs on the surface, and the latches have lost a little of their shine, but it is still in good condition, just as it had been when Tony sold it to me, second-hand, along with the Yamaha. I'd rushed into his shop after school that day with an envelope of cash in the inside pocket of my school jacket, my schoolbag bumping against my legs, and my tie stuffed into my pocket. I'd removed it from my throat as I had half walked, half run from the school, worrying that the shop would have closed early for some reason, and reciting sequences of numbers as I hurried. But there'd been no reason to panic, even though I had been a bit flustered by events during the last lesson with my old Latin teacher, who we called Satan. His houndstooth sports jacket, grey flannels and brown brogues rise into my memory as I remember this. His voice with its accent from somewhere down South sounds in my mind, and I remember, as though no time has passed, the conjugations, declensions, rules for formations of comparatives and superlatives of a dead language which is still alive in my memory. *TIMEO TIMES TIMET*, I recite to myself. Even a strange, almost meaningless mnemonic is still there: *Please Bring The Crown Derby Gently*. And a snatch of epic poetry: *CONTICUERENT OMNES INTENTIQUE ORA TENEBANT. INDE TORO PATER AENEAS SIC ORSUS AB ALTO.* All these snatches of things continue to reverberate along the corridors of my past.

    I imagine that the frontage of the little shop must still look the same, although it's possible that in the last two years it might have changed. In my head, though, its red, black and white image carries a sense of permanence and solidity. When I used to frequent it on after school visits to stare at the glowing bodies of the guitars and touch the silken metal of the strings, the barred shop windows on either side of the narrow, glass-paned door, and the primitive design of the signage, all looked like left-overs from the late 60s or the 70s. The shop had the appearance of always having been there, and now I find it impossible to think that changes could have occurred.

After showing me four or five new guitars and getting me to play chords and arpeggios, Tony had eventually taken the second-hand Yamaha down from a bracket on the wall. And, although with the case, some picks, a set of replacement strings and a book called *The Great Songs of the 60s* it was more expensive than I had expected, Tony had let me take the lot for the contents of the envelope in my pocket. And I had walked, self-consciously imagining everyone I passed to be admiring my fledgling rock-star status, down the long straight road to the railway station, named with the ambition and optimism of an earlier era: Paragon. And that was how I felt.

And I had taken it back to the house to show it.

101, 131, 151, 181, 191, 313, 353, 383, 727, 757, 787, 797, 919, 929,10301

Leaving the tent, I check the path in both directions. It is deserted save for a distant figure coming from the east, an unidentifiable human shape, a deeper greyish brown amid the greys and browns of the riverside landscape. The sky above is its customary grey, heavy and low, stretching monotonously across the brown water over the flatness of Lincolnshire to the south and the higher ground of the Wolds to the north. The figure is still a long way distant and there is plenty of time to push the guitar case and rucksack into their hiding place. One of the thorns catches against my skin as I withdraw my hand, scoring a line of red. Little globules of bright blood well up like knots on a length of thread. I lick them away, tasting the metallic tang and sweet saltiness. A memory threatens tautly.

101, 131, 151, 181, 191, 313, 353, 383, 727, 757, 787

I secure the tent's flap, reassuring myself further with the ritual fastening sequence, and feel a soothing calm begin to descend. It's less than a ten minute walk to the station. I clamber up onto the path. The figure has drawn closer, but there is something unusual about the way it is moving. Something disarranged about the way that the coat billows outwards around the body which seems to be turning from side to side with barely controlled twists. It looks as though the figure is pivoting from the waist upwards as it moves forwards, while the coat billows and swirls.

She has come close enough now for me to see that it is a woman, an old lady wearing a winter coat which is unbuttoned and blown by the gusts over the water, revealing what is obviously a nightdress underneath. Her pale hair, whipped by the wind, and a pair of ankle high wellington boots complete the picture of disorder and confusion. Incongruously, she carries a black patent leather handbag in the crook of one arm. Now that she has drawn nearer I can see that the pivoting, swivelling movement is her turning from side to side as though she is seeking something, or trying to work out where she is and how she has got here. She hurries forward, pauses and looks about her with a hesitating, stuttery motion of her head and shoulders.

Then she comes towards me, calling a name in her quavery, old lady voice.

"Harry? Have you seen Harry?"

*   *   *

Joan isn't daft, you know. She might be getting a bit forgetful, but she's not daft. And that doctor might have been a bit brusque in his manner, but he wasn't daft either, though it did come as a bit of a shock when he used the words Dementia with Lewy Bodies or DLB and talked about the forgetfulness eventually getting worse over time, and maybe having to go into a home. He gave Joan some helpful advice about how to remember daily matters like what day of the week it is; that sort of thing. He said, get yourself some bits of card, Mrs Fettes, and write things down in big letters. Joan's always been an organised sort of a person. People like that don't need to go into a home. Twenty years as a secretary at the factory after Bob died, and another twenty keeping minutes for the Women's Institute in the village, until it started getting a bit too much. So that was what she did. She went down to the Post Office and bought a packet of card – all different colours – and one of those felt tip pens with a thick nib – and wrote out the days of the week. They're on the thing over there, behind the cut glass fruit bowl. Every day, when she gets up, she changes the day so she knows which day it is. See? Today is Monday.

Then, when she started having trouble with remembering what some things were called, Joan took that doctor's idea further, and wrote down the names of things on little squares of card, and stuck them on with bits of that blue tacky stuff they invented. The thing over there with the cut glass, it's called a sideboard, and if Joan forgets, which she does sometimes, we all do, but that doesn't mean you have to go into a home, she can always read the card. She hasn't forgotten how to read, though it is more tiring these days. Joan's always enjoyed a good book, so long as it was real, not those daft things about goblins or ghosts or wizards. Joan liked to read about real life and real folks.

Things that could happen, not just something made up. Which makes the DLB thing all the worse, not just the forgetting what you're about and who people are, because another scary thing he said was that Joan might start having hallucinations, seeing things that aren't there, like fairies in the garden, that sort of thing. Joan told him that didn't sound like her at all. She's always been a very down-to-earth kind of person, as everyone knows. So she now has a list of important words she mustn't forget, which is on the pantry door in the kitchen. And all the keys have got labels on, so anyone can tell what they're for.

It's funny, though. Remembering things about now can give Joan all sorts of trouble, but when she thinks about things that happened donkeys' years ago, they're all there as clear as a bell. As clear as that cut glass fruit bowl that she and Bob were given for their wedding just after the war, the first war, mind, when he was back on leave before he went off on another of his trips with Harrison's, the shipping line. And he would always bring something when he came back, wherever he'd been – a bit of china, some jewellery. There's quite a collection around the house. He used to sail to all those far-flung places: Singapore, Hong Kong, the West Indies; but Joan has never been outside England. No, that's not true. Together, they went to the Isle of Man on holiday once and saw the Laxey Wheel and the Fairy Bridge, and the TT. Joan remembers it all, clear as a bell.

"It's good to be back, Joan," says Harry from his spot by the fireplace in the dining room. Joan lit the fire earlier that morning to take the chill off the air. Now the coals are glowing red, and a comfortable warmth radiates out. Harry gives a low growl of pleasure which rumbles from deep in his throat.

"It's nice to have you back, Harry," replies Joan. "I didn't think I'd be seeing you again." She smiles across the fireplace into the dark, intelligent eyes looking up at her. "You always loved it by the fire on a cold morning, didn't you?"

"I did and I still do," Harry says in a voice reminiscent of the actor, Sean Connery's.

"We can go out for a walk later, if you like," continues Joan. "We used to have some lovely times down on the riverbank, you and me. Do you remember?"

"Of course I do, Joan," answers Harry. "I remember everything just like it was yesterday."

"It seems like it was just yesterday to me as well, but it must have been, what, the nineteen seventies when I got you."

"That's right, Joan, nineteen seventy-four." Harry's eyes gleam with a look of faraway dreaminess, as though he is drifting away, watching scenes from the past unfold in his mind. There is a long, comfortable silence, disturbed only by the sound of the fire as the coals burn redly in the grate.

"Would you like a cup of tea, Joan?"

"That's a nice idea, Harry." Joan rises from her chair in a slow, crabbed movement. "Ooh, I am stiff this morning. That walk will do me good. We'll go out after we've had the tea."

"I'll come and help you make it," says Harry.

"You are a love."

"Maybe you've got some of those nice biscuits you used to have for me," suggests Harry, as Joan moves with cautious steps towards the door.

"We'll get some from the shops later, love," says Joan. "Now you're back, you'll want feeding properly, eh?"

"You spoil me," growls Harry, contentedly.

Joan pauses in front of the sideboard, a long piece of functional post-war furniture, whose top holds ornaments and a black and white wedding photograph of a girl dressed in the fashions of the nineteen twenties standing beside a young man in a morning coat. They both stare unsmilingly into the camera.

"I nearly forgot to change the day, Harry." Joan picks up the stack of coloured cards propped behind the cut-glass fruit bowl and removes the topmost card. The stack goes back behind the bowl. The top card now reads 'Tuesday'.

"There we are. I'd forget my head if it was loose," chuckles Joan, and opens the dining room door. Harry rises and goes through the door ahead of her, turning right to go into the kitchen. Joan follows.

"See," she says, indicating a list of neatly printed words affixed to the pantry door. "There's that list I was telling you about." She takes the electric kettle across to the sink and begins to fill it from the tap. The plumbing clanks gently as the water begins to flow. Harry hovers at her elbow, watching the level in the kettle rise.

"Don't get in the way, love," says Joan kindly. "You'll have me spilling it."

Harry floats away, upwards towards the ceiling.

"I don't know how you do that," says Joan, not looking at him as he hangs in the air.

"I can do lots of things I never used to be able to do," says Harry from above and behind her head.

Joan laughs, a tinkling, contented laugh.

"You are a clever dog," she says, shaking her head as she goes to plug the kettle in. "And these past few years I thought you were dead."

"Oh, I'm not dead," says Harry. "How could I be dead when I'm here for all to see."

"But it is a bit unusual, you've got to admit. I can't imagine what Muriel will say when I tell her." Joan stands and looks at all the things around her, kitchen things, and then, quite suddenly, there are other things too, the things from her dining room, and Joan isn't sure where these things have appeared from. She was in the kitchen one minute, but now she's here with Harry, flitting in and out of her line of vision, appearing at the foot of the dining room door at one moment, and then worrying at the long curtains which are half-drawn across the garden doors. The October morning light filters into the room through the panes in their metal frames, heavy with white gloss paint accumulated over almost sixty years since the house was built. Harry scrabbles briefly at the base of the doors before trotting over to the fireplace to look up at Joan with quizzical brown eyes. His tongue lolls from the corner of his mouth.

"I'm not as young as I was," says Joan. "And it takes me a while to get myself ready." She looks down at her nightdress, patting at the fabric around her hips. "You'll have to be patient." Harry gazes up at her, panting gently. Joan smiles. "I'll be ready in a minute." She pats at the nightdress again as if feeling for something in the hip pockets of an overcoat. She moves across the room to the sideboard, where the card propped against the cut-glass fruit bowl reads 'Tuesday', and runs a vague hand over the surface. "I can't seem to remember where I put those whatchamacallums." She picks up the wedding photograph, looking down fondly at the young man and the girl she once was, tapping at the glass with a gentle finger. "A girl and a boy," she mutters. "Not much more than children." She repositions the picture to stand in the centre of the sideboard facing straight into the room.

"I do wish people would leave things alone," she says.

Harry murmurs something to himself about forgetting and loose heads, while Joan tries to remember where she has put the things she is searching for. She must have had them when she went to the shops the day before, she thinks. They always sent her to the tobacconist's for father's tins of snuff. Tiny little things full of powder, and smelling of wintergreen. He said it cleared his passages. But it wasn't a nice habit. And, of course, she remembers being sent to the butcher's, Mr Partington's, by the entrance of the Garden Village Shopping Centre to buy ox beef, and the unpleasant sinewy coldness of the package as she carried it home. She remembers the young man in the photograph undressing in front of her, and guiding her hand towards a white bulge in his underwear which made her think of a package of ox beef but was shockingly warm to touch. She remembers asking what she was supposed to do. Something, it must be Harry, floats up from behind her and nuzzles at her neck.

"Harry?" says Joan, glancing around the room where the fire has burned low in the grate. She runs her fingers across her forehead, blinking away the thoughts of the past.

"What was I looking for?"

"You were looking for your keys, Joan," says Harry in his Sean Connery voice. "Let's go through all the places where you could have put them. Sideboard? Handbag? Coat pocket? In the kitchen?" Harry lists all the possible places he can think of while Joan stands in front of the sideboard, gazing out of the garden doors, trying to recall where her keys with their oversized cardboard label could be.

"Oh dear, Harry." Joan's voice quakes with the beginnings of a sudden panic. "I hope I didn't leave them in the lock." Thoughts of an intruder discovering the keys hanging invitingly in full view on the front door fill her mind. One of her friends from the Women's Institute, who lives not far away down a similar cul-de-sac in the village, was once burgled. With a sense of dread rising in her chest, Joan totters out into the entrance hall. The front door with its leaded panes is closed. She reaches for the Yale, turns it, pulls open the door. There, in the lock, are the keys.

Joan fumbles to extract the little jingling bunch, and stands helplessly as she feels a brief commotion around the hem of her nightdress. She looks down confusedly, and then out from the porch and down the short front garden and into the street.

"Harry?" she mutters. The cul-de-sac is empty. The windows of the houses opposite stare back with blank panes. One or two cars are parked at the side of the road, but there's no-one about, as usual. Joan hovers in the doorway, her worries about the keys supplanted by a new set of concerns for Harry's safety. He must have run from the house when she opened the door, excited by the prospect of the walk by the river. Joan scolds him quietly.

"Oh, the naughty dog," she says.

There's no point standing and staring helplessly down the street, though. She has to go after him. She turns to go back into the house to get her coat and to put something on her feet for the muddy path by the river. As she moves, she catches sight of a flash of motion in what appears to be a window in the wall of the hallway. Joan doesn't recall a window like that in the hall, a strange silvery window with an ornate frame. An old woman is watching her through the strange window. Joan speaks to the woman querulously.

"You gave me an awful turn peering at me through that window like that."

The woman says nothing. She and Joan look at each other. Harry must be well on his way to the river by now, thinks Joan.

"I wish you'd stop staring at me like that," she says. The woman's face seems familiar, as she stares and stares.

"Are you my grandma? How did you get here?" Joan asks, but before the woman can answer, Joan has left the house, as panicky thoughts about Harry flood into her mind.

"Harry?" she calls quaveringly, as she walks along the familiar avenue where she has lived for so long. "Harry?"

TWO

When he woke up on his fourteenth birthday that September morning, Cat knew that concentrating through the boredom of the eight lessons of the school day was going to be more difficult than usual. The prospect of choosing and buying his own birthday present independently on his way home from school filled his chest with a swelling feeling of excitement which radiated down his arms and into his fingers. Despite an exuberant need to throw off his duvet, though, he remained motionless, fixing an unblinking stare on the row of books which occupied the shelf at the side of his bed: *Grimm's Fairy Tales*, *The Chronicles of Narnia*, two volumes of *The Earthsea Trilogy*: stories which had accompanied his childhood before reading had started to become a painful chore. He counted through the first fourteen prime numbers. A voice, smaller than his, but his own nonetheless, quietly whispered to him, warning him that to leave the bed before he had counted a prime for each of his fourteen years would be to invite disaster. Something would keep him from going. The shop would be closed. No present. Or worse.

He ticked off the first fourteen primes under his breath, and hurried out onto the landing, pausing at the threshold of his bedroom door to tap the toes of his right foot twice inside the bedroom. He entered the bathroom, toe-tapping twice again as he went in, showered, made his way back to dress (toe-tapping at each threshold in the manner prescribed by the small, persuasive voice), and, having heard the loose floorboard at the head of the stairs creak, went down for his birthday breakfast with his parents. At the bottom step, he stopped, went back up three steps, and then continued purposefully into the dining room without hesitating.

From behind him, his mother kissed the top of his dark head, as he took his seat at the dining table, which stood before a set of long windows. Through them, a long stretch of lawn rolled down to a line of well-established trees at the far end of the garden. His mother wrapped her arms around his neck and nuzzled her cheek against the side of his head.

"Happy birthday, Christopher darling," she cooed into his ear.

"Thanks, mum," he smiled, looking down at the place mat in front of him, on which lay an interesting pile of envelopes.

"Happy birthday, Cat," said his father, roughly aspirating the aitch in an accent which was not quite English, but impossible to place after almost twenty years of living in Yorkshire. "There's something for you in those envelopes."

His mother released her hold on him as he slit the first envelope neatly open, extracting a card: *Happy 14th Birthday to our darling son, Christopher, with lots of love, Mum & Dad xxx*

He set the card, with its embossed number 14 and a picture of a boy playing a guitar, upright in front of him, and opened the next envelope. A fat wad of banknotes nestled inside.

"It's money," said his father, unnecessarily. "Like you asked. Enough for a guitar, we hope."

"I'm sure you'll find one you like, Chrissie," said his mother. "But we can always arrange to come with you to buy it, if you like."

Cat shook his head, smiling at both his parents.

"Thanks, dad. Thanks, mum," he said. "But it's OK. I'd rather go and look by myself on my way home from school this afternoon."

"Just make sure you don't let them con you," said his father, taking a slurp from his mug and spooning cereal into his mouth.

"Don't worry," Cat replied. "The guy at one of the shops is really cool. He wouldn't rip anyone off. He really loves guitars."

"You never know," warned his father.

Cat opened the two remaining envelopes before him, netting a further twenty pounds and two more cards from god-parents he had never met. As he set their cards neatly beside his parents' card, and tidied the empty envelopes into a stack with edges aligned, he silently recited his mantra of prime numbers to ward off the possibility of Tony, the proprietor of Music Workshop, overcharging him and selling him a dud.

101, 131, 151, 181, 191, 313, 353, 383, 727, 757, 787, 797, 919, 929, 10301

He repeated the progression to himself, and Tony's face in his mind's eye, resumed its benevolence and enthusiasm for musical instruments, as he went through the reassuring, calming sequence. His mother placed a bowl of cereal on his place mat and poured tea from the rotund brown teapot into his mug. Cat added milk and sugar, and set about eating.

After breakfast, he collected his schoolbag and pulled on the jacket of his school uniform, stowing the envelope of money, supplemented further from his secret stash of savings, into the inside pocket. It felt satisfyingly substantial rubbing against his chest whenever he moved his left arm. Grey-suited and red-and-black-striped-tied, he opened the front door, calling to his parents who were still at the table in the dining room.

"I'm off to the station," he shouted. "See you tonight." He performed the toe-tapping ritual and stepped over the threshold, just as his mother emerged into the hallway. The ghost of a frown passed over her face before she spoke.

"Let me kiss you goodbye," she said. "You're not too old for a goodbye kiss."

"'Bye, Cat," called his father's voice, as his mother approached. "Have a good day."

His mother came out to join him on the straight path which led down to the front gate. Overhead, the big trees obscured the sky.

"Have a lovely birthday at school, Cat," said his mother. "And don't spend too long choosing your present. We'll see you at tea-time."

Cat smiled at her. He liked it when she used the nickname which his father always called him. He turned from her. The path led away to the gate and out onto the gravelled way which connected the house to the main road.

"And Cat," his mother's voice behind him said, "go straight to the gate. You don't need to stop on the path. Just go."

A tight feeling of misery lodged itself behind Cat's eyes. "OK," he said, and he set off down the path. At the third, fifth and seventh steps, a horrible sensation permeated his body as he did not hesitate on his way towards the gate. He pulled it creakingly open, and went out onto the gravel. Behind him, he heard the front door close. Slowing his steps, he glanced over his shoulder at the house. Its windows stared back blankly. The door, black in the morning light and shadowed by the trees overhead, was firmly shut. No-one was watching as he turned, quietly re-opened the gate, and went back to the doorstep. Once again, he made the journey down the path, but this time he stopped, as required by the protocols, at steps three, five and seven. Then, he continued on his way to the railway station to catch the 8.10 train into the town.

By 3.30 that afternoon, he was able to reflect that he had been right about how difficult concentrating was going to be with thoughts of guitars in his head, but he had made it through, suffering the dullness of his teachers and classmates in the lessons and break-times of the school day. There was still half an hour to go before the bell would ring, but the end of his final lesson, Latin, was in sight, and he would be able to race through the school gates and out into the bustle of the world to visit Music Workshop and, if necessary, the other music shop further down the long straight road on the way to the train station.

From his desk on the raised platform at the front of the classroom, Mr Hellyer, the Latin teacher, was grinding through Demonstrative Pronouns. Known secretly to his pupils as Satan, perhaps because of the first four letters of his surname, his approach to teaching was unwaveringly traditional, centring on recitation and repetition, with strictly enforced standards of discipline. Cat and his classmates all had battered hardback books open on their desks, and were following a tabulated list of Latin words as the teacher read aloud.

"Now," he said in a voice which still reverberated with Devonian vowels despite years spent at one of the ancient universities and in teaching at a variety of minor public schools around the North of England. "You repeat after me: *hic haec hoc.*"

The boys' voices droned monotonously, repeating the alien syllables. Cat looked from his book out through one of the tall mullioned windows on the first floor of the school building. His desk stood at the edge of the classroom right next to a window with a tempting view of the horse chestnuts outside, which were larger versions of the trees in front of his own home. The thickness of their foliage was blocking the late afternoon September sun from penetrating into the classroom. Cat did not need to concentrate on the mindlessly repetitive task, having read through the table of words once. The sequence had fixed itself in his mind, and he could allow himself to follow the chorus of voices without thinking. From far away he heard Satan's voice as the recitation ended.

"It's getting dark in here. Boulton, switch on the lights, will you?"

There was a pause, as a gangly boy levered himself out of his desk in the front row and went to flick the light switches by the classroom door. Six fluorescent strip bulbs hanging on chains from the high ceiling flickered into life.

"That's better," said Mr Hellyer. "Now we can see what we're doing. Once again: *hic haec hoc.*"

Boulton had returned to his seat and again the droning chorus began. Cat's Latin text and his exercise book sat squarely in the centre of his desk with his pen, a pencil and a twelve inch ruler lined up in a precise pattern in the right hand corner of the desktop. He repeated the words with the rest of the class, continuing to watch the leaves of the trees through the glass which now held a vague reflection of the room's interior. A movement, glimpsed simultaneously from the corner of his eye and in the dim mirror of the window, made Cat turn his head. The boy who sat in the desk next to his had reached across to nudge Cat's ruler out of alignment. The pattern of his writing implements had been disturbed, so, as the class continued to recite and repeat the Latin words, Cat patiently replaced his ruler so that it lined up precisely in relation to his pen and pencil. The boy's profile stared straight ahead, but his lips curved in an amused line as they moved in time with the recitation.

At the front of the room, Mr Hellyer rose from his desk, and turned towards the whiteboard, beginning to write with a black marker pen in neat block capitals.

"In your exercise books," he said, when the boys had finished reciting the last of the Latin words, "write a neat title DEMONSTRATIVE PRONOUNS, colon, THIS." As he spoke, he wrote the words on the board, and underlined what he had written, his back towards the class. Cat's neighbour again reached over in a swift movement and pushed the ruler slightly.

"Stop it, Gadsby," muttered Cat through clenched teeth. He realigned the ruler, then opened his exercise book and picked up his pen, writing the title as Satan had instructed.

"We are going to copy down a table of all the forms of the Demonstrative Pronoun, HIC," continued the teacher in his formal, measured voice with its countryman burr, "and your homework will be to learn them for a test on Friday." He began to write out his own version of the table on the board, and Cat followed his example, making sure that his words were evenly spaced and aligned on the page under his pen. The class, engaged in its mind-numbingly dull task, was silent save for occasional shuffling and sighs as the boys worked. Mr Hellyer, inscribing the Latin words with slow precision, seemed oblivious to the thirty boys behind him. Cat's neighbour reached suddenly over with his ballpoint pen and drew a ragged pattern of dots across the page of the exercise book.

"Gadsby!" snarled Cat, and lashed out at his tormentor's arm, incensed by the violation of his book. "You –" His anger and infuriation were making words evaporate from his mind. He struggled for a suitable epithet. "You idiot." The word burst from him as an elongated screech. He realised that he had stood up from his desk, and was looming over Gadsby who was cowering away from him.

"Thomas!" bellowed Mr Hellyer, turning from the whiteboard to face the class. "Get away from Gadsby. What do you think you're playing at? What is the meaning of this outburst?" His intonation imbued his final word with a mixture of horror and disgust.

"But, sir," pleaded Cat, brandishing his exercise book and displaying the evidence of Gadsby's vandalism. "Look. He's put dots all over my book."

"Stop being such a *'histrio'*. An actor. Histrionic. Sit down and get a grip of yourself, lad."

Sobs were swelling in Cat's throat, forced upwards by a sense of intolerable abuse and injustice.

"He's an idiot, sir," Cat gasped, and then, losing control of himself, "An idiot!" he shouted.

"Thomas," snapped Mr Hellyer. "Enough. I will not have boys shouting insults in my class. Get out. Go and stand outside the door."

Cat stood for a moment at the side of his desk, hesitating, then threw his exercise book onto his desk and marched across the classroom to the door.

"When you have calmed down, I shall consider allowing you to rejoin us," said Hellyer, as Cat opened the door and stepped outside. "Now, the rest of you get on with copying down these pronouns."

Outside the classroom, Cat felt a terrible urge to slam the door as he pulled it shut, but resisted and closed it with exaggerated care. He stood with his back to the wall, breathing deeply, and regretting throwing down his exercise book. The derangement of his desktop pressed heavily on his thoughts as he tried to calm himself by reciting the primes at a measured pace.

2, 3, 5, 7, 11, 13, 17, 19, 23, 29, 31, 37, 41, 43, 47

As each number rose in his mind like a link in a restraining chain, he felt that he was regaining control, and gradually his breathing became gentler. From inside the classroom, the muted sound of Mr Hellyer's voice addressing the class reached him, but he did not try to make out what was being said, allowing himself instead to drift, borne away on a calming sequence of inviolable numbers. It was better to be outside on the quiet corridor, removed from the unpredictability of the interactions of the class. A bank of tall lockers ran along the wall facing him, painted grey, each with an identifying number stencilled onto its door. Along the classroom side of the corridor, ancient-looking, scarred benches like the pews of a church were positioned where boys would leave books and bags unwanted during lessons. Cat went and sat on one of them, staring across at the locker numbers, fixing his gaze on number 131, pleasing for its symmetry and wholeness. He continued to count off the prime numbers in his head as the minute hands of the clocks throughout the school climbed against the pull of gravity towards the hour.

Suddenly, at the sound of an approaching, slow tread ascending the staircase at the end of the corridor, Cat threw himself to the floor and, crawling, crept under the bench he had been sitting on. He lay, his back hard against the wall, his eyes half-closed, and watched a pair of polished black Oxford shoes come to a halt in front of him. Beneath the bench it smelled of dust and old wood. The floor under Cat's body was varnished, but the shine became more and more faded until the wooden boards were a matt grey in the middle of the corridor, worn away by generations of schoolboy feet. The shoes, which stood about a yard from Cat's nose, belonged to Mr Pole, the Headmaster. Like any boy sent out onto the corridor, Cat had decided that it would be better not to be discovered standing ignominiously outside the classroom door.

"And who do we have under there?" enquired Mr Pole's deep baritone. The voice was quiet, but filled Cat with fear. Tad, the Head's predictable nickname with the boys, was known to have little time for foolishness. Hiding under benches, it occurred to Cat, probably fell squarely into that category. He recited the first ten prime numbers under his breath before speaking.

"It's me, Thomas, sir," he said. "I'll come out, shall I?"

"I think that would be an excellent idea, Thomas," said Mr Pole, calmly. "Then we can have a civilised conversation, face to face, rather than face to bench."

Cat counted off another ten numbers in his head,

"Come on, lad," bellowed the Headmaster, suddenly. "We haven't got all afternoon."

Cat scrambled out from under the bench and rose to his feet in front of the suited figure who stood about a head taller than him. Mr Pole was looking down over half-moon glasses at Cat's dishevelled appearance. The dust from the floor had streaked his jacket and trousers with bands and patches of greyish white deposit. The Head reached out a large hand and batted Cat's shoulder gently, making him flinch.

"I must speak with the Porter about the cleaners," he said, removing a smear of dust from Cat's lapel. "It's disgraceful that boys cannot hide in this school without becoming filthy." He raised his eyes to look Cat in the face. "What were you playing at, Thomas? It's not like you to be such a gorp."

"I'm sorry, sir," answered Cat, fixing his gaze on the Headmaster's tie which was striped with a pleasingly symmetrical sequence of lines in three shades of blue. "Mr Hellyer sent me out, and when I heard you coming up the stairs, I was scared of what you would say. So I hid." There was a pause, as Mr Pole allowed the foolishness to hang in the air. "Under the bench." The foolishness continued to hover, like a cumbersome bird flapping slow wings behind Cat's head. He felt himself blushing.

"And why did Mr Hellyer find it necessary to send you out, Thomas?" The Head's voice held a note of genuine enquiry, as though he felt it important to understand. Cat felt a similar need to explain, although usually he did not relish talking about his motivations.

"I had a …" He searched for the right word. "I had an outburst, sir. Someone did something, and I called him an idiot. In a loud voice." He looked up from the Head's tie and saw the man's calm, grey eyes looking down over the tops of his little glasses. There was a benevolence and sympathy in his regard as he gave a sigh and looked at his watch.

"Sit down, Thomas," he said, taking a seat himself on the bench over Cat's hiding place. He patted the space next to him with the flat expanse of his hand. "There's still some time before the bell rings, and I'd like to have a chat with you."

He sat back, stretching his legs out in front of him, crossing his ankles, and folding his arms across his chest, as though he were taking a rest on a bench in one of the municipal parks around the city. Cat sat next to him, hunched forward with his forearms on his thighs and his hands clasped together. He jigged his feet up and down nervily.

"They call you Cat, don't they, Thomas?" asked the Head. "Why is that?"

"It's my initials, sir," Cat answered. "Christopher Andreas Thomas."

"Ah, yes, of course," drawled the Head. "But it could have been because you seem so nervous always. Like a cat on hot bricks."

Cat was suddenly aware of the movements of his legs, and set his heels on the floor. The jigging stopped.

"I suppose so," he said. "I'd never thought of that."

"You know what some of the boys call me?" asked the Head, conversationally. Cat felt nonplussed. He had not expected to be discussing nicknames when he had been discovered in his ridiculous hiding place.

"No, sir," he lied.

"Tad," laughed the Head. "Because my surname's Pole. Quite amusing, and perhaps inevitable. But it doesn't really say anything about me – my character, or even my appearance. A really good nickname should have some wit about it, I always think. Wit, as in intelligence, I mean. And Cat is an intelligent nickname for you, Thomas, because you are like a cat on hot bricks. I've noticed this, and your teachers have mentioned it before at meetings."

Cat was beginning to feel an uncomfortable, hot embarrassment, thinking that he had been the subject of discussions at 'meetings'.

"Your teachers have commented," continued the Head, "on some peculiarities ..." He corrected himself. "No, that's wrong. Some unusual mannerisms which they have noticed. They tell me that you like everything to be – just so. And that you can get flustered when things are not. Is that a fair assessment?"

Cat could feel unaccountable tears welling in his eyes, and a kind of hot fullness in his throat and nose, which made speaking difficult. His feet started jigging again, but he did not try to quell the movement.

"It's true, sir," he said. "I do want things to be in order, and it bothers me when they're not."

"And there are things you do to try to control this disorder." The statement had the inflexion of a question, and Cat had the urge to share with this benevolent, relaxed-seeming man some of the torments which harried his mind. His jigging intensified.

"Things need to be in order," he said in a small voice. "Because if they're not, bad things might happen. But if I do other things, they won't. I know it sounds stupid when I say it, but inside, it's real. Really real."

A voice, indistinct through the classroom door, said something and there was a burst of muffled laughter and the sounds of movement. The Head looked again at his watch. He made a quietly reassuring murmuring noise of encouragement.

"Mmhmm?"

"I think that if I repeat things, or if I count in a certain way, bad things won't happen. When I was little, I needed to recite my times tables over and over to prevent things happening, but now I count prime numbers a lot. Or palindromic primes. Or sexy primes. It can get very tiring."

"I'm not a mathematician, Thomas," said the Head. "Though I believe your father is. Palindromic? Sexy primes?"

"Prime numbers which read the same backwards and forwards, sir. Like 101, 10301. And sexy primes are primes which differ by six – from *sex* in Latin – like 7, 13 and 19. If I recite these sequences, it makes things …" He paused again to search for a suitable word. "Safer."

"I see," said Mr Pole. "Or at least I think I see. And you've learned about all these things from your father?"

"Yes, sir. We've always liked doing maths things together. Puzzles, games. You know."

The sounds of movement inside Mr Hellyer's classroom had increased, as desks were being moved, and chairs scraped along the floor in anticipation of the four o'clock bell. The Headmaster stood up, and Cat followed his cue.

"Very interesting," Mr Pole said. "I'm going to think about what you have told me, but first we are going to see Mr Hellyer, and you are going to apologise for your outburst. No matter what the provocation, it is never acceptable to shout insults. You know that, Thomas."

"Yes, sir," answered Cat. "I'm sorry, sir."

With sudden shrillness, the electric school bell sounded, making Cat jump, despite its predictability. The classroom door opened almost immediately and a stream of boys began to emerge. Other doors further along the corridor also opened, each sending forth a flood of grey-suited, noisy adolescents. Their voices dropped as they passed Mr Pole and Cat, who were waiting for the last of Mr Hellyer's students to leave, but swelled again after a few strides. The last of the boys, two child-sized businessmen carrying briefcases which were too big for them, left the classroom, wishing Mr Hellyer a respectful goodbye, and Mr Pole propelled Cat gently through the doorway with a guiding hand on his shoulder. Hellyer was facing the board, erasing his neatly formed Latin pronouns with meticulous wide sweeps of a whiteboard duster.

"Mr Hellyer," said the Headmaster. "Could we have a moment of your time?"

Hellyer turned around, a look of surprise on his face. "Of course, Mr Pole," he began, just as the surprise changed to concern when he saw Cat at the Head's side.

"Oh goodness," he blurted. "Thomas, I'd forgotten all about you." He looked over to Cat's place where his disarranged books were still occupying the desktop.

"Never mind," said the Headmaster, overlooking the teacher's neglect. "I believe there was some trouble in your lesson, Mr Hellyer? Thomas has something to say to you." Mr Pole appeared to have been distracted by something outside the window, and he wandered over to peer through the glass as he spoke. "Thomas?" he said.

"Sir, I'm very sorry for my outburst in your lesson," said Cat, looking at the floor around Mr Hellyer's shoes. One of the laces had come undone, and was trailing on the ground like an emaciated reddish-brown worm. The teacher made a humphing noise in his throat.

"You know I will not tolerate disruption in my class, Thomas. We have much to get through this year. We can't afford to waste time on foolishness. I want you to promise that this will never happen again." He shuffled his feet as he finished speaking, and the brown worm wiggled a little. Cat stared at it.

"Well, Thomas?" demanded Mr Hellyer. "Can you promise me that?"

Cat continued to watch the worm. "I don't think I can, sir," he answered thoughtfully. Mr Hellyer shuffled again and the shoelace wriggled.

"What?" he said with an angry inflexion in his tone. Cat continued quickly.

"I can promise to try to never let it happen again, sir," he said.

The headmaster turned from the window. "I think that's a reasonable promise, Mr Hellyer, don't you?"

"Yes, I suppose so," said the teacher. "And very honest – *probitas laudatur*, as Juvenal has it. Right, Thomas. Get your books and off you go."

"Thank you, Mr Hellyer," said the Head, who was on his way towards the door, as Cat scurried over to collect his books and writing implements from his desk. "Oh, and Stanley," Mr Pole added as he reached the doorway, "your lace is undone."

Hellyer looked down; then went to sit behind his desk as the Headmaster left the room.

"Thank you, Mr Pole," he said to the Head's back. "Come on, Thomas," he continued to Cat. "Get a move on, lad."

Cat had arranged his things in a neat pile and was following the Headmaster.

"Goodbye, sir," he said. "And I'm sorry again."

"Humph," said Mr Hellyer from his bent posture behind his desk.

Cat left the classroom, quickly toe-tapping twice as he went across the threshold out onto the corridor. Mr Pole was there waiting for him.

"One last thing, Thomas," he said.

"Yes, sir?" He had not realised previously how humane the man with his forbidding demeanour could be. It was not difficult to speak to someone who created a space in which to talk.

"Why the prime numbers? The – what did you call them – palindromes and *sexy* primes?"

"I don't know, sir," Cat answered. "They're kind of – pleasing – complete – safe."

"Perfect?"

"Yes," agreed Cat. "I suppose so."

"You're a perfectionist, Thomas. That's not a bad thing in itself. But, it's also fine to make mistakes, if you learn from them in the end. And a bit of chaos is sometimes a good thing too." He began to walk away. "Bear that in mind, if you can."

"Thank you, sir," said Cat. "I'll try." Clutching his books, he rushed to the staircase. It was well after four o'clock, and he would have to hurry to have enough time in Music Workshop before they closed.

* * *

It had been a cool and wet July so far, but Joan was at last wearing her summer dress with the white pleats which fell just below the knee. Her double-breasted, waist-length jacket with the sailor-style flap collar was, admittedly, making her slightly too warm as the temperatures had at last risen into the high seventies, but she would not dream of taking it off, and anyway it looked so modish, so true to the jaunty mood of the fashions of the first year after the end of the dreadful war. She was aware of her own vanity as she walked along the pavements, trying to catch a glimpse of herself in the windows of the houses she was passing. Although many of the buildings were not even ten years old, built soon after the founding of the Garden Village at the end of the first decade of the new century, their gardens had already become established, and opportunities to admire her increasingly womanly figure were scarce through the shielding foliage. But occasionally, between the hedges and trees, reflected in the panes of a bow window, there she appeared, a simple but pretty straw hat on her head, which she held high and proud. She slowed her pace to prolong the image; then walked on, round the curving bend of Maple Grove, past the long straight walk of Elm Avenue, flanked by trees in full leaf, onto Village Road and right into Cherry Tree Avenue.

The street names were evocative of the Arcadian idyll intended by the founders and architects of the unexpectedly rural area of a severe Yorkshire city, sitting on a neglected reach of the county. It was a privileged place to have grown up, in easy proximity to the busy central streets, but far from the rougher areas to the West, and right next to the green expanses of the nearby park. The wide areas of grass and trees had been Joan's playground for as long as she could recall. The boating lake, which she remembered being built when she was seven or eight years old, still drew her with its promise of adventure: the idea of taking the oars herself and not having to rely on her brother Henry was an ambition she still entertained, even though it would be unladylike.

On that July day in 1919, Joan was particularly aware of being ladylike, amid the dignified architecture of her village-in-the-city, as the sun shone down propitiously from an unusually brilliantly blue sky. She was fourteen and would be starting a secretarial course at the end of the school year which was just around the corner. A whole new era of her life would be opening up, away from the confines of the local school's two crowded classrooms. She would be meeting exciting new people, and would be one step closer to becoming one of the ladies she admired so. And, in addition, on that particular day, she was hoping to catch a glimpse of the young man in his nautical uniform.

Up ahead, standing in the shade of the archway which led into the Garden Village's Shopping Centre, Joan's best friend, Muriel, was waiting. Although there were very few shops and their stock, on the whole, held little for two fourteen year olds interested in the fashions of the day, this was an attractive place to meet and walk and share confidences. A colonnade ran along the three sides of the building, giving the place a continental air of elegance and sophistication, although the shops were typically Yorkshire. Ox beef, proclaimed the sign in Mr Partington's window, which made Joan shudder whenever she read it and thought of the sinewy meat. As she drew level with her friend, she noted with a twinge of shameful satisfaction that Muriel's flap collar was not sitting as neatly on her shoulders, nor did it emphasise the slenderness of her neck as well as Joan's did. Her greeting, though, was fervent with friendship.

"Hello, my dear." Joan enunciated the words in the style of the older girls she knew from around the Garden Village, carefully aspirating the aitch so as not to sound common. "Have you been here long? It's not five yet."

As if to prove her wrong, the clock in its domed turret on top of the arched entrance to the Shopping Centre just then began to strike the hour. The coincidence set the girls to giggling, and Joan linked her arm through Muriel's, leading her further into the shadows and then out into the cloistered court with its central shrubbery and flower beds.

Arm in arm, the girls turned to the left as they emerged from the archway, preferring to stand in front of Hammond's drapery shop rather than Mr Partington's, the butcher. From this vantage point, there was a clear view right across the courtyard to the streetlamp on the corner of Beech Avenue, a favoured place for nautical young men to congregate before they headed home for their tea. Joan and Muriel stood, unspeaking, scanning the courtyard, but although there were a few women leaving the shops and a handful of men looking as though they were on the way home from work, there was nobody who the girls were keen to look at.

The clock finished its chiming of the hour, just as, in the distance but clearly on their way to stand at the foot of the lamp post, there appeared three young men in the nautical uniform of the Trinity House School in the Old Town of the city. Muriel's elbow nudged Joan unexpectedly hard in the ribs; then Joan's arm was squeezed tightly.

"Look, Joan," muttered Muriel, but no encouragement was needed for Joan already had her gaze fixed on the tallest and handsomest of the three. A more impartial observer would have been hard pressed to distinguish between the boys' heights; they all looked tall in their long bell-bottomed trousers and waist-length mess jackets with their smart lines of buttons running upwards to each tiny lapel. Beneath their peaked sailor caps, which they wore with self-assured dash, two of the boys were just as handsome as each other, and were obviously brothers, sharing strong straight noses and broad mouths. The third of the trio was irrelevant to the estimations of the two girls. His only claim to a meaningful existence was in his role as friend of the two brothers.

From their vantage point under the over-hanging balcony running around the three sides of the Shopping Centre, Joan and Muriel continued their surveillance of the young men. Two of them had been occupying most of their thoughts for the past few weeks. They knew that they lived on Village Road, and that their names were Robert and Arthur. The boys' mother they knew to be a member of the Garden Village aristocracy, recognised and greeted with respect whenever she walked out. Their father, the girls also knew, since it had often been mentioned in adults' conversations, had been killed in the war, and had been given an important medal by the King. Joan and Muriel agreed that the boys' tragic loss of their father and the noble fortitude of their mother made the entire family all the more attractive.

"They're looking over here," observed Muriel, in a panicky whisper, and pulled Joan back against the wall of Hammond's shop.

"They can't see us, silly," said Joan. "We're in the shadows."

"What if they can, though," asked Muriel. "I'd be so embarrassed if they saw us watching them. What would they think?"

"They'd think there were two very pretty young ladies looking at them, and they'd ask us to walk out with them on Sunday in East Park," answered Joan. Muriel batted her playfully on the shoulder, but wore a serious expression as she did so.

"Do you think they would?" she asked, in a quiet, awe-struck voice.

"Let's go around the courtyard," suggested Joan. "Then we can cut across the shrubbery and walk straight past."

"Do we dare?" asked Muriel, but Joan was already leading her past the little shops under the cloistered walk. Although they were walking away from the young men, they would soon make a turn, walk across the shrubbery which filled the centre of the courtyard, and make another turn to bring them within ten yards of where the boys were standing. The girls said nothing as they walked arm in arm; each was concentrating on her posture and gait. As they made their approach, studiously avoiding looking at the boys and seemingly fascinated by the vista of houses on Beech Avenue, the faceless, nameless third of the trio bade the brothers goodbye. He passed Joan and Muriel, tipping his cap slightly while they in turn made bobbing motions with their heads. Muriel stole a glance at Joan, just as Joan turned her head towards her friend. In unspoken agreement, their postures stiffened, and they bustled past the two tall boys by the street lamp.

"Good afternoon, ladies," the elder brother greeted them, as they processed past. Both young men had raised their caps in greeting, but the girls did not halt. They continued along the pavement of Beech Avenue leaving the Shopping Centre behind. There was a brief pause and both girls experienced a filmy sense of anti-climax attaching itself to their shoulders like a grey bridal train. But then there came a polite shout from behind them.

"Excuse me." The cloak of disappointment detached itself from their shoulders, to be replaced by a white, diaphanous feeling of light hopefulness. Joan and Muriel paused and waited flutteringly as the boys caught them up in a few hasty strides.

"I think one of you might have dropped this," said the younger of the two. He was holding out a piece of pencil, no more than a stub, in strong-looking fingers. The girls looked at him, confused. His brother retrieved the pencil stub from him, pocketing it swiftly.

"My brother is mistaken," he apologised. "It was I who dropped the pencil. We are sorry to interrupt your walk."

The girls remained silent, neither of them knowing what to say, and Joan's heart was thumping so hard in her chest that she did not trust herself to speak in any case.

"Perhaps you would allow us to accompany you by way of apology for disturbing you?" asked the younger of the brothers. They were both smiling, but their eyes under the peaks were serious, giving them an air of shyness and vulnerability.

"That would," began Muriel, squeakily, "that would be very kind. We are just on our way home."

"I think you live on Laburnum Avenue, don't you?" said the elder. "My brother, Arthur, and I can walk with you. It's on our way."

Joan and Muriel caught each other's eye as he made his offer. He knew where they lived, which was certainly not on the way to Village Road. The implications of this knowledge and the boys' willingness to walk out of their way for two girls they had just met were thrilling. The young men placed themselves at the girls' sides. Arthur joined Muriel, and the other, older one positioned himself at Joan's shoulder. The pavements of the Garden Village were broad enough to allow four to walk abreast.

"By the way," Joan's young man announced," my name is Robert. Robert Fettes."

"How do you do?" said Joan. Her voice floated from between her lips into the warm, late afternoon air. The heat of the day had been lessening, but Joan's cheeks were hot as she spoke. The foursome began to walk, mindful only of the present, the summer smell of the trees over the Macadam of the road, and the alien, heavy scent of another's clothing in unfamiliar proximity. They were, at that important moment, heedless of history, and unthinking of the unlived years ahead; all that existed, for each of them, was now.

THREE

Cat's bedroom was dark, but a line of yellow light showed at the foot of the door, illuminating the first few inches of the carpet. He sat on the edge of his bed, loosely cradling the guitar, which after two years of dedicated, daily practice had become almost a part of himself. With his left hand, though, he was holding down an A minor inversion hard at the fifth fret. His arm was beginning to ache, and the strings were biting deeply into his index finger which spanned the Yamaha's neck. The joint of his thumb was burning with the unceasing pressure. His tiny, interior, me-not-me voice warned from the dark that he must hold the shape until his mother called again. The aching increased and he bit down on his bottom lip. It was strange how the sensations of pain, those in his arm and fingers, and that in his lip, were so different. And then there was the exhausting pain of the whispering voice with its threats and admonitions. His mother called up the stairs, insistent and frustrated.

"Christopher. This is the third time I'm shouting you. Come on." She emphasised the final word, elongating the syllable and biting down on the consonant. Cat released the pressure from the neck of the guitar and felt a tingling throb permeate through his arm, hand and fingers. He lay the guitar aside on the bed and stood up.

"OK, Mum," he called. "I'm coming. I'm ready anyway."

"It's nearly seven and a half," his father's voice called. "The reservation is for eight. We're going to be late, if you don't hurry."

Cat imagined his parents standing side by side at the foot of the stairs, his father in a dark suit and sober, tightly knotted tie, his mother in some kind of neat, pretty dress with a single string of pearls at her throat. They always dressed the same when going out for dinner to celebrate their wedding anniversary. Cat always wore jeans and one of his crew neck sweaters. They always went to the same pub-restaurant in a local village about half an hour's drive from the house. They always told Cat how his father had proposed to his mother in that very place. This year they would say it was nineteen years ago, three years before Cat was born. The conversation would be reassuringly predictable.

"It's half-past seven, not seven and a half, dad," he shouted as he opened his bedroom door, pausing at the threshold and tapping the toes of his foot twice. It was infuriating how his father, who spoke English fluently in almost every way, insisted on 'and a half' instead of 'half past' when telling the time. Cat went to the top of the stairs, sensing the loose floorboard move beneath his weight. His mother and father were no longer in the hallway, so he jogged down, stopped at the bottom step, and went back up three steps before continuing to the bottom. His mother was standing just inside the dining room doorway, watching him.

"I wish you wouldn't do that thing on the stairs, Chrissie," she said, a note of exasperation in her voice. "We're in a hurry and we haven't got time for messing around."

Cat stood at the foot of the stairs, a feeling of hot shame suffusing his neck and shoulders at having been discovered performing one of his rituals. He knew and understood his parents' frustration at what they saw as his weird behaviour.

"Well? Are we going then?" he asked combatively. "Come on. I'm not holding you up, am I?" He opened the front door and stood at the threshold, waiting for his parents. His father emerged from the dining room, wearing, as Cat had predicted, his dark suit and a plain tie.

"Hi, Cat," he said. "Come on, Mrs Thomas. Your carriage awaits." He jingled his bunch of keys in the air, and led his wife out into the drive at the front of the house. "Shut the door, Cat," he called over his shoulder, as they walked towards the car. It glowed a yellow-white in the evening gloom, reflecting the streetlights on the main road beyond the trees. Cat's father unlocked the doors, and he and his wife got in.

"Come on, Christopher," called Cat's mother.

Cat toe-tapped at the threshold, and pulled the front door shut, hearing the Yale latch snick into place. He pushed at the door and pulled the handle again. There was a brief toot from the car. His mother's face stared palely from the passenger side window. Her mouth moved, forming the words 'Come on.' Cat took a few steps towards the nearside rear door of the car and hesitated. There was another toot and a sharp tattoo on the window. He threw himself towards the car, opening the door and settling himself untidily into the back seat. As he pulled the door shut, his father released the handbrake and the car jerked forward out of the driveway, down the little lane, and onto the main road.

They drove in silence through the village, out onto one of the winding roads which threaded between the fields and low hillsides of the surrounding countryside. Black banks of trees loomed at the side windows, and were illuminated with a ghostly greyness briefly in the car's headlights as a bend approached. Occasional signs whizzed towards the windscreen: Slow Vehicles Turning. Farm Entrance Ahead. In the back seat, Cat sat, his right knee jigging nervously up and down, a feeling of distress and unease creeping along his limbs, as a quiet but insistent voice sounded in his head. Hedgerows flashed past as the car travelled further from the house and closer to the pub where they had booked their table. A mysterious triangular sign bearing only a bold exclamation mark appeared and disappeared. Cat's leg jigged with increased violence.

"Dad," he said. "Dad, can we go back? I don't know if I shut the door properly."

His mother made a tutting noise with her tongue against the roof of her mouth.

"Dad. I really need to check that I shut the door."

"I saw you close the door, Cat," his father intoned. "We don't need to go and check."

He continued to drive.

Cat leaned forward in his seat, intruding his head and shoulders into the front of the car. Both his legs were jigging now.

"I need to check the door again, Dad," he insisted. His voice was trembling. He reached a hand towards his father's shoulder. "Dad, please."

His mother turned in her seat slightly.

"Christopher. Sit back. Leave your father alone while he's driving."

Cat's hand between the two front seats grabbed at his father's arm, pulling at the jacketed sleeve.

"Cat. Let go," his father shouted, trying to free himself. There was a flurry of noise and movement inside the car, a sudden brilliance as headlights appeared around a bend in the road, followed by an intense compression of sound and space. A sweetly metallic tang filled Cat's nose and mouth.

* * *

Mrs Kershaw had come to live with her son, Harold, his wife, Mary and their infant daughter, Joan, after her husband, and the trawler he captained, had been lost somewhere in the icy seas off Iceland. After another couple of years, the family was added to by the arrival of Joan's younger brother, Henry, and the three generations of Kershaws lived comfortably together in surroundings designed to evoke a forgotten rural idyll. As Joan was growing up, old Mrs Kershaw's heavy Victorian mourning and her quiet air of resignation steadily made her appear more and more ancient in the eyes of her grand-daughter, as she went placidly about her business of helping run the household, seldom offering an opinion and forever deferring silently to her son's wife. People had always commented that her grand-daughter took after the old lady in looks, but, as she reached her teens, Joan became appalled at the possibility of ever being like someone so alien, dark and shut away.

Despite the reserve which surrounded her as a constant throughout Joan's childhood, in 1923 the old lady suddenly became unexpectedly interested and almost animated about matters outside the walls of 57 Laburnum Avenue, on the announcement of the wedding of Prince Albert and Lady Elizabeth Bowes-Lyon. Joan's own wedding to Robert Fettes was scheduled to take place just a fortnight after the royal match. Mrs Kershaw extended her interest beyond the royal wedding to include the preparations and proceedings of Joan's nuptials, and would only relapse into her withdrawn placidity once the ceremony at St Columba's had concluded and the Kershaw family had returned, without Mrs Joan Fettes, nee Kershaw, to the gabled house with its swooping pitched roof.

In one of her uncustomary pronouncements, Mrs Kershaw expressed her regret that Bob would not be wearing his Merchant Navy uniform at the ceremony. Prince Albert had worn full RAF dress in the rank of Group Captain, and looked splendid at the side of his bride in her fashionable, Italian-style gown. But Joan wanted her groom to wear morning dress, although it had had to be hired for the occasion, and Bob agreed with her, less interested in how he would look than in pleasing his young bride. Joan would, however, imitate royal precedent, and her veil would be secured by a chaplet of leaves picked from the trees of the area and fashioned by the hands of her grandmother just before the wedding. Everyone agreed that, as Joan left the house to walk along Laburnum Avenue to St Columba's Church near the corner of Holderness Road, she looked as lovely as the pictures of the royal bride in the newspapers.

Early in the morning of the happy day, before Joan began the process of dressing in her simple, drop-waisted wedding gown, Mrs Kershaw summoned her to her chair by the fireside of the front room. The grate was empty since the weather was warm. Joan sank to her haunches next to her grandmother, resting her palms on the arm of the chair.

"Yes, granny?" she asked. It was unusual, almost unheard of, to be so close to the old lady who normally hovered out of the way in the background, and took little part in the conversations and human interactions of the household. But for the past few weeks things had been different. Joan had begun to see that there was more to her old relative than the black carapace had always suggested.

"I wanted to have a little word with you before everything gets hectic, my dear," the old lady said, smoothing away invisible creases in her lap. It made Joan feel hot just to look at her in her heavy, dark dress. "I know you'll be keen to be getting ready, so I won't keep you long. I remember what it's like to be a bride. All the excitement of the day. And looking forward to being a wife. Your Robert seems like a lovely boy, and I hope he'll be good to you when he's home. Your grandfather was at sea, you know, and there'll be times when you'll miss him terribly when he's away. And worrying if he's safe. But that's what your life's like when you marry a seaman."

The black beads of her grandmother's tiny eyes scrutinised Joan as if expecting her to say something.

"I know, granny," answered Joan, smiling her most reassuring smile. "My friend Muriel is engaged to be married to Bob's brother when he comes home on leave in the summer." She patted the veined hands in the old lady's lap, noting the beginnings of liver spots and vowing, as she often did, never to forget her nightly ritual with the tin of Nivea. "We know what to expect." She made as if to rise, but her grandmother was beginning to speak again, and she sank back down.

"Your grandfather was taken from me." Mrs Kershaw continued to look down at her hands. "We had expected to go and live by the sea when he retired. Scarborough maybe, or Brid, but that wasn't to be. We had a good life together, though, and he always stayed home when his ship was in. Not like some of them on the trawlers, I can tell you."

Joan hoped that granny was not about to break the habit of all the eighteen years of her grand-daughter's life and begin to tell stories of the debaucheries of the trawler crews when they came home. "But what I wanted to tell you is this," she went on. "Whatever time you have together, make the most of it. You don't want to be thinking back in thirty or forty years, regretting things you did – or even worse - didn't do." The grey head sank a little in contemplation of the hands. There was a silence in the room, although muffled noises could be heard coming from elsewhere in the house. A voice, upstairs and distant, called Joan's name.

"How old are you, granny?" Joan asked, realising that she could not put a figure on her grandmother's age. The old lady's answer was predictably Yorkshire.

"I'm as old as my tongue and older than my teeth." But then she capitulated. "I'm sixty-one this year."

To Joan it sounded like a great age. She could not imagine being alive for so long.

"I'm grateful that we had this talk," said Joan. "And I promise, I will make sure Bob and I don't have any regrets."

"Children are a blessing," added Mrs Kershaw. "I don't know what would have become of me if I hadn't had your father to look after me. Especially after your grandad's ship was lost."

The voice from upstairs called again, more importunately.

"I was so thankful he didn't want to go to sea, and went to join Reckitt's after school. It would be a blessing if you could persuade your Bob and his brother to find something ashore, you know."

Joan straightened. Her legs had started to cramp from squatting beside her grandmother's chair.

"I don't think that will happen," she said jauntily. "I've got to go now, granny. Muriel's upstairs calling me to go and get ready."

She dipped her face towards Mrs Kershaw's head and planted a tiny, dry kiss on her cheek. The surprise at how soft the old skin was shocked her, and she gave an involuntary gasp.

"Go on with you," says Mrs Kershaw. "Don't go all soppy on me."

Muriel appeared at the door of the front room, carrying something white and flouncy in her arms.

"Joan," she said, impatience and importance mixing equally in her tone. "Come on. We have to get ready."

Mrs Kershaw remained immobile in her chair, her eyes fixed on the thin band of gold on her left hand which bit into the skin below the knuckle. The two girls hurried away to climb the staircase with its runner of Persian-patterned carpet secured by arrow-headed brass rods on every step. Their footsteps made a subdued, rapid tapping sound as they ran.

And then time flooded past, and a few hours later, having signed the register in St Columba's Church, and having bidden goodbye to their families after a brief reception in the Garden Village's Clubhouse, Mr and Mrs Robert Fettes set off to Hull Paragon Station where they caught a train on the Yorkshire Coast Line to Bridlington. Unknown to Joan, a three night stay at the Alexandra Hotel on the sea front had been booked for them.

They arrived late in the afternoon, both marvelling at the expanse and height of the hotel's frontage. They had been to the resort together on day trips while they had been courting, and Joan's family took regular holidays in the resort, staying in apartments at Mrs Maw's in Windsor Crescent near the sea front for many years, but neither of them was used to the opulence and luxury of the Alexandra, which faced the white-topped, grey-blue waves of the North Sea with aristocratic aloofness. When they arrived, they stood before the short, semi-circular flight of steps leading up to the pillared portico of the entrance like two peasants at the gates of a French chateau. Then, as they checked in,

Joan's excitement and gratitude gave way to nervous, concerned whispers to her husband who looked over-awed by the formality of the hotel's concierge as he inscribed their details in the ledger on the front desk.

"Can we afford it?" she asked, reaching her lips up towards Bob's ear. She could smell the macassar oil he had untypically used that morning for the ceremony at the church. Bob's head turned towards her and he gave a reassuring smile and nod.

"It's my god-father's wedding present to us," he said, and Joan felt a sense of relief and relaxation flood through her.

They followed the bell-boy up stairs and along corridors, eventually finding themselves waiting self-consciously as he unlocked the door to their room. It swung open and the bell-boy stood aside. Bob hesitated, seemingly unsure what to do next. Then he wrapped one arm around Joan's waist, hooked the other arm behind her knees and hoisted her lightly into the air. The bell-boy watched, an indulgent smile on his face.

"What are you doing?" laughed Joan.

"Carrying you over the threshold." Bob's voice was taut with a note of self-conscious doubt. Taking care not to collide with the jamb of the door, he manoeuvred Joan into the room and set her down next to the double bed. The bell-boy had brought in the bags and set them down.

"There are bathrooms down the corridor, sir," he announced. There was a pause. "And there is a lovely view of the sea-front from your window." The three faces in the room all turned to look at the window. With a sudden movement, Bob's hand went to his pocket, and he pulled out a coin which he proffered to the bell-boy.

"Enjoy your stay, sir. Madam."

The coin disappeared. The door closed, and Mr and Mrs Robert Fettes were alone.

"He's right," observed Bob, going across to the window. "It is a lovely view." Joan joined him, resting her head against his upper arm and looking out at the grey-blue water. White waves were ruffling the surface. White sails of yachts stood out against the horizon with geometrical sharpness. White clouds moved slowly high in the sky. Joan and Bob stood looking.

"We should go for a walk on the front," suggested Bob.

"Oh," said Joan. She removed her head from his arm. "Alright. But I'll have to change into something more comfortable."

"That's alright." Bob loosened his tie and threw it onto the bed. "I'll wait for you downstairs in the lobby." He went to the door. "Don't be long." He left the room and the door closed behind him, slowly and carefully. Joan looked around the room, at the double bed where the tie lay like a streamer forgotten after a children's party. She observed the two suitcases by the wardrobe. Then the door opened again, and Bob's head appeared.

"Don't forget the key," he said, and the door closed again. Joan experienced a strange sense of disappointment and loneliness, although she did not have the words to explain it to herself. She picked up her suitcase.

Twenty minutes later, Bob was looking up from the copy of the Yorkshire Post he had been reading in the lobby, as Joan approached. She had finally selected a pink gingham frock to change into, with a nautical style blazer over the top. Bob was levering himself out of his chair as she came towards him, holding out the key on its heavy fob.

"You look lovely," he breathed. "Very sea-sidey." He took the key from her hand and walked over to the front desk, setting it down in front of the concierge who was slowly turning the pages of his ledger.

"We're going out for a stroll," Joan heard Bob's voice telling him.

"Enjoy yourselves," the man answered, pushing the key to one side and returning to his task. Bob rejoined Joan, smiling an uncertain smile, and they stood together irresolutely, side by side.

"Where shall we go?" Joan asked, placing her straw boater on her head and pushing loose strands of hair away from her face. Bob picked up his own hat from the table where he had been sitting, and took hold of Joan's hand.

"We'll walk along the front and see what there is to do." He pulled her towards the hotel entrance. Outside, the wind had picked up slightly, tousling the sea into choppy waves beyond the stretch of lawn leading down to the steps to the beach promenade. Gulls wheeled overhead, making their mournful, shrill keening.

"Don't they make a racket," Joan observed. "It's like they're screaming and crying at the same time."

Bob answered with a laugh. "You're right there, love. Not the happiest sound for a honeymoon. Let's go down to the pier like we did the last time we were here, and then we can have tea at the Floral Hall or at the Coliseum."

They set off along the sea front promenade in the direction of the distant pier. Joan hooked her arm in the crook of Bob's elbow, and was starting to feel more at ease. The awkwardness of the past half hour since they had arrived at the hotel was gradually lifting. The breeze buffeted them as they walked along, and they both had to hold onto their hats which were in danger of being blown away. The seagulls' shrieking provided a constant accompaniment to their stroll, with the vast sea to their left and the crowded buildings of the town to their right. Joan began to find the insistence of their noise silly rather than disturbing as her mood continued to lift, freshening with the stiffness of the breeze. When they reached the pier, a late afternoon crowd was there, taking the sea air. Joan pointed to where a small group of people were gathered about half way down.

"Look, Bob," she said excitedly. "It's the weighing man."

For a penny each, the man on the pier allowed them to stand on his machine and see the large needle on the scale swinging round to record their weights in stones and pounds. Joan watched with pride as her new husband stood, tall and broad-shouldered on the platform, and the needle came to a juddery rest just beyond the marker for fourteen stones. Bob stepped down, patting his stomach above the waistband of his trousers.

"It's all muscle, you know," he told Joan. He grasped her wrist in his long, strong fingers. "Feel," he said, guiding her hand. Joan's palm encountered the hard, slightly yielding muscles of Bob's abdomen through the fabric of his shirt, and felt herself begin to blush in front of the weighing-machine man.

"Bob," she said, half-laughing, half-scandalised. "Not here." And she pulled her hand away, although her blood had quickened and she could feel her nipples hardening under her clothing.

"Your turn," said Bob, handing her up onto the platform of the machine. The needle traveled a fraction of its previous course and came to a halt halfway between the seven and the eight stone markers.

"My goodness," Bob laughed. "You're as light as a feather. We'll have to be careful that you don't blow away in the wind." Joan was laughing too, thanking the man, who raised his straw hat to them as they walked on towards the end of the pier.

"And you'll have to be careful one of those gulls doesn't take a shine to you and carries you off in its beak," continued Bob. Joan was smiling back, still thinking how light and lissom she must appear to Bob, to the weighing man, to all who saw them. Then, there flashed into Joan's head a sudden image of herself whirling away into an empty sky, her arms and legs flailing as fearsome wings beat above her.

"Oh, don't," she gasped, hooking Bob's arm again. "What a scaring thought." Holding on to Bob, and feeling his bicep taut in her grip, she felt a sensation of groundedness, as though with him she could never be taken or lost. He felt solid, full and safe. They stood for a while, arm in arm at the end of the pier, watching the water and the triangular sails of yachts and the slow, steady motion of a pleasure steamer making its way towards Scarborough to the north. They did not speak for some time, but it was a comfortable silence, filled with the sounds of the crowd on the pier, the strengthening breeze which would then relax, and the constant shrillness of the gulls. At last, Bob suggested that they make a move.

"How about some tea and a bite to eat?" he said. "We can go to one of the cafes at the Coliseum, and then they have dancing in the evening."

"That would be lovely," said Joan.

The Coliseum boasted in its advertising that it offered the finest ballroom in Yorkshire, and cafes which served throughout the day. Bob and Joan ordered tea, and ate a fish supper, taking their time and watching the Bridlington weekend people come and go until the ballroom opened at half past seven. Joan had always enjoyed dancing, allowing herself to be whirled lightly around the dance floor in Bob's confident arms. In the ballroom, she felt sure that all the other patrons were watching them, the bright, young, newly-wed couple, as the evening passed. Resting between dances at their table, Bob instructed Joan about what he knew about the Coliseum. He had read about it when it was newly opened the previous year.

"The floor you were just dancing on," he informed her, "is made of rock maple, you know."

"It is lovely," observed Joan. "And so comfy to dance on, like dancing on air."

"That's because it's laid on two thousand little springs," he explained, looking at his watch. "It's half past nine, Joan. If you're tired we could be getting back?" His statement ended with a question mark, making it sound like a request.

"Let's have one more dance first."

Taking Bob's outstretched hand, Joan followed her husband out into the centre of the floor. In her mind, she imagined the hundreds and hundreds of little springs bouncing up and down beneath their feet, yielding and then returning to their original positions, over and over again, lifting them up into the movement of the music. It felt reassuring to know about the springs. There was nothing mysterious about how they danced so lightly. Everything was real, and solid, and reliable.

The dance came to an end, the dancers standing and clapping the little orchestra on their dais at the end of the room. Bob led Joan out of the palatial building into the May evening where the breeze from the sea had grown to become a wind, and the sea gulls had disappeared from the darkening sky. The sun had set some time ago, although there were still vestiges of light in the margins of the sky, and it was not yet night. They walked briskly along the promenade, arriving back at their hotel, out of breath and cold, hurrying up the flight of steps from the beach. They quickened their pace across the expanse of lawn, and finally ran up between the pillars of the portico to issue into the lobby, panting and rubbing their arms against the chill.

"That sea breeze is definitely bracing," laughed Bob.

Joan waited while Bob retrieved their room key from the concierge. Then, arm in arm, they climbed the staircase towards their room. As they ascended, Joan found it difficult to catch her breath, and her heart was beating hard in her chest. Bob, too, seemed flushed from their walk, the chill of the sea air, the climb up the stairs. They arrived in silence at their door. Bob fumbled with the key and turned the handle. Standing aside, he allowed Joan to enter.

"After you, Mrs Fettes."

The chandelier in the centre of the ceiling cast an even light over the room. Bob's suitcase was still sitting where the bell-boy had placed it, and Joan's case was lying open on the chaise longue by the dressing table, displaying the clothing she had neatly folded when she was still Joan Kershaw a few hours ago. Someone had turned down the bedclothes while they were out, and a freshly cut sweet-pea flower had been placed on each of the pillows. One of the flowers shimmered a pale pink; the other glowed a deep magenta. It looked like a stain of blood on the pillow-slip. Joan picked up the pink flower, and held it to her nose, taking a deep draught of its airy, honeyed scent. It reminded her of early summer mornings in the park next to the Garden Village.

"Smell," she said, holding the flower out to Bob. He lowered his face towards her hand and inhaled, raggedly as though breathing was difficult.

"Lovely," he whispered, and embraced Joan, pulling her in towards his chest. She felt his hand find the back of her head, and tilted her face upwards so that he could kiss her. They had kissed before, many times, but now there was a forceful urgency in the way that he crushed his mouth against her lips. She felt his other hand move into the small of her back, as he pressed his groin against her hip bones. Then, he took a step back, saying briskly, "We'd better get ready for bed."

Unmoving, the sweet-pea in her hand at her side, Joan watched as Bob quickly pushed off his shoes, unbuttoned his shirt, and unfastened his trousers, which fell around his ankles, the braces looping like reins on a tangled black bridle. He kicked them away, and stood before her in his cotton singlet and underwear, slightly off-white, in contrast to the deep black of his socks, which were held in place by a pair of suspenders. He reached for Joan's hand, drawing it towards him, towards a swelling bulge in the front of his shorts. Joan thought of the packages of ox beef her mother used to send her to collect from the butchers'.

"What do you want me to do?" she whispered.

He took her hand, guiding her and she flinched in surprise at the heat of him, half expecting a cold flabbiness, but encountering a hot and sinewy hardness. She pressed her palm firmly against him, with a slight massaging motion. His hands were gripping her shoulders tightly; there was a sudden, jerking movement, and he pulled her hard towards him, holding her fast to his chest; he shuddered; and then let her go.

"Oh, Joan," he mumbled, turning away. "I'm sorry."

* * *

The reeds at the water's edge are thrashing in the gusting wind as Joan stumbles along the path, her coat ballooning about her. Harry must have raced ahead of her, always just out of sight, but she knows he is there leading her on to the river bank where he loves to walk.

"Oh, you naughty thing," she mutters to herself as she goes, breathless and worried. Where has he got to? Where is he? She looks around, from side to side, just in case he has run off the path and is hiding in the grasses, teasing her, ready to rush out, barking joyously at this opportunistic game of hide and seek. He isn't in the reeds. She knows he has run on ahead, and at any moment she will catch sight of him bounding along, coming towards her down the long, straight path with the grey expanse of water at its edge. The wind whips about her ears, making them ache with cold. Two gulls arc overhead, calling in their plaintive voices. The promenade is very empty for the time of day. Joan has been expecting many more of the weekend visitors to be out taking the air. There's Bob, waiting for her on the prom, ready to walk to the Coliseum again, and strangely, there's Harry too, sitting patiently at his feet.

"Bob?" Joan mumbles quietly. Something's wrong. Didn't Bob die, long before she ever got Harry?

"It can't be Bob," she says under her breath, and passes her free hand across her eyes. Her other hand clings to her handbag where the keys have been safely stowed away. Of course, it isn't Bob on the prom. It's the weighing man, who has found Harry. The good, obedient boy is sitting expectantly at the man's ankles, waiting for her. His tongue lolls from the side of his grinning mouth, and he looks up at her with intelligent, mischievous eyes. She quickens her pace as she draws nearer.

"Harry," she calls, as she approaches. "Oh, Harry. How did you get here?"

*   *   *

The old woman is calling 'Harry Harry' in her quavery old lady voice. She's not dressed to be out on the river bank – she's not really dressed to be out in public. Even though her coat covers her body, her pale nightdress billows in and out above her little wellies. If I had to imagine a weird old woman, she would be pretty close to what I've got in my head. She looks as though she is about to lose control of herself as she pushes against the gusts, turning distractedly from side to side, repeating the name, 'Harry, Harry'.

101, 131, 151, 181, 191, 313, 353, 383, 727, 757, 787, 797, 919, 929, 10301

If she doesn't take care, she will lose her footing and find herself crashing down into the bushes to her right or floundering among the mud and reeds to her left. Her frail limbs and torso do not look as though they could take much of that kind of rough treatment. She needs help, protection from herself, and there is no one here but me.

101, 131, 101, 131, 101, 131, 101

"Harry," she says, coming to a breathless halt, and looking down at my legs. Then she looks me in the face with an expression of empty distress in her eyes. Her mouth moves as if she is forming silent syllables. The skin of her face has a tired, stretched quality, greyish-pink. She clutches a shiny handbag in front of her, and fumbles with the clasp, trying to open it or close it, I'm not sure.

"Are you alright?" I ask.

"I thought you were Bob at first," she answers. "But then I saw you had Harry with you, and of course you couldn't be, because I got Harry long after Bob ..." Her voice drifts away, blown by the wind into vagueness. "But you can't be the weighing man either," she adds puzzlingly. She looks up and down the path. "And this isn't ..." There's a catch in her voice, the sort of sound people make when they're about to give in to a bout of tears.

"Where am I?" she says, and I feel a terrible wave of sadness flood through me, because I recognise her confusion and disorientation.

101

"You're at the river," I say in a reassuring tone as if speaking to a lost child. "Do you want me to take you home? It's cold out here. Where do you live?"

"I was looking for Harry," she says. "He ran off and I came after him. I thought he was with you." She scans the area again, tilting her head like she is trying to see around my legs in case I am hiding this Harry behind me.

"Harry is your dog?" I ask.

"That's right. And he ran off ..." Again, her words trail away on the breeze, and her face becomes vague and introspective. "But that can't be right," she continues. "Harry died. So how can he be here asking for biscuits and floating?"

I'm feeling a bit out of my depth, and I'm not sure how I can help her. I run through a couple of sequences of chords before I try another question.

"Maybe you've got your address written down somewhere in your bag?" I suggest, pointing at the shiny black handbag she is holding against her ribs. She looks at me uncomprehendingly. I've heard of old people losing touch with reality and becoming forgetful, but I've never experienced it face to face. It's quite scary to look into the vague emptiness of this woman's expression and watch her struggling to make sense of where she is. Or even who she is. I try again.

"Do you think it might be written down somewhere?" I nod at her bag. "In there?"

"I don't know what you mean," she says. "I thought you were going to weigh us. But I'm not sure I've even got a penny. Bob used to carry all the money." She starts to look in her bag, fiddling ineffectually amongst the contents and finding a purse. She opens it and her fingers fumble with an assortment of silver and copper coins. She extracts a two-pence piece, and holds it up to me.

"Is this a penny?" she asks. "It doesn't look right."

"No," I answer. "It's a two pee piece. Let's look in your bag and see if you've got your address. Maybe there's an envelope? You know, with your address on it?"

She is still scrutinising the coins in her purse, looking at them in puzzlement. She snaps the purse shut, and places it back in the bag. I can see that there is a lot of stuff in there. Paper and cloth, a bunch of keys, and some unidentifiable paraphernalia of old age. I try again.

"Do you want me to look in your bag and see if there's a letter?" I reach out towards the bag. Tentatively. I don't want to scare her or make her think I'm going to steal something. "I'll just look inside, and see if there's a letter."

"A letter?" she asks. "Who from?"

"I don't know. Your bank? Maybe a friend? If you've got your address, I can help to get you home. You do live round here, don't you?"

"My friend Muriel writes to me," she tells me, before her voice fades into the tones of reminiscence. "We were sisters-in-law when she married Arthur. They were away at sea a lot with the Harrison Line, Arthur and Bob, so Muriel and I used to write."

"And have you got a letter? With your address?" I feel like grabbing the bag and rifling its contents for something helpful.

"Muriel and Arthur lived in Bridlington," she informs me. "On King Street, but they moved later on when he came home for good. That was long after the war. His ships never saw action. Bob used to call him a deck ornament. And he called Bob a brass tap polisher. All in good humour, you know. But Bob's ship went down during the war, you know." She stops, and looks at me. I decide to try a different approach, because it's getting horribly cold standing in the wind.

"Look," I say. "Let's walk back towards the village, and maybe you can tell me where you live as we go."

"What about Harry?" she asks.

"Oh. Yes," I falter. "What does he look like?"

"He's a Border Collie," she says. "Black and white with a blue collar." She gives a confused shake of her head again. "But it's a funny thing, you know. I thought he died but then he was there in the house. And it was all very strange." I still don't follow what she is telling me about her dog.

"Maybe we'll see him on the way. Or I can come and look for him later, once we've got you home."

"This is the river," the old lady says, as if struck by a sudden epiphany. "How silly. I thought it was the sea."

"Do you remember where you live?"

She looks at me, and something takes place in her eyes, an acknowledgement of where she is standing and a realisation that I am not whoever she has been thinking I am.

"I live in the village," she answers. "Why are you asking? Who are you?" It is not a question born of confusion any more, but a genuine request for information. Her tone has changed since she first stumbled towards me a few minutes ago.

"I'll walk back with you, if you like," I offer. "To make sure you're alright. My name's Christopher. But people call me Cat."

"That's a funny name," the old lady says in what is now a conversational tone, not the stricken voice of her previous strange announcements and questions. "We never had a cat, but I did have a dog, Harry, for years."

"I know," I say. "You were looking for him, but I think it's better if we start back towards the village, and see if we can find your house."

I take a couple of tentative steps and thankfully she turns to join me. We set off at a painfully slow pace in the direction of the village. Miles away across the grey-brown flatness of the river the Lincolnshire landscape runs in a thin line along the horizon. The two gulls describe slow arcs in the sky and their voices call in outraged complaint.

"Bob always said that seagulls sounded as though somebody was torturing them," the old lady comments as we totter along. It requires a concentrated effort to maintain such a pace and not race ahead of her. "But I thought they sounded silly, like whiney children."

"Bob was your husband, was he?" I ask.

"That's right. We moved to the village when we bought the house after Bob got his Chief Engineer's ticket. That was in 1936. We'd been married – oh - thirteen years by then."

"Where is your house?" I venture casually, and she gives me the name of a road and a house number.

"I know where it is," I say. "Just off the main road. We'll be there quite soon."

It takes a lot longer than it should because of the pace we are going, but eventually we leave the river path, take a short cut down a wooded lane, and find the main road which runs through the village. There are few people about and only occasional vehicles. We've been chatting companionably as we've crept along. She's informed me her name is Mrs Fettes, and asks me to call her Joan. Joan's been telling me about how this part of the village has changed since she and Bob moved into their house, which, she says, cost £535 in 1936. Though she still seems a bit vague and disoriented, when she's talking about things in the past, she's quite coherent.

"This is your road," I say, as we come to the mouth of an avenue of neat bungalows leading down to a cul-de-sac where there are a few larger, semi-detached houses. "Which is yours?"

"Down at the end," she answers. "One of the semis. You can see it from here."

"I'll walk you to your door, Joan."

"Thank you, love. You are a kind lad. What did you say your name was again?"

We're walking along one of the narrow pavements, passing neatly trimmed privet hedges and little gates which lead through tiny front gardens to front doors flanked by bow windows. Most are screened by net curtains, and have similar looking ornaments sitting on window ledges looking out at rose bushes and shrubs. Most of the doors are painted white, although an occasional householder has chosen something more adventurous, a sunshine yellow or a sky blue. The door to Joan's house is white, or at least it had once been white.

"People call me Cat," I tell her again as we approach the brick and pebble-dashed frontage of her house. The bow windows have little stained-glass panes along the top, and the front door has matching stained glass in a kind of arty pattern. It obviously hasn't been changed since the house was built, and the woodwork and frames haven't been painted for a long time. "It's my initials," I explain. "Christopher Andreas Thomas." She's fumbling in her bag for the keys. "Here. Let me help you." I take the jangly bunch from her and insert the only Yale on the ring into the lock. I push open the door, and stand back to allow her to enter. An old smell drifts out through the open doorway, a mixture of well-used carpeting and upholstery, trapped, cold air, and tinned food. There's an undertone of soot too, a kind of railway smell from long ago.

"There were some Thomases who lived in the village," Joan observes as she takes back her keys. "I don't remember what happened to them. I think they went away."

"Will you be alright?" I ask. "By yourself?"

"Oh yes," Joan answers. "I'll be fine. Thank you, Christopher." She pushes the door shut, and I am left looking at flaking white paint, and a rather beautiful stylised flower in rose and honey glass shapes, held together by dark seams of lead. I wonder if I should knock on a neighbour's door, or call someone.

After a moment, I turn from the door, and realise with a sudden sense of strange vacancy that I cannot remember reciting a sequence or performing a ritual in all the time I have been with Joan.

101, 131, 151, 181, 191, 313, 353, 383, 727, 757, 787, 797, 919, 929, 10301

I set off up the avenue to go back to the tent.

FOUR

The house was flaunting its mid-1930s newness from the gleaming sheen of the slates on its roof to the pristine pink and yellow Art Deco panels in the windows and door at the front. The brickwork glowed redly in the May sunshine. The pebble-dashed upper third of the building was as clean as a beach newly washed by the outgoing tide. Bob and Joan stood in the unplanted patch of front garden and looked up at their new home. Bob jangled a bunch of keys; then threw them in the air and caught them safely in an outstretched hand.

"Well?" he asked. "How does it feel to be lady of the house?"

Joan laughed. "There'll be plenty of skivvying before I can call myself that. And you're going to be more of a gardener than lord of the manor for a long time, my lad," she said playfully.

Bob was smiling happily as they walked towards the front door. He separated one of the Yales on the bunch from the rest of the keys and inserted it into the lock. Joan watched in anticipation. The door swung open, revealing bare floorboards and a narrow, steep flight of uncarpeted stairs rising to the first floor. The smell of new wood, paint, and the cold odour of fresh plaster floated over the couple on the threshold.

"So much for a relaxing three weeks of leave," commented Bob, as he and Joan entered the house they now owned. "An Englishman's home," he said.

"Is his castle," concluded Joan. "But it's mine as well. After all, I'll be in it a lot more than you ever will, when you're away at sea." She contemplated him archly. "So it'll have to be an English*woman*'s castle."

"It can be whatever you want it to be, love. So long as you're happy here."

Bob strode into the front room whose big bay window looked out onto the empty front garden and the other new houses around the cul-de-sac. He deposited the keys on the mantelpiece above the fireplace, and stood proprietorially in front of the grate, beckoning Joan to join him by opening his arms for her. They stood together, Joan's head against his chest, looking out of the windows at the vacant houses where the clouds in the sky above were reflected, white on silvery blue. A memory of white waves and the sails of yachts flashed in Joan's mind.

"I wonder who our neighbours will be?" she mused.

"I don't know how many of the other houses have been sold yet," said Bob. "Not everyone can afford a house like this. Especially these days. And ours was the most expensive, because of the size of the garden."

"Five hundred and thirty-five pounds," breathed Joan in awe. "It's a lot of money."

"A Chief Engineer can afford it," boasted Bob.

"Don't you get too big for your boots, Bob Fettes," Joan warned, freeing herself from his embrace. "Remember, you and Arthur are going to be manual labourers for the next few days. You'll regret that big garden you're so proud of."

"Never," Bob laughed. "It'll be worth it when the fruit trees grow, and the vegetables – and the rose beds. No regrets about that when I'm ashore, I promise you."

Joan was smiling at his enthusiasm, pulling away from him to explore the rest of the house which was now home to the two of them after thirteen years of marriage, living first with Bob's mother and then in a rented terraced house in a quiet side street of an almost fashionable area in East Hull. Now that they had moved to the small but expanding village whose railway station was only twenty minutes from the big terminus in the centre of the town, they were feeling almost like country gentry.

"When Arthur and Muriel get here, they'll have the back bedroom," said Joan, climbing the stairs. "Our room is the front – the master bedroom." She opened one of the doors off the landing. New furniture clustered in the middle of the room, a bedroom suite in pale, limed oak. The double bed looked enormous, daunting, and dominating the space. There was a silence as they contemplated the room.

"I'll get Arthur to help me rearrange the furniture when he gets here," said Bob. "I expect the removals men have left the back room in a similar state." They left the master bedroom and went to inspect the other rooms on the first floor where furniture from the old house had been left, waiting to be arranged. A second, big bedroom overlooked the large back garden; a tiny box-room sat in a corner at the front of the house like an afterthought; a cold bathroom, tiled in black and white, completed the set of upstairs rooms.

"We'll need a paraffin heater in here," said Bob. "Especially in the winter." They descended to the ground floor again, Bob leading the way, and passed through the little hallway into the kitchen which led through a scullery to the back door. Bob patted his pockets in search of the keys.

"You left them on the mantelpiece in the front room," Joan told him. He tapped his forehead with the flat of his hand, and went to fetch the keys. Joan waited patiently by the back door and surveyed her kitchen, the scullery, and the little downstairs lavatory. A heavy chain hung from the cistern high on the wall. A damp smell of fresh water and new plaster hung in the air. Bob returned and opened the back door. The back garden seemed enormous, a dark brown expanse of roughly levelled earth with a wire fence running round it, marking its perimeter. A similar, but smaller patch lay off to the right, the garden of the adjoining semi next door, while to the left, and straight ahead to the north, farmland stretched away, open fields and dark stands of trees with occasional distant buildings on the skyline. In a huddled group just outside the back door, an assortment of trees and shrubs, their roots swaddled in coarse sacking, was waiting like a stunted platoon of emaciated, disgruntled soldiers. A selection of garden tools, spades and forks, rakes and hoes, a pick-axe, and some smaller, hand-held implements had been piled in a large green wheel-barrow.

Bob exhaled a long, whistling breath as he scanned the extent of the land before them.

"The farmer at the back levelled it with his tractor," he told Joan. "But there's still a lot of work. Look at it." He picked up a clod of earth, rich and dark, and crumbled it between his palms. It was soft and moist, like the muscovado sugar Bob had seen in consignments shipped from the West Indies, and had once brought back for Joan to taste. "We've got our work cut out for the next few days."

A boyish enthusiasm bubbled in his words, which Joan recognised, knowing that he was not complaining but looking forward to the challenge and working with his younger brother. She remembered watching their strong bodies standing on opposite sides of a tennis court in the centre of the Garden Village, and remarking the serious joy in their faces as they had exchanged shots across the net. More than a decade might have gone by, but Joan was certain that Bob and Arthur remained the same strongly physical, driven boys, despite the passage of the years. She took hold of his right arm above the elbow, feeling his bicep tighten under her touch. A sensation as of standing in the swell of a warm sea flowed over her, until a colder current of undefinable sadness made her shiver suddenly.

"Are you cold, love?" Bob asked.

"No, I'm fine," Joan answered quickly. "I was just wondering who our neighbours will be. You know, if we'll like them? If they'll be company?"

Suddenly, an exuberant rapping on the front door carried through the house and out into the back garden where they were standing. They heard a loud male voice calling, "Hellooo!"

"They're here," exclaimed Bob, leading the way through the scullery, kitchen and hallway to the front door where the outlines of two human forms loomed through the stained glass. Joan followed in his wake, excited to see her childhood friend and her brother-in-law. Almost a year had passed since they had last met in person, although they had been regular correspondents by post. Bob pulled open the door, and the two brothers greeted each other with boisterous laughter and handshakes at the threshold. Muriel pushed past the pair and embraced Joan.

"How are you, my dear?" she breathed, and the two women stepped back, joined at the hands, looking one another up and down.

"It's lovely to see you, Muriel," said Joan. "It's been such a long time. How was the journey?"

"A bit of a wait at Hull Paragon," answered Muriel, "and a stuffy compartment on the way here, but otherwise fine."

Bob and Arthur had been collecting suitcases and holdalls from the front porch, and were hauling the luggage up the stairs, their treads reverberating like heavy thunder in the hallway.

"It's nice to see you, Arthur," Joan called after them.

"Hello, Joan," he replied, his voice ringing clearly down the stairs as though issuing a command from the bridge of his ship. "I'll say hello properly when we've stowed these bags."

"Hello, Muriel," Bob's voice called from the landing above. "Welcome to the Fettes residence."

"Let's find the kettle and some crockery," suggested Joan, "and we'll make a nice pot of tea."

Half an hour later, having rummaged through boxes to find the necessary equipment and ingredients, Joan and Muriel had poured cups of tea for all four of them, served with condensed milk from a tin until fresh milk could be arranged. The men had taken their tea into the garden and could be seen standing in the centre of the plot, pointing and nodding as they sipped the hot liquid from their cups. Joan and Muriel watched their husbands through the French windows, standing shoulder to shoulder, sipping their own tea.

"It's going to be lovely, Joan, when you're settled in properly and the garden's established. I love being in Brid near the sea, but it must be wonderful to have all this countryside to look at." She made a gesture which included the garden, the fields beyond, and the dark trees on the distant wolds.

"We're very lucky," said Joan. "We've both got a lovely place to live, and a handsome, successful man." She gazed out at the garden, past the two men who were now pacing with exaggerated long strides, obviously measuring something. They resembled a pair of amateurish tightrope walkers, each holding his teacup carefully as if balancing as he moved along an invisible wire. Joan gave a strange yap of a laugh.

"Is everything alright?" asked Muriel, turning to her friend.

"Oh, Muriel," replied Joan in a suffocating voice. "Bob's wonderful. He's caring and lovely. He can't do enough for me. He's always attentive and …" She searched for another word; then repeated herself, "… and caring. It's just this new house. All this space. You know."

"I know, dear," said Muriel. "It's been thirteen years. How are we ever going to fill it all?"

*   *   *

With an overwhelming sense of embarrassment, Joan thinks that she has been a bit daft. Thinking things, like Dr Blaine had said. She worries about what that nice young man must have thought. Fumbling about in one of the drawers of the sideboard, searching for her pad of Basildon Bond writing paper, she thinks she should tell someone, in case it happens again. Or maybe she should telephone Muriel. She thinks she put the light blue pad back in the drawer the last time she used it. She tries to think when that was. It's so hard to think straight sometimes. Eventually, she tracks the pad down. It is sitting on the seat of her chair, with a ballpoint pen resting on top of it, ready to be used.

Joan settles herself into her chair, and, resting the pad on her knee, begins one of her more or less regular letters to her friend Muriel in Bridlington.

October, 1991

Dear Muriel,

I hope that all is well with you and Arthur, and that the weather in Bridlington is not too blustery. It's been windy here, especially down by the river, and cold, but not wet, though it has looked like rain. I've been having fires on and off since mid-September when the weather moved into autumn. I'm sorry if I haven't written for some time. I have lost track of when I last wrote to you – I'm also sorry that my handwriting is becoming spidery and difficult to read, but I suppose that is only to be expected.

The DLB seems to be getting worse just recently, and some worrying things have been happening, which I should probably tell Dr Blaine about. I've been thinking that Harry, my old Border Collie, has been with me, and even talking to me. It sounds so daft when I write it down like this, but I really thought it was happening at the time, even though he was doing very strange things like floating in the air and talking in a deep voice like Sean Connery's. I do feel such a fool, saying it like this. People will say I'm a mad old woman, and I don't want to go into a home.

When I was thinking that Harry was with me, I followed him down to the river, and it was all ever so confusing. But a nice young man was there who brought me home. I think he might be the son of a family who lived in the village – the Thomases. There was something in the news about them a few years back – something happened to the mother and the father. I remember thinking how dreadful for the little boy, being left all alone. I think they sent him away to the grandparents. I had a lovely chat with him as we were walking home. I was telling him all about how the village has changed over the years and he listened like you imagine your child or grandchild would listen, hearing about the past, about where and who he has come from. Such a nice young man.

My own grandma lived with us for years in the Garden Village, you remember. She never said much though, but she did say that children were a blessing. We didn't have that, of course. Neither you nor me. This house was always too big for just me and Bob, though I often had people to stay, especially during the War when there was all the bombing. It would have been a lovely house to raise a family in, with the big garden. Do you remember your Arthur and Bob playing tennis when the lawn had grown – with the washing line as a net? Just like when we were courting in the Garden Village – two strong, strapping lads in their whites. It would have been lovely to have had our own boys to play on the lawn and climb in the trees. It's all a bit overgrown now and sad-looking and I don't go out there very much but that wasn't going to happen for any of us and then the war came and we dug up half the lawn to plant more vegetables and the chickens my little Periwinkle

Joan has been writing for a long time, and her wrist and fingers have begun to ache. She puts the pen aside, and closes her eyes, as she feels the writing pad slipping from her knee.

*   *   *

The air stewardess with the make-up and hair scraped up into her little pill-box hat was watching with mild concern from her seat at the front of the cabin as the Cyprus Airways flight from Manchester banked to make its final approach over the sea and come in to land at Larnaca. The old man and his teenage grandson who were sitting in the first row of seats had been no trouble throughout the five hour flight. Since the old man had drawn her aside after boarding and had muttered with her in the open doorway to the flight deck, she had been watching the boy with regular, covert glances, looking for signs of 'agitation'.

What did he mean 'agitation'? she had asked the old man, who had explained that his grandson had been through a traumatic time a few months ago. And then, when it transpired that Maroulla, the stewardess, and Kyrios Thoma, the old man, came originally from neighbouring villages of the Limassol district and knew members of each other's families, he had narrated quickly the tragedy which had befallen his son, his son's English wife, and their sixteen year-old son. How they had been travelling by car for an evening out to celebrate their wedding anniversary; how the car had swerved into the path of an oncoming lorry on an unlit country lane; how his grandson had been under medical care for stress since the accident, but was now well enough to travel and live with his grandparents, since there was no one in England prepared to take the poor child in. The doctors had given the boy medications to keep him calm, but there was always the possibility that Christophoros might start behaving strangely, reciting numbers, and being 'agitated'.

Maroulla had tutted sympathetically, but as they now were coming into land, and the boy continued to stare blank-eyed into the blue air beyond the Perspex of the cabin porthole, it did not appear that there was going to be a problem.

The aircraft's wheels' striking the tarmac and the juddering of the cabin were greeted with a ripple of applause from a group of passengers, but other than that, there was no reaction from anyone in the cabin. The engines made their customary howl, and the big plane slowed to begin its protracted taxi-ing towards its resting place. As he unfastened his seatbelt, Kyrios Thoma wondered, glancing back at the unflustered looking individuals rearranging their belongings in the rows of seats down the long tube of the plane's body, how many of them had played out terrified scenarios of carnage as they had come in to land. Thankfully, his grandson had not become agitated, and was continuing to stare blankly out of the window. Kyrios Thoma patted his arm in gentle reassurance.

"Bravo, *Christophore mou*," the old man said. "You did very good, *re*."

The boy did not respond, and after a few more pats, the grandfather sat back in his seat to wait for the plane to end its taxi-ing. At the front of the plane, the stewardess reached for the telephone handset mounted at the front of the cabin, and announced their arrival at Larnaca, first in Greek and then repeated in English. It was, she informed the passengers, 11.15 local time, and the temperature was a pleasant twenty-eight degrees.

When the majority of the passengers had left the cabin, stepping out into the glare of the late morning sun and picking their way down the steep flight of moveable stairs which had appeared at the plane's side, Maroulla approached the remaining pair in the front row.

"*Ela, mana mou,*" she said to the boy. "*Na se voithiso?*"

"*Then milai ellinika,*" the old man said, rising from his seat. "*Ma prepei na mathei.*"

"Let me help you," said Maroulla. "Your granddad says you don't speak Greek. But you'll learn." She unclasped the seatbelt in the boy's lap. The two straps fell apart, but he gave no indication of preparing to move. The grandfather had taken two pieces of hand luggage from the overhead locker. He slung one of the bags, a small rucksack, over his shoulder, and carried the other, a holdall, in his hand. With his free hand he reached out to the boy who allowed himself to be pulled upright.

"Come, *Christophore*," said the old man. "Let's go and find your *yiayia*. She will be waiting us with uncle Pambos." He turned to Maroulla, as he led the boy towards the cabin's door. "*Thank you, Maroulla mou,*" he said in Greek. "*Greetings to your family.*" He and the boy went out into the sunlit air and the hot reek of aviation fuel, while Maroulla bade him goodbye, and joined the rest of the crew in their post-flight tasks.

Cat and his grandfather stepped carefully down the metal flight of stairs. The old man, whose heavy shoes clanged at every step, held one of Cat's arms in the deeply tanned grip of a work-scarred hand. They descended slowly, Cat's limbs moving as though through some viscous fluid. His eyes were screwed up against the glare of the sun. When they finally reached the bottom of the staircase, one of the airport staff in a fluorescent waistcoat pointed them in the direction of a long, low shuttle bus, scuffed and faded from years of service, which was waiting for them. A line of impatient faces stared from the side windows as the old man and the boy crossed the stretch of tarmac and, at last, stepped up into the body of the vehicle. The electric doors closed behind them with a rattle, and the bus set off with a jolt.

Cat was thrown into one of the vacant seats by the sudden motion. His head lolled sideways and struck against the window with a bump.

"Grandad," he said, tightly. "*Pappou.*" One of his hands rose towards his temple, as his grandfather sat swiftly beside him, laying reassuring hands on his shoulders. "Grandad," Cat repeated, his voice louder and more strained. "My head." He began to call out a sequence of numbers while his grandfather repeated, "Is alright, *Christophore*," and put his arm around him. The passengers on the bus looked on as the vehicle rattled its way towards the terminal building, following some mysterious, circuitous route past ranks of parked aircraft, occasionally crossing paths with security vehicles whose yellow lights flashed palely in the bright sun. Cat continued to call out numbers, and his grandfather continued to hold him in a reassuring embrace.

"Is alright, *Christophore*," he repeated. "We'll stop soon. Is alright."

A small, roundish woman came tic-tacking towards them in wooden-soled sandals.

"Is he alright?" she asked, looking over the old man's shoulder at Cat's tortured face. He had started to recite his times tables.

"Is there anything I can do?" the elderly woman offered. She was pushing her face closer to the pair of entwined bodies, gently intruding herself into their space. "I was a nursery school teacher," she added with an apologetic smile.

"No, thank you, *kyria*," said Cat's grandfather over his shoulder. "He will be OK. He need calm."

The woman pulled back, hovering uncertainly, smiling and looking concerned, but then withdrew to rejoin her husband who had remained with their hand-baggage and duty-free carrier bags on the other side of the bus.

Someone among the passengers commented, "Poor lad." There were a few sympathetic tuts and mumbles.

Just then, the bus pulled up outside the terminal building, and there was a sudden lull, as another voice added, "What a nutter," in tones made loud by the silence of the bus. The doors rattled open, and the passengers covered their embarrassment with noisy movement and bustle, pushing to disembark and scurry across the pavement into the shade of the arrivals hall.

Cat and his grandfather were the last to alight from the bus, making their way slowly across the few metres of pavement to the glass-panelled doors of the airport building. After his outburst on the bus, Cat had relapsed into a state of disengaged quiet, soothed by his grandfather's gentle reassurances. He shuffled along beside the old man who kept his hand on the boy's arm. Inside the arrivals hall there was shade, but the air was still oppressively warm, and the passengers in the lines were fanning themselves with hats or the documents which would allow them to go on to the next stage of the process of entering the country. The elderly woman from the bus was looking over from her place in one of the queues, and made a sympathetic gesture, a kind of ineffectual half wave in the pair's direction. Cat's grandfather gave her a smile in return.

"You come and stand along with me, Christophore," said the old man. "In the Cypriot line. I explain him your British passport." He was holding two similar-sized dark blue booklets, one embossed with the royal coat of arms, the other with the crest of the Republic of Cyprus. There was also a rectangle of card which they had filled in on the plane with Cat's details and reason for coming to the island.

Gradually, the queue moved forwards until they were standing looking through a sheet of Perspex at a blue-shirted policeman who took the documents, glancing uninterestedly at the photographs inside the booklets. There was a rapid exchange of words during which the official stared at Cat.

"You should be in the other queue," he said to Cat after a pause.

Cat's grandfather raised his eyes upwards to the ceiling of the arrivals hall.

"*Panayia mou*," he breathed in an emphatically exasperated tone, and launched into a long explanation. The policeman looked at him, glanced at Cat occasionally, but remained silent. Eventually, without a word, he picked up a rubber stamp, pressed it against an ink pad, and brought it down with two solid thumps, once on Cat's passport and once on the grandfather's.

"*Efharistoume*," said Cat's grandfather as he guided Cat on past the little Perspex-shielded box towards a sign proclaiming baggage reclaim with a black arrow pointing the way. The policeman said nothing, beckoning with a laconic hand the next in the queue.

"We must wait our bags, Christophore," said the old man as they reached the luggage carousel, which stood motionless in front of them. There was a sudden mechanical clanking and the conveyor belt jolted into life. A solitary suitcase emerged through an aperture draped by strips of thick, rubberized plastic. Then nothing appeared for a long time until two skeletal folded pushchairs came through, followed closely by a black, hard-shelled guitar-shaped instrument case. As it came towards the spot where Cat and his grandfather were standing, Cat reached out towards it with slowly moving hands. His grandfather took hold of the case's handle and lifted it off the belt, handing it over to Cat who held it before him, cello-like, his arms around it in an embrace. After that, more and more items began to nose their way out, parting the plastic strips. The waiting passengers darted forward as they recognised their possessions, and hauled suitcases and hold-alls away with them. Eventually, Cat's grandfather had one small and one larger suitcase at his feet, while Cat remained motionless, the instrument case still held before him.

"Now we just wait your big bag, your *racksack*," he told Cat. Almost immediately, a large, overstuffed rucksack nudged the strips of plastic aside, and was borne along the conveyor belt towards them. Cat's grandfather hoiked it with difficulty from the belt, and placed it with the other bags. Apart from when his guitar case had appeared, throughout the procedure and the wait, Cat had stood staring blankly as the various items of luggage had paraded past. Now, guitar case in his grip, he allowed himself to be led away once his grandfather had loaded their bags onto a trolley.

"Now we go to meet your *yiayia*."

They made their way through a series of scuffed corridors, past a tiny room with plastic chairs and formica-topped tables where a couple of travellers sat smoking and drinking from polystyrene cups. Then they emerged into the sunlight and a wave of heat to be greeted by a shout from a deep male voice.

"*Re Thoma!*" an enormously fat man boomed. "'*Po'tha, re goumbare!*"

The man, silver-haired and sweating through a light-blue shirt which strained at its buttons, strode across the concrete to clasp Cat's grandfather's hand in a huge brown paw. His face beamed with pleasure as his greeting was returned, but then creased with lines of concern. Glancing at Cat, he asked, "*Pos paei to moro mas?*" And to Cat in heavily accented English, he said, "How are you, my boy?"

Behind him, emerging from the shadow of his huge bulk came a small, elderly woman, dressed simply but smartly for a trip to the airport in a black linen dress, a long row of buttons down the front. She approached Cat, her presence causing the two men to step slightly away from the boy in deference to her sympathy and concern. She reached a calm hand towards one of Cat's cheeks, making a reassuring, stroking gesture as one would still a nervy colt.

"You come to live with *yiayia* and *pappou* in the village, Christophore?" she asked. "*Sto vouno.* On mountain." She spoke rapidly to the two men who set about wheeling the trolley with the suitcases and rucksack in the direction of the airport carpark. Then, taking Cat's arm in hers, she led him in the wake of the men, one mountainous and ebullient having taken command of the cart, the other quieter walking at his side. As they went, each occasionally glanced back at the woman and her charge. Although she asked occasional questions, sometimes in Greek, sometimes in broken English, Cat remained unresponsive until they reached their vehicle which had been parked in the shade of a slender tree at the margin of the car park.

"Here is Uncle Pambos' *diplo-cambino*," said the old lady. "He takes us to the *horio*."

Pambos and her husband were already transferring the baggage into the open rear section of the double-cabin pick-up truck, a long, rugged piece of machinery with wide tires and an air of practical serviceability. Cat's grandmother opened one of the rear doors and pushed Cat gently towards the back seat. With slow movements, impeded by his guitar case, Cat slid along the upholstery and sat passively, staring with dull eyes out of the window at the rows of cars in the car park. The air in the truck was hot, and a sheen of perspiration had broken out on his forehead. Taking her place at his side, his grandmother used a square of cotton fished from the pocket of her dress to wipe his face.

"*Ela, mana mou*," she said. "Soon we go home. In the village is *droshia*."

"Cool," Uncle Pambos translated over his shoulder, squeezing behind the steering wheel and starting the truck. "In the village it is cool."

The journey from Larnaca - along dusty sub-urban roads, towards a two-lane motorway through an arid landscape, brown and scarred, and then onto a final, protracted climb up mountain roads which wound through a series of tiny, unremarkable villages - took about an hour. The khaki coloured landscape flashed past the half-open side windows of the double-cabin pick up, as hot air buffeted the faces of the passengers. The old people talked and asked Cat questions throughout the trip, but, apart from accepting a drink of water from a plastic bottle, the vague-eyed boy said nothing for the whole of the ride. As the pick-up entered the village, passing a sign of welcome which bore the scars of serving as target practice for double-barrelled shotguns, Cat's grandfather made an attempt to explain the village to his grandson.

"Village is small. Only fifty people. Our house up there." He pointed through the windscreen to a rise at the side of the road. A low building stood at the top of the hill, its roof, a deep terracotta red against the burning blue sky. Light blue painted shutters screened windows set in whitewashed plastered walls. "You remember house? No? Is no shop. Is quiet. You be OK here, Christophore."

Uncle Pambos turned off the road onto a track which rose steeply towards the house. At the edge of the track huge pad-like leaves of prickly pear bushes swelled outwards. Some had had geometrical shapes carved into them: a square, a triangle, a heart. The engine of the pick-up strained a little, and the vehicle jolted over the rougher surface. Black-trunked trees with slender leaves overhung the track. Cat began to mutter under his breath, as the pick-up came to a halt outside the garden of the house. Within the garden, a latticed metal gate set in a low wall gave onto a central courtyard enclosed on three sides by the wings of the building. One side looked very old, while the other two seemed to have been added later. The engine died and there was silence, except for the blurred sounds of insects and birds in the trees.

"You no remember this place?" asked Cat's grandfather. "You come here when you were little baby. But your daddy not bring you again for a long time."

"Thoma," said Cat's grandmother in quick admonition. "*Siopi.*"

One of Cat's knees had started to jig up and down, banging gently against the guitar case. He continued to mutter quietly to himself, a frown of pained concentration on his face. Uncle Pambos opened his door and began to manoeuvre himself out of the truck.

"Come, Christophore," he said in a loudly encouraging voice. "We get bags. You go in house with your *yiayia*."

There was a bustle of activity, and eventually the little party stood in front of the metal gate which Cat's grandfather pushed squeakingly open. He took hold of one of Cat's elbows and guided him into the courtyard. As they passed through the gate, Cat hesitated, tapping his foot twice on the threshold before going through. He seemed to be moving with increasing reluctance. His grandfather took out a little bunch of keys and manipulated a large, ancient-looking padlock which secured the front doors of the house. They swung open to reveal a dark interior which smelled of earth and old wood.

"Welcome to your new home," said the old man with studied seriousness, pulling Cat's arm gently, but his grandson resisted, holding himself back, unwilling to step into the cool darkness.

"Ten thousand, three hundred and one," he said.

"Come, Christophore," his grandfather encouraged him. "Is cool inside. You have drink and take another pill like the doctor said."

"I don't want another pill," Cat announced. "I don't want to go inside. I can't," he stuttered.

Pulling his arm away from his grandfather's grasp, he turned and pushed past his grandmother and Uncle Pambos. The three old people followed him patiently out of the courtyard, where they watched impotently as he lowered himself to the ground and hugged the guitar case against his chest. With his eyes closed, he continued to recite a sequence of numbers quietly to himself.

Behind the house, distant mountains topped with golf-ball radar installations shimmered in the blue haze. Brown, terraced hillsides, on which olive trees and groves of citrus grew, dropped precipitously into dry river beds. Overhead, the tall sky burned a deep, uniform blue, arcing towards the distant sea. The air was full of the scent of hot, dry earth and the thrumming, insane music of the *ziziri*. Outside the walls of the little house in an insignificant village, a tiny, incomprehensible universe of dread seethed.

*   *   *

Suddenly I am awake, and the light is doing its seeping through the fabric of the tent thing. I can hear the jangly thrum of the stays of the yachts moored further up the river. The air on my face is cold, colder than the previous morning, though the rest of me is comfortable in my cocoon-like bag. I feel haunted by a lingering sense of disorientation because, for the first time in a very long time, I have dreamed. Or rather I have remembered a dream, since people tell me that we all dream. The Limassol doctor, who saw me for a long time, was very keen to hear my dreams, but I couldn't help her. Until last night, it has been as though when sleep comes, everything in my head shuts down. I recall an extract from something at school. A boy's voice, it could have been mine, reciting something learned: *Sleep – the innocent sleep. Sleep that knits up the ravelled sleave of care.* Then, other snatches return to me: *Tomorrow and tomorrow and tomorrow creeps in this petty pace from day to day.* And a teacher's voice, insisting "Put the emphasis on the *and*s – see what happens to the meaning, Thomas." And then, *Who would have thought the old man to have so much blood in him?*

101, 131, 151, 181, 191, 313, 353, 383, 727, 757, 787, 797, 919, 929, 10301

I drag my mind back to my dream, and the strangeness of the way the mind works. Dr Angela, as she told me to call her when *pappou* and *yiayia* first took me to see her, tried to explain what was happening in my head, but I don't think she really knew. I don't think anyone knows. That's why it's easiest to give you the clomipramine and the Prozac.

The dream. I replay the events while I still remember them. I am standing in front of the old lady's house, Joan's house, with the stained glass roses in the front door and I see my hand moving very slowly to knock. There is no sound, but the door opens immediately, and Joan is standing there in her coat and little boots. "Come in, Harry," she says in her wavy voice, and I pass straight over the threshold like a ghost. No toe-tapping and no dark, me-not-me voice whispering the warnings. Inside the house, it is not Joan's house, unless her hall and the rooms off it are an identical match for the house I lived in before the dreadful thing.

101, 131, 151, 181, 191, 313, 353, 383, 727, 757, 787, 797, 919, 929, 10301

I travel comfortably from room to room, again without hesitation at the thresholds, and Joan's voice calls to me, "Come into the kitchen, Harry. See what I've got for you."

I go through and see that the door which leads to the garden is standing open. I go outside and I am in the courtyard of the mountain village with a blinding Mediterranean sun in my eyes. Two dark figures are standing in the glare, obscuring something behind them which I don't want to see. Each is holding something out to me.

"Here, Christopher, eat something." "*Ela, Christophore, fae kati, mana mou.*"

The two voices speak simultaneously. They belong to Joan and my *yiayia*.

Then, I had woken up to the sounds of the river and the vague morning light.

But the strangest thing, throughout the whole of the dream as I passed from room to room, was that I felt no sense of suffocating dread, nor any need to perform my rituals or recite the sequences. Even when crossing the thresholds; even when faced with whatever the two old ladies were shielding. There had been no me-not-me whispering.

I wonder what Dr Angela would have made of that.

The lingering feeling of disorientation remains with me as I struggle into clothes while still in the sleeping bag. It's an unusual experience to recall the events of a completely different life lived during the hours I've been asleep. There are things I like about my dream-self – his freedom from ritual and his ability to cross thresholds without dread – and there are things I would like to ask him. For instance, what did *yiayia* and Joan give him to eat. I realise that I'm hungry for some breakfast. And what was the awful thing they were hiding from him. Breakfast first, though. And later my postponed trip into town, revisiting places which were important to me. I think about using the train station's facilities to clean myself up.

As I assemble a rudimentary breakfast from my provisions store, I find myself thinking about Joan: what she might be doing alone in her musty smelling house, whether she has found her dog, whether she has any family.

And if she is alright.

FIVE

Joan was sitting in front of the long mirror of her dressing table, applying a few dabs of Nivea to her face and working the silky cream into her skin. Although she and Bob married over thirteen years ago, she had still kept her youthful looks: her eyes remained bright and her complexion undimmed by the passage of time. She was proud of her looks, even though her lips were thinner than she would have liked, and she was proud of the elegant bedroom suite which Bob and Arthur had positioned in the master bedroom, setting each of the pieces of furniture according to her directions. The oak shimmered a very pale yellow, slightly streaked with white from the liming process. There was an enormous wardrobe which contained drawers and compartments labelled with their intended contents – a drawer for collars, one for gloves, another for lingerie. In the end, she and Muriel, unpacking and distributing clothes and accoutrements, had ignored some of these labels: a whole drawer for collars? So, some things had had to double up. Still, it all possessed a very elegant air.

There was also a heavy chest of drawers, on top of which stood Bob's hairbrush and comb, and the Spanish leather shaving kit with his initials embossed. And there was her dressing table, a beautiful piece of modern design with a seat, three little drawers and the long mirror, all-in-one, where she sat in the alcove of the bedroom's bay window. The curtains, which Muriel had helped finish and finally hang on the last day of her and Arthur's stay were drawn. The room, despite being lit from the centre of the ceiling by a pendant bulb, which cast a uniform light over all the surfaces, felt cosy and comfortable. Over her shoulder, reflected in the mirror, Joan could see the limed oak headboard of her and Bob's big double bed.

From across the landing came the noise of the lavatory being flushed, and then the gentler sound of water running into the hand basin, accompanied by Bob's soft whistling of a tune, something by Jack Buchanan, Joan thought, one long drawn out note, followed by five jaunty shorter notes. Joan sang the words quietly under her breath, and finished rubbing the Nivea into her skin. In the mirror, Bob's broad shouldered figure appeared in the doorway. He was wearing his corded dressing gown over plain pyjamas.

"Well, I think we've achieved an enormous amount over the last two and a bit weeks," Bob announced. "You and me, Arthur and Muriel, we make a fine team."

"So you keep saying," replied Joan. "It's sad that they've gone back to Brid. The house seems empty without them." Bob was making vigorous use of his hairbrush. Its bristles on his still full head of hair created a hushing sound. "And you'll be going back to sea in a few days' time as well."

Bob continued to brush, then stopped. There was the clink of metal on wood as he set the brush gently down on the top of the chest of drawers. In the mirror, Joan saw him approach and felt his comforting, strong hands on her shoulders. His face appeared beside hers in the mirror.

"I know it's hard for you when I'm away, love," he said. "And, honestly, I am thinking of coming ashore for good, you know. There are lots of opportunities for an engineer with my experience – motor cars, motorbikes, aircraft. Lots of openings. A few more years at sea, and then we'll see." He gave a little laugh. "Or I could become a poet."

Joan smiled weakly at him in the mirror. Guiltily, she noted that her eyes betrayed sadness, and she tried to make them bright again.

"It's always hard when you first go away. And just now it seems worse because of everything."

"You mean the move? The new house?"

"Yes, the move. But all the things in the news, as well, you know. Palestine – the Jews and the Arabs. That Mussolini in Italy, and that horrid Hitler in Germany. I worry there might be another war."

"The Prime Minister and the new King would never let it come to war, Joan. Not after the last time. And anyway that Mr Hitler doesn't seem too bad. He's been doing a lot of good things for the German people to get them back on their feet."

"I don't like the look of him, Bob. Always in uniform and surrounded by soldiers. It's not nice."

"He's been proposing a new peace treaty. And he's built that new motor car, which all the Germans are supposed to be able to afford. We should have something like that over here. We could do with a motor."

"Maybe we could get one when you come ashore for good? And especially if we ever start a family."

Joan's eyes were looking down at her hands as she spoke, and she felt rather than saw Bob's body stiffen. He inhaled a slow, silent breath, and pushed himself gently against her back, still gripping her shoulders in his palms. Through their night attire, she could feel the swollen hardness of his erection pressing between her shoulder blades. She raised her hands, crossing them in front of her, and lay them on top of Bob's hands on her shoulders, her right over his left, her left over his right. Then, she drew his hands down to her breasts, feeling her nipples, under the lace of her nightdress, harden against his fingertips. Against her back she could sense his tension. He stood, statue-like, as though he dared not move. She too kept herself motionless, matching his tenseness, since she knew what might happen if she were to move herself against him. Delicately, she leant her body forwards, releasing his hands, and stood upright. She looked into his face in the mirror, and sensed his passion. Then she turned to face him and took his hands in hers again.

"Come on, Bob," she whispered to him. "Quickly. Take off your things. I'll lie down on the end of the bed."

They moved with dispatch, like performers with a rehearsed sequence of moves in a crucial scene. Bob unknotted his dressing gown and let it fall behind him, while Joan climbed onto the bed where she hoisted her nightdress up around her waist. Bob allowed his pyjama bottoms to fall around his feet and stepped out of them. He positioned himself between Joan's legs, his groin with its swollen member standing up level with her body on the high bed. Hitching his arms behind her knees, he pulled himself towards the dark triangle between Joan's thighs.

"Please, Bob," whispered Joan. Her arms reached out as though to guide him in to her. She could feel the muscles in his arms hard and tense behind the backs of her knees, straining as if he were holding an insupportably heavy weight. She felt his hardness against her, just before he slumped forward, burying his face in the lace which covered her breast. There was a hot wetness between their naked bellies, which very quickly cooled.

Bob mumbled something into Joan's nightdress, but his words were indistinguishable. She stroked the back of his head gently with one hand, and stared up at the light bulb. It burned into her eyes, but she didn't blink. She wanted to see how long she could stand the intensity of the glare.

Eventually, patting Bob's shoulder in a business-like manner, Joan squirmed under his weight.

"Come on, love," she said matter-of-factly. "Go and wash up a bit. Then I'll go."

Bob pushed himself up, and Joan turned her head to face Muriel's curtains, but not before she had glimpsed his flaccid cock with a long, rope-like dribble swinging from its tip as he went to leave the room. Muriel really had done an excellent job with the curtains, Joan thought. She pulled her nightdress over her head and used it to wipe away the mess on her abdomen.

When Bob returned, Joan had already pulled on a clean nightie, and was lying under the covers. She slept on the side of the bed nearest the window, lying on her side with her back to the door. She heard Bob's quiet return.

"You're already in bed," he observed.

"Mmm," Joan mumbled, as though sleep had almost taken her.

"I'll turn the light out, then."

"Mmm. Goodnight, love," muttered Joan, indistinctly.

"Goodnight, love."

In the darkness, as Bob inserted himself carefully between the sheets, trying not to disturb his wife's immobility, Joan stared at blackness, thinking for a moment of dictators and wars, but then of more immediate threats to her future happiness. Gradually, as her eyes grew accustomed to the dark, she could make out a vague line of very dim light where the curtains had not met. The moon must be full, she thought, imagining its pale, bone-like face staring from the barren coldness of space into her world.

*   *   *

After two days of refusals, starting with excessive toe-tapping and ending in hurried withdrawals to the rear of the building which overlooked a steep, terraced hillside and deep valley, it became clear to the old couple that their grandson was not going to cross the threshold into the dark interior of their house. Although he would enter the courtyard from the surrounding garden, even that involved cautious negotiation. And so, he had slept on the soft earth of one of the terraces, on a sheet which they had brought him and surrounded by saucers of vinegar which his grandmother had insisted would keep any snakes at bay. They had brought him food and water, and had tried to get him to take some more of the medications which he had in his bag, but he had refused, saying only that he did not want to feel funny. He had sat in the shade of the almond trees and the large pines which grew on the hillside, fingering the guitar he had brought with him and occasionally getting up to walk with vague, directionless steps down the zig-zagging path which led from terrace to terrace. After some time, he would climb breathlessly back to his place in the shade. The two old people and an assortment of visitors, who came to see how the *moro* was getting on, were confused and worried.

"He cannot live outside when the weather changes. It will soon be October, you know," *kyrios* Thomas told his wife as they went about their morning chores on the third day. She stopped sweeping the flagstones of the courtyard for a moment and watched her husband directing a gentle stream of water into a line of potted basil plants. The soft green and purple foliage disturbed by the watering gave off a clean, peppery aroma.

"What can we do, *re Thoma*?" his wife asked. "He will not take the medicines they sent. He will not come in the house. He only eats a little – and he seems so –" She paused while she tried to think of suitable word. "So 'wound' – you know, like a spring, all coiled up. But far away, as well." She began to sweep again. "I don't know. It's very strange. And very sad."

Her husband laid down the hose pipe he was using, allowing the water to flood into a large terracotta pot containing a miniature olive tree. He took his wife into his arms and pulled her head gently against his chest.

"Certainly, it is very sad," he said. "We shall always be sad that we never saw our boy again." They stood silently in the embrace for a long moment, as he gulped back his own tears. "After we lost him to the English girl. But we have Christophoros with us now. And we must try to help him through all this –" He made an expansive gesture, releasing his wife from his hold.

"Maybe we should take him to a doctor in Limassol." Hastily, his wife laid down her broom, and bustled over to the gate in the low wall, wiping her hands down the front of her black dress.

"Christophore," she said brightly. "Good morning, my boy," she added uncomfortably in English.

Cat had been standing, unnoticed, in the shadow of a tree at the entrance to the courtyard for some time, watching his grandparents going about their tasks and finally embracing each other. One of his feet moved, tapping at the ground in front of the gate.

"Good morning, *yiayia. Pappou*," he said. "I'm sorry." He tried a phrase, unused for years, since he had never regularly spoken Greek. "*Signomi*."

"Christophore, you don't say sorry," said his grandfather. "Is no need. You have done nothing wrong." The two old people stood before their grandson, separated by the invisible line of the threshold to the courtyard. "You try come into the house again?"

Cat shook his head. His eyes flicked from one lined face to the other, as though he feared for the couple's safety and was unwilling to lose sight of either of them. His lips moved soundlessly as he ran a sequence of numbers in his head. His grandparents watched helplessly until he had finished.

"I'm hungry," he said, finally.

"*Etsi, bravo,*" said his grandmother. "You go sit. I bring you *proyevma.*"

Cat performed a toe-tapping ritual and crossed the threshold into the courtyard. A low bench stood against one of the walls of the house, shaded from the early morning sun. He sat and watched his grandmother hurry into the house. Soon, the aroma of toasting bread began to drift into the courtyard and there was the sound of plates and cutlery rattling from within. In the bushes and trees around the garden, the *zizeri* were beginning a hesitant prelude to their daily symphony of noise.

"I finish watering the garden," Cat's grandfather told him. "One day, you help too. When you feel OK. Yes?"

"Of course," Cat replied. "I want to help." He looked down at his knees which were jigging up and down. He stilled them with his hands. "It's just. You know."

The noise of a pick-up truck approaching distracted the old man and the boy from their uncomfortable conversation. A car door slammed as the engine died, and a loudly familiar voice greeted them from beyond the boundaries of the property.

"*Kali sas imera*," boomed Uncle Pambos' voice. "See what Pambos brings for you, Christophore!"

Through the green shadows of the garden came Uncle Pambos' large bulk, waddling, impeded by some sausage shaped bundles he carried before him. Cat's grandfather went to the gate to meet him and the two men exchanged rapid sentences which ended in laughter and a series of firm pats on the shoulder for Pambos.

"*Ela, re Christophore*," Cat's grandfather called to him. "Come to see. Uncle Pambos has *doro* for you. A present." The two stood side by side in the gateway, one like a beardless Santa Claus, bearing gifts, the other, his much smaller, dark-shirted helper. They both looked pleased. Uncle Pambos extended his arms to display his burdens. Cat raised himself in a stuttering movement from the bench, and crossed the courtyard. His grandfather was making beckoning motions and smiling.

"These I have in my *apotheki*," Uncle Pambos said, lowering his voice to a gentler volume than his customary bellow. "An Englishman came to live in the village. He give these to me." He began a halting explanation of how he had come to possess a sturdy A-frame two-man tent and a well-insulated sleeping bag. Both appeared to have been well-used, but also well-cared for. The Englishman, who had given Uncle Pambos the equipment in exchange for a supply of winter firewood, had spent a year in one of the village houses before suddenly leaving in the early eighties. No one knew why he had come, nor why he had left. He had only been known as the *Englezos*, although he had got on well with the local people, speaking Greek with a soft Athenian accent and keeping himself to himself. He had always greeted Pambos amiably when the pick-up had passed him on the dirt tracks around the village. As the big man was telling his tale, he unpacked the tent from its canvas bag, laying out the various items on the ground. There was an assortment of pieces of strong-looking fabric, orange and khaki like the bag they had come in, some aluminium poles with plastic connectors in another bag, and some metal pegs and guy-lines in a drawstring pouch. Then, Pambos unrolled the silky sleeping bag.

"I think the *Englezos* was a *stratiotis*," he said. "You know, army-man. He like walking everywhere. Now you have this, Christophore. You live in tent. You like *Englezos*. Strong man. Live *monos sou*. By yourself."

Cat had dropped to his knees to join Pambos in the laying out of the equipment. Each of the pieces had a precise place in the structure of the tent, complementing each of the other pieces, fitting together to create a coherent whole. His mind thought of factorisation, of individual musical notes, and then of combination, of building a complex entity, a number, a chord. He thought of permanence and impermanence, of continuity and flow, of legacy, of independent self-reliance. The tent seemed to embody all these things in some symbolic, talismanic way. The enormous Cypriot villager looked up at his *goumbaros*, and the two men smiled at one another over the bowed head of the boy.

Later, Cat's grandmother eventually tracked down the menfolk, bearing a tray with Cat's breakfast arranged upon it, a plate of village bread, its spongy texture lightly toasted to make the surface crisp and crunchy, some slices of halloumi cheese, brilliant white, but flecked with tiny shreds of mint, some chopped tomato and thickly cut cucumber. The men had left the courtyard, making their way through the green shade of the garden, and taking the steep path which led down from terrace to terrace, carrying the various components of the tent. The brown terrain was patched with greens, dark areas of shadow from the carobs, lighter clouds of dusty olives, viridian clusters of the towering pines. While Cat's grandmother had been preparing the food and then searching for the men, they had chosen a space just beyond a little grove of olive trees. Now, something orange and green was laid out on the ground in amongst the trees, and three figures were kneeling, engaged in the task of construction. It was only when the tent had been erected that Cat's grandmother finally managed to persuade him to eat from the tray she had brought. She watched with satisfaction as he crunched the toast and bit into the slices of cheese and vegetables.

"*Efharisto, yiayia,*" Cat said, chewing and smiling at her. "Squeaky cheese." He pointed to his mouth and continued to chew. His grandmother's eyes filled with tears as she watched her grandson eat.

"I think he likes the tent of the Englishman," observed Uncle Pambos in Greek.

Cat spent the next half hour ferrying his belongings from the house to the tent, which stood solidly orange among the dusty khaki of the olive trees. He arranged everything inside, then brought a metal framed chair from the garden and positioned it outside the entrance where the olives cast their dappled shade. Then, he spent the rest of the morning sitting on the chair's thin cushions, gently fingering the strings of his guitar. For some time, his grandparents and Uncle Pambos watched him from a distance, hearing the foreign-sounding arpeggios repeated again and again over the constant drone of the *zizeri* in the trees.

*   *   *

I know breakfast should be more than a Mars Bar and a carton of milk. Now that I have checked at the station for times of trains into the town, and have over an hour to kill before a mid-morning service, I can do some shopping in the little village supermarket. The row of shops in the centre of the village has not changed since I have been away. In fact, it has not changed since I was a little boy. These are familiar landmarks: the Post Office in its red and gold livery, a dark off-licence, a butcher's shop with a comically smiling pig in the window, a bank – not mine – and at the end, the supermarket. Each presents its own difficulties, and I stand on the opposite side of the road from the arcade, counting the people who go in and come out. Soon, I will be able to cross the road. The seventh customer since I began counting crosses the supermarket threshold, and it is safe for me to scurry across the road. I reach the other side before she makes it past the bank, and all is well. I have to wait for three more people to use the supermarket doors, making them swish open and closed, and then I can enter, number eleven, safe and elegantly symmetrical. A slight, stutter toe-tap, and I'm in.

But shops, and supermarkets in particular, are dreadful places, or rather places full of dread. The aisles and rows of shelves require much negotiation, and I have often given up in the past, leaving without making a purchase, rather than disturb the order of the goods on the shelves.

Although the shop is small, not one of those sprawling, high-ceilinged places with a bewildering selection of brands and products, it is well-stocked and the shelves are neat and organised. I take a little wire basket from a stack by the door, and the labour of shopping begins. It is time-consuming and painful to perform the repetitive rituals, checking the labelling and sell-by dates. Sometimes it is impossible to place an item in the basket because the numbering is wrong. Sometimes I cannot take an item from the shelf because a pattern would be disturbed in the display. Sometimes the ghostly me-not-me voice simply forbids a purchase. I have been standing in one of the aisles, reading the ingredients and checking numbers and dates on a packet of fruit and nut cereal bars, when a woman's voice interrupts my calculations.

"Are you alright, love?" she asks. "Can I help? You're taking a very long time." She looks down critically at the basket at my feet. It contains two cartons of milk, lying side by side. Two cartoon cows are leering up at me and the woman. I'm not sure how long I've been in the supermarket. I don't want to miss the mid-morning train into town.

"I'm sorry," I say. "I'm not good at deciding. I'm not very good at shopping." I give her an apologetic smile.

"You're just like my husband," she laughs. "Always comes back with the wrong things. It's quicker if I do it myself. What have you got on your list?"

In the end, after explanations of not really having a list and then a flurry of activity as I follow her bustling, tabarded figure from aisle to aisle, we end up at the cash till where a bored-looking boy in his late teens is sitting, staring at a display of pet food.

"Are you sure that's all you want?" says the woman, whose name is Julie, according to a plastic oblong on the breast of her tabard. "You haven't forgotten anything?" Julie asks.

101, 131, 151, 181, 191, 313, 353, 383, 727, 757, 787, 797, 919, 929, 10301

I know that I did not come in only to buy seven Mars Bars, three pre-packaged sandwiches, and the two cartons of milk. I know that I cannot explain that I only want to buy items in batches of prime numbers. I know that I cannot explain that I don't like to buy a single item since, technically, one is not a prime. The dreadfulness of the shopping process is becoming too intense. Of course I have forgotten something. I look around in agitation.

101, 131, 151, 181, 191, 313, 353, 383, 727, 757, 787, 797, 919, 929, 10301

"Oh. Yes," I say, following the bored check-out boy's gaze. "I'd better have some dog food. For Joan's dog. Three tins."

Julie obligingly fetches three cans from the display, and three over-enthusiastic dogs join the leering cows on the shop's miniature conveyor belt. The boy has an oblong too, which says Dean. Dean begins to ring in my purchases and Julie and I begin to pack the items into one of the flimsy plastic carrier bags with the shop's logo on them. I pay and start to leave.

"Bye bye, love," says Julie. "You take care."

The electronic doors swish open for me. I toe-tap. I go back to the check-out.

"What's the matter, love?" asks Julie. "Did you forget something?" Dean is looking at me with blank, black eyes.

"My change," I say. "Did I get my change?"

I can feel Dean's malevolence radiating from the eyes.

"You put it in your pocket, love."

I go back to the doors which swish open for me again. I toe-tap. I go back to the check-out.

"Just checking that I didn't leave anything," I say scanning the conveyor belt and the bagging area. Both are empty of forgotten items.

"We put it all in your bag, love," says Julie with that patient tone people often begin to adopt after a while. "Off you go, now. And take care."

I go back to the doors. They swish. I breathe, toe-tap, and step onto the pavement outside the shop. The doors swish closed, just as I hear Dean's voice laugh and, with a musical inflection, say to Julie, "Nutcase."

101, 131, 151, 181, 191, 313, 353, 383, 727, 757, 787, 797, 919, 929, 10301

Standing indecisively on the pavement outside the shop, I want to go back in and explain to Julie and Dean that I'm not a nutcase, not really, but I know that I could not manage to put into coherent sentences all the logical but irrational persuasions, the intrusive exhortations, all the unspoken compulsions and the unspeakable consequences which crowd into my head. I know that what they have just witnessed certainly looks a bit nutty, but then to go back in again and to try to explain it all would only make it seem nuttier. I want to go back in and tell Julie that I always take care, and that taking care is a huge part of the problem. If I did not take care to perform the rituals and recite the sequences, the consequences could be dreadful. Or so I am warned. They say never go back, and I won't. Even though I have, because here I am.

And anyway, I don't want to miss the train into town. There is still time to return to the tent, leave the shopping and pick up the guitar which I'll take with me to Music Workshop. I run a quick sequence, and set off past the bank.

2, 3, 5, 7, 11

Past the butcher's pig.

13, 17, 19, 23, 29

Past the dark off-licence.

31, 37, 43

And then, coming out of the Post Office, looking down into a bag, fumbling with the contents, there is Joan. We almost collide, but I pull up just in time, and she too comes to a juddery halt.

"Oh my goodness," she gasps. "You almost had me over."

She's much more appropriately dressed than when I found her on the river bank path and I escorted her back to her house. She's wearing a proper pair of walking shoes, rather than the little wellies. A skirt of some kind of heavy fabric shows beneath her overcoat which is buttoned up all down the front. She does not have the windblown aura of chaos around her as she did at our previous meeting. Her wispy old lady hair is tied under a head scarf which is knotted beneath her chin. But, framed by the patterned fabric, at second glance, her face still bears an expression of vagueness. Something across her eyes suggests that she occupies a liminal space.

101, 131, 151, 181, 191, 313, 353, 383, 727, 757, 787, 797, 919, 929, 10301

"I'm sorry," I apologise, although our near miss was not my fault. "You're Joan, aren't you? I walked with you from the river yesterday. I'm Cat. Christopher."

She studies me with her transitional eyes.

"Cat? Oh yes. I remember. The Thomas boy. I wrote to Muriel about you. Such a nice boy. And we had a lovely chat."

"You were looking for your dog, Harry. Did you find him?"

"Harry's been dead for years," she says. "I'm not going to get another dog. Too much responsibility for someone at my time of life. I said so to Muriel."

"That's a shame. Because I've bought you some dog food. For Harry. But if he's –"

"That was very kind of you, but why would you buy him dog food now?" She is looking into my face with an expression which is both vague and piercing at the same time. "Have you seen him as well? I thought it was only me. Part of the DLB like Dr Blaine said. Was he floating?"

Once again, as during our first encounter, my exchange with Joan is taking a bizarre turn and I feel out of my depth. Momentarily, I wonder what Dean with his blank eyed stare would make of this conversation.

"No, no," I tell her. "I haven't seen him."

"So why did you buy him the dog food? He was never fond of tinned food, anyway. Did I ask you to buy some? I'd better give you some money." She starts to dig around in her handbag. "How much was it?"

"No, there's no need. I only bought it because … I'm sure we can find someone else to give it to. Someone who's got a dog."

Joan is not listening. She's rummaging around in her bag in the panicky, controlled manner of someone who has mislaid something important.

"I'm sure I put them in here when I came out," she says. "I wouldn't have left them in the door again, would I?" She's speaking into the bag, and I suppose this is one of those rhetorical questions, but I join in nonetheless.

"Is it your keys you can't find, Joan? Have you looked in your pockets? Your coat pockets?" I gesture towards the big squares of fabric with the button-down flaps on the hips of her coat.

"My pockets? I never put my keys in my pockets. I must have left them in the door again. Like I did before."

She seems to be getting flustered again, and has started to do her looking around thing, as though she were expecting someone to appear and make everything right. Despite her protestations, she pats ineffectually at the pockets, and the handbag bangs against her thigh. It gapes open like a slackly grinning mouth, just as the Post Office door opens and a wiry man wearing a similar grin and a baggy cardigan steps out to join us. He's flapping something in Joan's direction, and speaking with a kind of relieved breathlessness.

"Oh, Mrs Fettes. I'm glad I've caught you. You left these on the counter." He brandishes a pair of tan leather gloves and a jingly bunch of keys. "You wouldn't have been able to get in when you got home," he observes. "You'd have to sleep in the garden tonight," he adds, humorously. A laugh comes out of his grinning mouth.

Joan is looking blankly at the gloves and the keys which dangle from the man's hand.

"The garden's in a terrible state," she says. "I don't go out there much these days. And it used to be so lovely." The man is still dangling the keys.

"These are yours, aren't they?" he asks.

"I'll take them, Mr Greaves," I say. "I'll walk Joan home. She's a friend of mine."

The man looks at me inquisitively. Then there is a twitch of recognition in his eyes.

"You're the Thomases' boy," he says. "You used to live here."

Joan has started rummaging again. She doesn't seem to be properly with us. Mr Greaves hands me the keys and the gloves, and speaks quietly to me. "She seems a bit off. She was alright when she was getting her pension just now, but –"

He's right, and he doesn't need to finish his sentence. Joan seems to have crossed some kind of boundary in the past few moments, and now occupies a space which is tangential to the world where Mr Greaves and I are standing. I drop the gloves into Joan's open bag, and put her keys into my pocket. I snap the bag shut for her.

"I'll see her home."

"Thank you," says Mr Greaves. "Take care."

I hear the Post Office door close as he goes back inside. Joan is before me, looking disconnected.

"Let's get you home," I say in a mildly patronising, bright voice, offering her my arm in an old-fashioned, alien gesture, which nevertheless seems appropriate for the circumstance. She takes my arm and I abandon my plan of going into town on the mid-morning train as we set off on another snail-paced journey to Joan's house. When we arrive, I fish the bunch of keys from my pocket, but as soon as I insert one of them into the Yale lock, I know that something is wrong.

From somewhere in the house's interior, muffled by the wood and glass of the front door, comes a quiet susurration, but with a deeper reverberation behind it. I push the door open, and the volume of the sound increases with a sudden reminder of my Cypriot grandfather in the courtyard of the mountain house and a line of basil plants, brilliantly green in the sun. The noise of running water is accompanied by an earthy, wet smell of old damp fabric.

"Oh no, Joan," I gasp. "You've got a leak somewhere." My trainers squelch on the sodden hall carpet. "Wait there, Joan. Don't come in. The floor's all wet." I squelch nippily past the foot of the stairs, past two half-open doors, glimpsing a coal fire burning low in the grate of a fireplace through one of them, and come to the open door of the kitchen. The linoleum kitchen floor is awash and water is gushing from one of the taps over a Belfast sink. It cascades over the rim, falling in an unbroken torrent. I splash over, and switch off the tap. The susurrating noise stops, and after a moment the deeper sound ceases too.

"What a mess." I thrust my hand into cold water and remove the plug by its chain. The level starts to go down, revealing one or two pieces of crockery and a teapot. An unsanitary looking dishcloth has been stuffed into the overflow, and hangs into the receding water like a piece of grey seaweed left behind by the tide. But other than the mess on the floor and a general air of dilapidation, the kitchen is tidy and reasonably clean. Weirdly, there are little labels in old-fashioned black capitals affixed to many of the surfaces and pieces of kitchen equipment. On the door to the pantry, there is a long list of words written in the same hand.

Going back into the hallway, I see Joan has ignored my warning that she should remain outside. She is standing in the hall watching her feet squelching in the soaking carpet.

"You left the tap running in the sink, Joan. It's a real mess. If you've got a broom and a mop, I'll try to clear it up for you."

It doesn't seem as though Joan has heard me. She continues to take little splashing steps on the spot.

"It's just like the time we went to the Isle of Man," she laughs.

*   *   *

Joan is delighted when a bright black nose, a white muzzle and a lolling tongue in a pinkly grinning mouth emerge from the dining room, quickly followed by two intelligent eyes set in glossily black fur. Alert ears come next, and then the rest of Harry's body, his neat paws stepping carefully over the wetness on the floor.

"This is certainly a strange situation," Harry comments in a sentence full of soft sounds, just like Sean Connery.

"It's just like the time we went to the Isle of Man," Joan tells her dog, who is looking up at her with the faithful, interested expression he always wears. She reaches down to pat him, but another voice speaks before she can touch his silky coat.

"Maybe you should go and sit by the fire and take your shoes off," says the voice. "Your feet will be all wet." Joan's eyes follow Harry as he starts to float away towards the door he has just emerged from.

"Well, it's all your fault, Bob Fettes," says Joan archly. "If you hadn't insisted on wading in, I never would have jumped in after you. We are a pair." She allows herself to be led into a room where there is a comfortable chair by the fire. Harry is already here flopped down on the rug. "That fire could do with mending," Joan tells the nice young man as he removes her shoes and places them on the hearth to dry. She sits back in the chair and contemplates Harry affectionately. "I didn't think you were with us in Douglas that day, Harry." The young man's voice says something, but the words aren't clear. "It was just before the war, and we'd gone on holiday because Bob ..." Joan scans the room, a mildly perplexed expression passing over her face. "I thought he was here just now. How odd."

"This is certainly a strange situation," Harry repeats.

"Anyway, we'd gone because Bob wanted to see the TT races. A friend of his, Freddie Something was racing. I didn't like it. Too dangerous. And noisy too. Anyway. Freddie came third or fourth in his race, which Bob said was good, but he, Bob that is, was most excited because some German fellow won the race, and he was keen on the Germans. That was before war broke out, of course. Well, he was excited, full of enthusiasm for everything – you know how he was – and we were walking along Loch Promenade in Douglas, which was lovely, not nearly as windy as Brid can get. There was a long pool they'd built for the kiddies to sail their boats in. It must've been as long as our garden, but only shallow, about a foot deep. Well, as we were passing by, there was a little boy, whose yacht had capsized right in the middle of the pool. He looked on the verge of tears. I don't know where his parents had got to, but Bob just took off his shoes and socks and waded in to get the lad's boat for him, and – I don't know what came over me – I did the same. And there we were, paddling about like two daft kids, when I slipped and nearly went over, but Bob caught me just in time and held me up. Oh, we were daft – we must've been well into our thirties by then. But the little lad was ever so grateful to get his boat back. Bob would have made a wonderful father." Joan takes a gasping breath. She seems to have been talking for a long time.

"And you would have been a wonderful mother, as well, Joan." Harry makes a snuffling noise, as other strange noises start to come from outside the room.

"It's the water," Harry observes.

"What a funny swooshing sound," says Joan. "I suppose they have to drain the pool sometimes to clean it."

Joan sits in companionable silence for some time while the noises outside the room continue their swoosh swooshing. Eventually, a young man appears at the door. He is holding something, and saying words. Harry's ears prick up and Joan listens to the words.

"I'm going to take up the hall carpet and hang it out to dry in your garden," the young man says. "Is that alright?"

"Take Harry out with you. He could do with a walk. I'll stay here in case Bob comes back. He's gone to look at those motorbikes with Freddie Whatsisname."

The young man says something in reply, but Joan does not hear. Her eyes are following Harry who has floated up from the rug and is drifting through the glass of the long French windows into the garden.

"You'd better go after him," Joan tells the young man, "or he might float away into the sky."

SIX

Thirty years ago, according to one of the older ladies Joan chatted to outside the church on a Sunday, the year before the War (the first one) started, the local railway station had been honoured as 'Most Beautiful Station in Britain'. As Joan was waiting for the arrival of Muriel's train on a Monday morning in early June, she could not see much of beauty in the long straight rails which pierced the distance to the east, nor in the functional iron of the footbridge which crossed to the second platform and then led over to a goods siding. Before the station was expanded and developed, according to Joan's informant, there had been shrubs in planters, ivy on the walls of the Stationmaster's house, and, bizarrely, a large pond stocked with goldfish.

The train had been delayed at one of the smaller stations further down the line, Joan heard a porter tell someone, so she went along the platform to the Ladies' Waiting Room where there were polished wooden benches to sit on. A sign on the wall depicted a steel helmeted infantryman asking, "Is your journey really necessary?" I'm not going anywhere, thought Joan, and sat down on the bench looking out onto the platform. At one end of the room set into the wall was a little fireplace. The empty grate had been leaded recently. It gleamed blackly, but although the weather had been inclement, no fire had been laid.

The last few days had passed in a cool blur for Joan. She had tried to grow used to hearing dreadful news reports on the wireless; reports of dire events around the world. She didn't like to dwell on such things, and could usually occupy her mind with the everyday matters of life; looking after the house and the garden, her part-time work at the aircraft factory, meetings at the Women's Institute in the Village Hall. But since the previous week, she had found it impossible to distract herself from the terrible things that had happened.

Somewhere outside a bell rang briefly, announcing an approaching train. Joan rose from her seat, smoothing the skirts of her Utility-cut frock in an accustomed, unthinking movement.

"That'll be Muriel's train," she announced to the empty room.

On the platform, there were the porter, an elderly couple, and a young man wearing an RAF uniform. Their faces were all turned to the east, watching expectantly for the train to appear. At first, a dark shape appeared in the distance, which grew larger, and then, suddenly and noisily, the engine was upon them, gritty smoke huffing from its funnel and wheels slowing with a grinding squeal of brakes. Gouts of steam hissed and billowed briefly. The glass in the door of one of the compartments was lowered from within, and a hand reached out to turn the handle. And then, Muriel was there beside Joan, placing her suitcase at her feet and enfolding her in her arms and breathing welcome words into the side of Joan's head.

"Oh, Joan, dear, dear Joan. How terrible. How terrible," Muriel sighed. A bloom of affection for her friend, and sadness, and horrified, impotent anger enveloped Joan as she let herself be held and comforted for what seemed like a very long time. Somewhere, far away, there was the sound of doors slamming, a blast on a whistle, and the mounting noise of the train pulling away from the platform. Joan extricated herself from her friend's embrace, but Muriel was holding on to her arms as though fearful that she would drift away if she released her completely.

"Come on, dear," said Joan in an encouragingly bright tone. "Let's get back to the house. You must want a cup of tea after the train."

The porter had disappeared, and the little station, which had been awarded Britain's Most Beautiful Station 1913, looked deserted. There was no-one to collect Muriel's ticket. She picked up her suitcase, and the two women set off to make the quarter of a mile walk to Joan's house.

"It's so kind of you to come," said Joan.

"Don't be daft."

"I don't think I can bear to be alone in the house at the moment."

"I know, dear. I know."

Neither of them could find much more to say, and they hardly spoke for the rest of the way until Joan's patch of front garden, and the front door with its pale stylised rose patterned glass panels were before them. Then Muriel heaved a gulping sob.

"Oh. Joan," she gulped. "I promised myself I wouldn't cry, but it's too awful. To see your house and to think that Bob will never come back to it again."

Joan had taken the door key from her handbag and pushed open the front door. Something in her had been released by Muriel's tears, and she could feel her shoulders shaking and a strangling constriction in the bottom of her throat. There was wetness all down her cheeks and chin. Seating herself on the second step of the staircase, lowering her body in a long, slow descent, she hunched over, burying her face in her forearms like the people from the Civil Defence had shown them all to do in case of an air raid. She felt the gentle weight of an arm falling across her shoulders as Muriel took a seat beside her. The front door had remained ajar. There was silence outside and in the house, except for Joan's wet gasps punctuated by Muriel's sympathetic sobbing. Eventually, after the sobs and gasps had slowed and passed like a summer storm, Joan pushed herself upright.

"I never made that tea, did I? You must be parched."

She led the way into the kitchen, Muriel following. Each dabbed at her face and eyes with a square of handkerchief as they went. They busied themselves with the comforting familiarity of making a pot of tea, setting cups and saucers on a tray, and pouring a trickle of condensed milk from a tin into a jug. Seated at the table in front of the French windows looking out into the garden, the tea things set out between her and her friend, Joan narrated how she found out, and shared what few details she knew, about how Bob's ship had come to be lost in a U-boat attack sometime during May.

"But the news has been full of how German submarines aren't sinking as much shipping," said Muriel. "I was reading a thing about it in the paper on the train."

"That doesn't mean that they aren't sinking any though."

"But why did it have to be your Bob's?"

"Why does it have to be anyone's?" asked Joan. She could sense Muriel's fear from across the table. She knew that her friend was thinking about Arthur; on the bridge of his own Merchant Navy ship somewhere out in the world, part of a convoy, constantly on the alert for the hidden enemy beneath the waves.

"It doesn't do to think about it all, Muriel," she continued. "Such terrible things happen."

Thoughts of the children killed by a bomb as they had been eating their school dinners; thoughts of the civilians crushed as they descended into the London Tube to escape an air-raid; thoughts of the hollow-eyed people in the Warsaw ghetto; thoughts of the thousands of Germans whose homes had been swept away by the waters of a dam ruptured in a bombing raid just that month; all these thoughts crowded into Joan's mind, only to be displaced by the single, overwhelming thought of Bob's death.

"I'm so glad you're here."

"Don't be daft. Of course I'm here."

When they had finished their tea, and had installed Muriel in the back bedroom, the sky began to brighten a little. What had seemed as though it would be another inclement day, unseasonably chilly for the time of year, was turning out to be, if not exactly warm, at least pleasant.

"Do you want to give me a hand in the garden?" Joan asked Muriel as they were putting away the tea things. "We can do an hour's weeding and what have you before it's time for lunch."

Muriel pulled a scrunchy expression with her nose and mouth, but with some reluctance agreed. They went outside where the sun was struggling through the clouds, and the garden smelled earthy and damp.

"You've certainly got your work cut out," commented Muriel, as they opened the door of the shed at the side of the house to collect tools and work gloves. The salty shed odour of garden equipment, potash and engine oil rose to greet them.

"We dug up half the lawn to plant veggies. It is a lot to manage, but it's worth it – not having to rely on the rationing. And the hens are a godsend. Fresh eggs every day. I'll introduce you to my favourite."

"I'm not too keen on chickens," Muriel said with a shudder. "Horrible feathery things. But I like an egg."

Joan passed a long-handled hoe to Muriel, and handed her a pair of sturdy gardening gloves from the shed. Then she took a trowel and a couple of galvanised pails, peering into the shadows of the shed's interior in search of a second pair of gloves.

"I know we had another pair somewhere," she said.

"What's that?" asked Muriel from over her shoulder.

"What?"

"That. Under the cover." Muriel was pointing past Joan at a long shape shrouded in sacking at the back of the shed. Various tools had been leaned up against it. Whatever it was, it had the look of something heavy and unmoveable.

"Oh, that." Joan sucked in a breath of the earthy shed air. "It's ..." She took another breath, then continued, speaking with measured difficulty. "It's the motorbike Bob bought when he was last ashore."

"Well, I never knew ..."

"I'll tell you about it later." Joan had spotted the second pair of gloves she had been looking for. "Come on, dear," she said, making a shooing motion to move Muriel out of the doorway. "Let's sort out the hens first. Then we can do some of the vegetable patch." She latched the door of the shed and led the way towards an enclosure of high wooden posts and chicken wire in which a number of brown hens were scrabbling at the dirt and pecking enthusiastically at whatever microscopic bugs they had unearthed. Muriel gave a horrified shudder.

"Don't ask me to go in there, Joan. I can't bear the feathers."

"Don't worry. I'll go in. But watch this."

Joan unfastened a twist of wire which was holding the gate of the enclosure shut, and then slipped through into the chicken run.

"Chick chick chick," she said in a funny, chirpy voice. The hens, intent on their scratching at the ground, ignored her except one, which was smaller and looked somehow daintier than the rest. This hen darted over to where Joan was standing and began to fuss around her ankles, more like a cat or a dog than a chicken.

"This is Periwinkle," said Joan. "She stays at my feet all the time I'm in the run, and if I let her out into the garden, she'll stay with me. She's like a little dog."

Muriel watched suspiciously from outside the wire as Joan went to the henhouse at the far end of the run to check for eggs. When she came back, she had five brown eggs in her hands, and the little hen still at her ankles.

"You won't mind if Periwinkle comes with us while we do the veggies, will you?"

"She won't peck me?"

"No, you'll be quite safe." Joan unfastened the gate again for Periwinkle and herself to join Muriel, who took a few precautionary steps backwards.

"Why did you call her Periwinkle?" Muriel asked as the three of them were heading over to the green rows of vegetables which occupied half the garden.

"No particular reason. It's just such a pretty word."

"I like the word 'balloon'. It's such a round word."

While Joan and Muriel busied themselves in the vegetable patch, stooping to remove the weeds which had been starting to threaten the lettuces, peas and potato plants, they periodically called to each other, swapping words which they liked for one reason or another. After some time, Joan straightened, stretching her back. Periwinkle was still at her feet pecking among the pile of weeds Joan had been removing from around the stems of a row of tall bean plants.

"Have you noticed, Muriel, that a lot of your favourite words have to do with the sky?"

"Really?" said Muriel. "No, I hadn't noticed."

"Yes. You had 'cloud' and 'balloon' and 'float' and 'aeroplane'."

"'Aeroplane' *is* a lovely word, though. It makes you think of, you know, height and flying." She suddenly gave a little gasp. "Oo. I've just thought of my favourite word of all."

"What's that, then?" Joan stooped to remove another handful of weeds from the soil.

Muriel breathed the word, elongated and soft, in a gentle exhalation.

"Aerial."

Joan straightened again, and looked at her friend.

"How strange," she said.

"Why?"

"I'll show you."

With her hen at her feet, Joan led Muriel away from the rows of vegetables back towards the tool shed. She pulled open the door and Muriel watched her remove the garden tools leaning against the shrouded motorbike. Then, with a little difficulty and quite a lot of disturbed dust which made her cough, she pulled aside the sacking, revealing a silver, black and red machine. On the carmine paintwork of the fuel tank, white capitals blazoned in a black lozenge spelled out the motorcycle's name.

"It's Bob's motorbike," said Joan. "An Ariel Red Hunter."

*   *   *

Everything in the room was pale, as though all the colours had been gradually draining away over the years. The door, the bookcase, the desk were all made from a matching, very pale yellow wood, just a few shades darker than the magnolia emulsion on the walls and ceiling. The spines of the heavy-looking books on the shelves had been bleached by years of sunlight falling through the unshuttered window behind the yellow desk. Two, low armchairs which faced each other across the room were upholstered in bruised-looking, pale grey leather. On the wall behind one of these chairs, a large canvas of gentle pastel swirls had been hung, and opposite, at the side of the bookcase, a considerable area of the magnolia wall was covered by framed oblongs of parchment decorated with spidery gothic script. The largest of the frames contained the only bright colour in the room, a large scarlet seal. Sitting in one of the armchairs, with the pastel swirls behind him, Cat occupied himself reading for yet another time the many credentials which allowed Dr Angela to practise as a psychiatrist. He tried mouthing her polysyllabic surname again to himself as he read, but there were too many vowels pressed up against each other.

From the other armchair, Dr Angela's voice was speaking. Like the room, Dr Angela seemed to have had all the colour leached from her hair and skin, and as if to match her body's pallor she was dressed in the lightest of beige linen dresses and wore a pair of white open-toed sandals on slender, stockingless feet. And like its owner, Dr Angela's soft voice was pale and thin, her perfect English unaccented and uninflected. Cat forced himself to listen, although he knew what she would be saying. She had said the same or similar things each time his grandfather had brought him to visit her over the past six months.

"Doctors prescribe medicines for a good reason," she was saying. Cat let his eyes drift away from the diplomas, and watched Dr Angela's pale lips opening and closing. "If you had a cold or the 'flu, you would take something for it, wouldn't you?" Cat felt that he should nod at this point, so he did. "And then you would feel better. It's the same with the …" Dr Angela tapped her temple with the end of the ball-point pen she was holding. It had the name and logo of a big pharmaceuticals company printed along its side. The same logo decorated the cover of the notebook on Dr Angela's knee. Cat nodded again.

"So, I would really like you to start taking the medication again, Christopher," continued Dr Angela. "It will make it much easier for you to function. Maybe move into the house with your *pappou* and *yiayia*?" She looked inquisitively at her patient who nodded once more. "You've been making so much progress. Remember how you couldn't come in here to begin with? And now you almost leap through the door." Cat smiled a wan smile, suited to the room. "But maybe we should also talk about your compulsions again, and the reasons for them. Why they became so intense. Do you think we could do that, Christopher?"

"Maybe," said Cat. Silently, he recited a long sequence of palindromic prime numbers in his head, and surreptitiously tapped the toes of his right foot as the sequence unfolded.

"You see, the thing you are doing now. With your foot. Why do you think you are doing that?"

Cat finished the sequence and the tapping stopped.

"You know why. I've told you before."

"Yes, I know. And you said that you know it's not real. That there isn't somebody's real voice warning you. So, rationally, you could say to yourself, 'There is no voice; therefore, I do not need to do x, y, or z. Nothing bad will happen.'"

"I know there isn't really a voice. But it's still there, so it is kind of real. It's real to me at that moment, and I feel that I have to believe it. It's part of me – even though it's not. There's this strong urge, and unless I do it, I can't – you know – settle."

"But the bad things don't happen if you don't perform the – what do you call them? – the protocols?"

"Honestly, Dr Angela. I don't want to go back over all this again. It's really not helping."

"If you try to help *me* understand, maybe it will help you to understand yourself better, though."

"I do understand myself. It's who I am – if I don't do certain things, bad stuff might happen."

Dr Angela's wiry body seemed to tauten, but her give-away ballpoint was tapping nonchalantly against a papery cheek. Cat could sense what the next question was going to be leading towards. He ran a short sequence of primes.

"Is there a particular time that you're thinking about, when bad stuff happened? That you'd maybe like to talk about, Christopher?" The ballpoint descended very slowly and came to rest expectantly on the notebook balancing on Dr Angela's knee. Cat sat forward in his armchair. The leather made a soft, creaking sound as he moved.

"Look, Dr Angela," he began, "I know what you want me to talk about, but I don't see what good it would do to go over it all in words. I know that coming to terms with everything is what this – all these sessions - is all about. I know that you think drugs will help – and maybe they do, but they also make me feel like not me." Dr Angela's pale head was nodding along slowly as Cat was speaking, encouraging him to continue. "I think ..." Cat paused, looking around the colourless room as if seeking a physical representation of what he was thinking. "I think ..." He gave a little sigh. "I'm not sure what I think." He sat back in the chair. The leather creaked again. He played a progression of chords in his head, shaping the fingers of his left hand unobtrusively. Dr Angela nodded some more.

Outside the window, Cat saw the Cyprus summer sun flash briefly across the windscreen of a passing car. Over the street, an imposing Palladian building gleamed whitely behind a screen of towering palms, their fronds an improbable green. Overhead, the sky was fiercely blue. Everything seemed terribly bright compared with the neutrality of Dr Angela's room. Terribly bright and intense and alien. Dr Angela had stopped her nodding, and was waiting for Cat to say some more. He gestured towards the window, and she turned her face to look, squinting her eyes slightly against the glare.

"Do you want me to lower the blind?" she asked.

"No, no," said Cat. "You see that building? The old-fashioned, white one?"

"The library?" Dr Angela asked. "Yes. What about it?"

"Well, look at all the other buildings here. The shops and offices, the hotels down on the sea road. This house. The library looks as though it's kind of disconnected from everything else. Like it has nothing to do with all the other buildings."

"It used to be a private house, before it was a library. It belonged to a very wealthy man and his family, a Mr Pilavakis. He modelled it on a casino somewhere, they say. In the end, the municipality bought it. You're right, though, Christopher. There's nothing quite like it in Limassol." Dr Angela glanced quickly at her wristwatch, as though impatient with the architectural turn the conversation had taken. "We were talking about protocols, rituals, preventing …"

"It looks to me," continued Cat, ignoring Dr Angela's attempt to return to her theme, "as though that building …" His face made a scrunching expression as he searched for the appropriate word. "As though it's kind of *yearning* to reconnect itself somehow."

"You mean, go back into the past?"

"No, no, not at all," said Cat. "It's pointless thinking like that. What I mean is, to be itself again – it's obviously not really a library, though it does a good impression of a very impressive library. It's obviously something else, and it would like to be that again somehow. If you see what I mean," he finished lamely.

"Is that how you feel? About yourself?"

"Yes. No. I don't know. I don't know what I'm talking about really. I think I'll have to go."

Dr Angela looked at her watch again. "We still have quite a while left, Christopher. I'd like to explore what you were saying just now."

"No, I mean I think I should go back – to England. To make sense of everything. I can't do it here, even though *pappou* and *yiayia* are kind and very understanding."

Dr Angela began her nodding exercise again, but supplemented it with the pen-tapping routine. Cat wondered what she was thinking about. He also wondered why he had suddenly thought about going back to England. It was not something that he had considered at any time during all the months since he had arrived in Cyprus.

"Hmm," said Dr Angela. She cocked her head to one side, and repeated, "Hmm," watching Cat with a contemplative, peaceful expression on her pale features. Another windscreen flashed outside the window. "How does the idea of going back to England make you feel, Christopher?" she asked.

"How does it make me feel?" Cat repeated. "I don't know. I haven't really thought about it. I only thought of it just now."

"When you were thinking about the library?"

"Yes."

"Was there a library where you lived in England?"

"Just a very small lending library in the village. There was quite a big library at my school."

"Can you describe what it feels like when you think about those libraries?"

"I don't really think anything about them. I hardly ever went to them."

"What kind of books did you borrow when you did go to the library, though, Christopher?"

"Like I said, I hardly ever went to them."

"What kind of books did you read when you were younger? When you were growing up?"

A row of hardback books flashed into Cat's mind, their multi-coloured spines lined up along a shelf: a hefty volume of Fairy Tales, dark blue with gold on the spine, some wizard adventures, a sequence of stories set in a parallel universe. He remembered an imaginary zone where things were different. He remembered reading the books over and over again. And then not reading.

"I didn't read much, I suppose. Not after a while. Things in books kind of got in my head. And I had a compulsion to read words and sentences over and over. It made reading very tiring. And painful. I'm more of a Maths person."

Dr Angela's face took on a disappointed look, and she let the hand holding the ball-point pen flop over the side of her armchair. Her expression, the colours, the position of her body and the arrangement of pen and paper reminded Cat of a painting he had once seen: a man from the French Revolution, murdered in his bath while writing a letter. He raced through a panicky sequence of primes in his head. Dr Angela sat up straight in her chair, and took a breath.

"Christopher," she said. She let Cat's name hang in the air for a few seconds. Cat squirmed a little in his chair and sat straighter, prompted by Dr Angela's upright posture. "I am going to ask you a rather strange question." She had begun speaking very slowly, almost hypnotically. This is new, Cat thought to himself. Dr Angela continued after a protracted pause. "The strange question is this." She paused again. A windscreen flashed, but Cat resisted the impulse to glance away from Dr Angela's pale lips. She's trying something new, he thought, so I should concentrate. "After we finish our talk here today, you will go back to your grandparents', to the house in the village, and you will do whatever you need to do for the rest of today, such as helping your *pappou* in the garden, eating dinner, playing your guitar, and so on, all the routine activities of your everyday life." Dr Angela was taking her time, as though she were trying to immerse Cat in her words. "Later, it will become time to go to bed. You will go into the tent where you live. Everyone will go into their houses, and all will be quiet. You will be sleeping in peace." The sibilants in Dr Angela's gently expressionless voice were as quiet as the village night, and her face as pale as the moon, bathing the terraced hillsides in its white, reflected light. Cat felt drowsy. He ran some primes to keep himself from nodding off. "In the middle of the night, a miracle happens, and the problem that made you talk to me today is solved!" A note of quiet animation crept into Dr Angela's voice for a moment. "But …" The note went away. "… because this happens while you are sleeping, you have no way of knowing that there has been an overnight miracle that solved the problem." A longer pause followed. The ballpoint pen began to tap slowly at the papery cheek. A gentle smile stretched Dr Angela's lips and she looked deep into Cat's eyes. He felt a little uncomfortable.

"So," said Dr Angela, "when you wake up tomorrow morning, what might be the small change that will make you say to yourself, 'Wow, something must have happened – the problem is gone!'?"

Cat made his scrunching face, and tried to think of something to say.

"A miracle?"

Dr Angela nodded. "A small change – something which would help – and make you say 'Wow!'"

Cat scrunched again. "I'm confused," he said.

Dr Angela smiled her patient, stretchy smile. "I'm asking you to project into the future, Christopher. To imagine a scenario which could make a better reality for you."

"I don't know. Maybe if I go back and try to understand everything?"

"There would be difficulties about your going back, though, Christopher. You're still a minor – not yet eighteen, and I don't believe there is anyone to look after you in England, is there?"

Cat allowed his gaze to drift away to the brilliance outside the window. There was a colourless silence in the room.

"I'm confused," he said again.

"Maybe that wasn't the right thing for today," said Dr Angela, half to herself. "Christopher, I really think that for the moment medications will help you more than anything else." She scribbled something down, placed the ballpoint neatly on top of the notebook, and glanced at her wristwatch. "Well. It's time. Your *pappou* will be outside waiting for you." She stood up and walked over to the pale yellow door. "Ask him to call me to arrange our next appointment. And I can write a repeat prescription for you, if he needs one." She opened the door for Cat to go out into a little vestibule where there were more pale wooden doors. One of them had ΕΞΟΔΟΣ stencilled in white paint on it. Visitors left Dr Angela's consulting rooms by a different door from the one through which they had first entered. Cat assumed that the arrangement was to ensure that no two patients ever came face to face with each other. It seemed sensible and considerate.

"Goodbye, Dr Angela," he said as he prepared to leave. "Thank you for trying to help."

"Goodbye, Christopher," Dr Angela said in her inexpressive voice. She looked away, apparently distracted by something outside the window, as Cat negotiated his way through the doorway. Similar negotiations took place at the exit door before he found his grandfather standing outside in the shade of a dustily fragrant citrus tree. The old man gave a smile and a little wave. Across the road, guarded by its towering palms, the Pilavakis mansion gleamed under the intense blue of the tall sky. Cat wondered how and when he would be able to explain his idea of leaving the village and going back.

"*Entaxi, Christophore?*" his grandfather asked. "OK?"

"'*Entaxi*," replied Cat as he approached. "*Pappou*," he continued, "can we go and have a look in there?" He gestured towards the palatial building over on the other side of the street.

"The *vivliothiki*? You want to get a book?"

"No, I just wanted to have a look at the place – to see what it's like inside."

His grandfather laughed. "It's very high class – posh. The man, Mr Pilavakis, was very rich – very posh." Cat's grandfather laughed again. He seemed to like the word. "Come on, then, *paedi mou*. We will have a look. Maybe we need to be *meli tis vivliothikis*, members, to go in?"

He led the way across the street, pausing as a car sped past and Cat did his toe-tapping routine before stepping off the kerb. They walked up a long path flanked by the tall palm trees, and then climbed a flight of marble steps leading up to the grand front entrance. Its doors had been painted a muddy brown. There was a notice announcing opening times. Cat's grandfather tentatively pushed the door open and waited while his grandson peered into the cool dark of the interior, toe-tapped a couple of times, and finally crossed the threshold. As they entered, it seemed to Cat that they had stepped into another world.

"Wow," he breathed, as his gaze took in four enormous, white Corinthian columns which soared to a vaulted ceiling many metres above their heads. It reminded him of something he had once seen, a ritual, a sacrifice. Directly ahead, a grand staircase led upwards to a first floor balcony which ran around three sides of the hallway. "This is amazing." His eyes followed the sweep of the stairs to the top and a little landing where they branched away into two smaller flights. Beside him, his grandfather spoke in quiet admiration.

"You know, Christophore. I have never been in here. I did not know it was like this inside."

The old man seemed to have been affected by the grandeur of the library's interior. His face reflected a kind of astonishment as though he had just witnessed a feat of magic performed.

"Dr Angela was talking about a 'wow' moment this morning," whispered Cat. His grandfather looked at him uncomprehendingly. "This is very posh," Cat explained, simply, and his grandfather nodded smilingly. He took the old man gently by the arm, drawing him back towards the doors. One of the librarians behind a heavy counter was looking up from the sheaf of papers she had been sorting through, and was observing them expectantly.

"Listen, *pappou*," said Cat, speaking quickly, although his voice was still a whisper in order to preserve the quiet of the building. "I know you won't follow what I'm going to say. I'll try to explain properly later, but I want to tell you something now. I'm not sure that I understand it myself, but coming in here has helped me to see something." His grandfather squinted at him.

"You are speaking too quickly, Christophore. *Den katalaveno*. I do not understand."

"Nor do I," smiled Cat. "But this place reminds me of something I need to remember, or to understand – as though it's filled with some kind of meaning, a place of – I don't know what to call it – a place of hidden codes or messages which can explain things. Maybe the books are making me feel this way."

"I do not understand, Christophore. What was Dr Angela saying to you this morning? Are you having a problem?"

"No, *pappou*. No, there's no problem. Look, *kitaxe, oute ego den katalaveno ti thelo na sou po*. I don't understand what I'm telling you. I feel a sense of nostalgia, something from before. But I also need a way forward – like a plot in a book, or a map for the future. It might mean going back."

"Yes, *Christophore mou*," said his grandfather, fixing on the last two words and inspecting the heavy watch on his deeply suntanned wrist. "Your *yiayia* will be expecting us. We better be going back."

* * *

The young man is still in the house, and Joan is wondering what he has been doing all this time, making noise and popping his head around the door, and asking questions. She wants to tell him that it's just some days. It's not every day. And that she really couldn't bear it, you know, because she's heard about those places.

And anyway, it's not as though she's doo-lally or anything. He can see her lists. She's always been an organised person. You had to be. That's what they taught you at the commercial college – that and shorthand. Pitman's. From the age of fourteen, though she stopped when she'd got married. Until the War and then they were all expected to go back to work.

Joan isn't quite sure where the young man has come from. She hopes he's not one of those people from the council, because now all this has started happening, they'll be sure to be sending people round. They'll say she can't cope. And it's not every day. People like Joan look after themselves. Anyone can see her lists. She was brought up to be – you know – self-sufficient. She managed the garden, the hens, and the house, all by herself, as well as being part-time in the factory offices after the War.

The young man is still making those funny noises out in the hall. The hush-hushing sound goes on and on like a kind of whisper. Joan's own voice whispers along with the sound, saying things for the young man to hear, telling him how she couldn't bear it. Sitting around all day and the smell of wee. She's heard about those places.

And then Joan realises with a kind of horror that her voice has broken into sobs, although she's not weeping, not really. It's just weakness. She didn't weep when they told her Bob's ship was lost, though Heaven knows she'd felt like it. People like Joan were brought up not to show things.

Joan hopes the young man won't tell anyone about the water. It's not the sort of thing that happens every day. She can look after herself. It wouldn't do to tell anyone. Outside the door the sounds go on hushing and hushing.

*   *   *

From where I am in the kitchen I can hear Joan's thin, old lady voice muttering intermittently in the room where I placed her, as though she is in conversation with herself. The water has flooded the lino and soaked the hall carpet, which is a bit threadbare and smells old, but must once have been good quality. It's not one of the fitted kind, leaving varnished floorboards exposed along the skirting. It's thoroughly sodden. There's no way it will dry out where it is. And the kitchen floor needs the water to be swept away and mopped up. I can't leave Joan to cope with all the mess. My trip into the town, revisiting my old school and Music Workshop will have to wait.

There's a long-handled broom and a mop and bucket by the back door. The key is in the lock with a large tag hanging from it. BACK DOOR has been printed in block capitals. There's another label on the door itself with the same message. Most of the items in the kitchen have been labelled in some way. It reminds me of Alice in Wonderland. I open the door revealing a large, very overgrown garden. There's an uncut expanse of lawn with mature hedges and trees along its sides, and, beyond, unpruned fruit trees and what must once have been a vegetable patch. It hasn't been tended for a long time and looks like a wilderness. It must have been quite an impressive place in its day, but a lot of work for someone. I wonder if Joan has any family who help her with the house and the garden.

Taking the broom, I sweep and sweep the water from the kitchen floor, flushing it out through the open door into the garden. Then I manoeuvre the cooker, the little fridge and a bulky top-loading washing machine into the middle of the room to clear the edges. The broom makes a reassuring, hypnotic hushing sound as I work. From the other room I can hear Joan in conversation with herself.

What must it be like to live in the margins of reality, I catch myself wondering, while the broom goes back and forth and the water disappears through the door. The hall carpet will have to come up, I decide, but I'd better tell Joan before I start to dismantle her house. I finish the sweeping and mopping in the kitchen. Then, mop in hand, I go to talk to Joan, who is sitting by the guttering fire, a distant expression on her face. I tell her about what I've done in the kitchen – swept and mopped, removed everything and got it all reasonably dry, though the doors and windows should be left open for a while.

"I'm going to take up the hall carpet and hang it out to dry in your garden," I say. "Is that alright?"

Joan looks up at me with her distant look which is in some way a smile, but not a smile. It's hard to describe how she looks, kind of at a tangent to the rest of the world.

"Take Harry with you," she says. "He could do with a walk. I'll stay here in case Bob comes back. He's gone to look at those motorbikes with Freddie Whatsisname."

Not for the first time when I've been in Joan's company, I feel a sensation of disorientation. Harry is the dog. Bob was her husband, but he's dead. I haven't heard of Freddie before.

"Is it OK to take up the carpet? It won't dry otherwise. It's not a big job – just a few tacks along the edges. Have you got some pliers? Or a screwdriver?"

But Joan is not looking at me. She's focused on something outside the French windows which lead out into the wilderness at the back of the house.

"You'd better go after him," she tells me, "or he might float away into the sky."

"Joan," I say in one of those voices people use with small children and animals, kind of questioning and buoyant. "I'm going to take up your hall carpet because it's very wet. I need some tools – do you have anything?" She's still following some movement in the sky outside the windows, so I try again. "You know, Joan? Tools? A screwdriver? Maybe Bob had some tools somewhere. A tool-kit?"

The mention of Bob's name has drawn her gaze back into the room.

"I think he went to look at some motorbikes with his friend. Did you want him for something?"

"Did he – does he have any tools I could use?" I can hear stretched patience joining questioning buoyancy in my tone. "Maybe some pliers and a screwdriver?"

"Oh my," says Joan, smiling and shaking her head. "The shed's full of his tools. You should see them all. I don't know what half of them are for."

"Is it OK then?"

Joan smiles her distant smile and her gaze strays away to the windows once again.

"He's alright. He's just outside the window. There's not much wind by the looks of it."

I take this as sufficient go-ahead. There's a key, hanging from a nail in the jamb of the back door, labelled SHED in Joan's helpful block capitals. In a corner of the garden close to the house, a decent sized shed is tucked away behind a screen of overgrown bushes. There's a hefty padlock on the door which yields to the key. I pull the door open with a grating of unused hinges. Obviously Joan has not been in the shed for some time. The air is heavy with the smell of earth, treated wood, old metal and motor oil. Everything, and there is a lot of stuff in here, is coated with a layer of powdery dust. It's a bit like stepping into an unvisited museum exhibit: all the gardening implements have wooden handles; on a set of shelves, there are tins which had once contained products from long ago – custard powder, dried egg, gravy browning. I look in a tin banded with once-bright primary colours. It contains a selection of nuts, bolts and washers, discoloured with rust and age. On the bottom shelf sits a large, beautifully crafted wooden tool box, its hinged lid stamped with the initials R.W.F. beneath the film of dust. Inside are tools which look like the sort of things that antique collectors would want to get their hands on. I pick out a pair of heavy pincers and a flat-bladed screwdriver with a polished handle. Everything in the box looks craftsmanlike, made of wood and metal. Nothing is plastic. I think of a word to describe it all: authentic.

Closing the lid of the box and standing up, I knock against some of the garden tools, a spade, a rake and a long-handled hoe, which topple over onto a shape covered with sacking at the back of the shed. Another relic of the past, I imagine, pulling aside its shroud a little to reveal a pair of straight handlebars and the huge black and silver headlamp of an old-fashioned motorcycle. I can't resist having a look at the rest of the machine, so I strip away the rest of the sacking. The tarnish and discolouration of many decades cannot disguise the elegance of the piece of engineering which stands before me in the half light of the shed. I know nothing about motorbikes, but this looks like something special: red, black and silver, a cluster of circular gauges mounted on the petrol tank, a swooping chrome exhaust pipe curving along the entire length of the body. Its beauty exerts a sort of enchantment, and I read its name ARIEL in block capitals on a label on the fuel tank. It's almost as though Joan has been at her labelling work here too.

"Wow," I breathe, reverentially; then cover the machine with its sacking again. I feel like those archaeologists must feel when they unearth a cache of hidden treasure, half victor, half violator. From the amount of dust on the sacking, nobody has looked at the machine for decades.

Back in the house, I find Joan still sitting in front of the fire, which has almost burnt out. Her head jerks up as I appear in the doorway, and she gives a little gasp of shock.

"Oh my," she says. "You gave me a turn. What are you doing here?"

"It's me, Joan," I tell her. "Cat. Christopher. I brought you home from the Post Office. I've been clearing up in the kitchen. You left the water running when you went out."

Joan's face takes on a look which is both horrified and frightened at the same time.

"It's alright," I say reassuringly. "I'm here to help you. Don't be afraid. I'm going to dry out the hall carpet for you. Luckily there's not much damage. It could have been much worse – a real flood – and you'd have to move out." This does not have the effect I had hoped for, and she looks even more afraid. "It's alright, Joan," I repeat.

"It's just some days," says Joan in a small voice. "It's not every day. And I really couldn't bear it, you know. I've heard about those places."

I'm standing uselessly, antique screwdriver and pliers in hand, as Joan unfolds to me her fear of being taken into an old people's home because people will say that she can no longer look after herself. She's become much more lucid than she was before I went out to the shed, but she's terrified of being thought incompetent. She tells me how organised and self-reliant she is, and always has been. She asks me not to tell anyone about the flooding. Unbearably, she starts to cry in little sobs.

"Don't worry about it, Joan. I'll finish sorting things out; then we'll talk about the best thing to do. You sit there. I'll mend the fire for you, and I'll be back in a minute."

As I'm prising up the tacks from the floor and hauling the sodden carpet with its layer of brown underfelt out into the garden, I ponder what I should do about Joan. From what I've witnessed, she shouldn't be on her own, but I don't feel right about contacting the authorities. If she has family who can look after her I could contact them, but I've seen no photos around the house of children or grandchildren, just a wedding photograph on the sideboard in the room where she is sitting.

I eventually get the carpeting onto the length of washing line which sags alarmingly under the weight, and I can go back into the house to see what Joan has in her fridge and pantry.

"Here you are, Joan," I announce, placing a tray onto her knees. "I've made you a mug of tea and some Marmite on toast. It'll make you feel better. And I'll tell you what I'm going to do."

Joan fumbles with the things on the tray, but does not eat or drink. She's watching me intently, wondering what I'm going to say.

"I don't have anything to do at the moment, so I can pop round every day to check that you're alright. I really don't mind. That's unless there's someone else who can come and look after you – do you have any family nearby?"

Joan looks at me with an indecipherable expression. "It was only ever Bob and me. We didn't have any children."

"Well, that's decided then. I'll come round to look in on you every day for the time being. And we'll see how it goes. You're looking better already. More - well, you know, better already." I give a reassuring nod and smile, and Joan takes a bite of her toast.

"You have been very kind. I feel awful to be such a bother."

"Honestly, I don't mind. I'll lock up at the back, and I'll come round tomorrow. I'll knock on the front door – three raps so you'll know it's me."

"You've been so kind. I feel awful. I should give you something." Joan looks helplessly around herself, searching for something to offer me.

"Honestly, Joan. There's no need. I'll tell you what – tomorrow, if you can remember, tell me all about the motorcycle in your shed. It's a beautiful machine."

Joan's face takes on the indecipherable expression once again.

"What, that old thing? I haven't thought of that for donkeys' years. I'd forgotten it was still there."

"You can tell me about it tomorrow when I come back." I give the room a quick glance over to check that Joan will be alright. The fire is burning gently behind a sturdy guard. She seems more with it, and is sipping at her tea. I go to secure the back door, leaving the key with its oversized label swinging in the lock. Then I bid Joan goodbye and leave the house. I'll go back to the tent since I've missed the chance of going into the town today. I'll go in tomorrow after I've checked on Joan.

Walking back towards the river, I 'm once again struck by the realisation that for the past three or four hours I have felt no desire to perform any of my rituals. It's as if being around Joan kind of blocks out the compulsions, as though her greater need has in some way eclipsed mine. I wonder what Dr Angela would have to say about this. It's not as though I've been taking any of her drugs or doing anything she suggested during any of the sessions. But, as I come to the kerb of a road that I must cross on the way back, the insistent me-not-me voice returns, whispering in the shadows, and I go through the toe-tapping protocol before stepping off the pavement. And then, making my way onto the riverbank path, with the sky low and grey above and ahead of me, I see a dark figure waiting, standing level with the tent.

101, 131, 151, 181, 191, 313, 353, 383, 727, 757, 787, 797, 919, 929, 10301

"Is this your tent, son?" the figure asks as I draw near. There is a burst of static from the walkie-talkie fastened to his chest, and a distorted voice relays some kind of incomprehensible message. "You can't camp here. You'll have to take your tent down and move on."

SEVEN

Sitting at the top of the stairs with his shoulder against the newel post, sleek and shiny with its thick coat of white gloss paint, Cat could feel a troubling sense of disquiet building. He shifted his position slightly, and the creaky floorboard under the thick pile of the carpet moved beneath his buttocks. He tried to think of what his dad had told him, that he was a big boy now, and ten-year-old boys didn't get scared by silly things. He took a breath, and started to read the words in his book again, but it was no good. It was difficult to concentrate with the sound of his parents' voices floating up through the half-open sitting room door, and he didn't like the look of the words coming up in the paragraph he was reading.

He usually found this a comfortable place to read, somewhere he could still feel connected to the rest of the house and his parents, not shut away in his bedroom, yet private enough to get on uninterrupted with his story. Usually, the background noises from downstairs, the dialogue or laughter of the television set in the living room, the snatches of conversation between his parents, were all filtered out, and he could find himself immersed in the narrative. But this evening, his parents had been talking for a long time with a different tone in their voices, and something he had just read, although this was the third or fourth time he was reading this particular tale, had troubled him in a way which he could not quite understand.

Cat closed the book, and looked at the decorative dust-cover. A line drawing with deep shadows around the edges depicted what appeared to be a ritual of some kind. Under a vaulted roof, supported by tall columns, dark, hooded figures looked on as another, white-robed figure wielded a long sword. When he had first been given the trilogy, of which this was the second volume, he had imagined the illustration showed a monarch knighting someone, but on closer inspection, and having read the story, he knew it was a scene of sacrifice. He preferred to think of the knighting ritual, though, and that was always his initial impression when he looked at the picture. Strange, he thought, how I know it's a sacrifice, but I always think it's a knighting. It was as though two realities could exist at the same time, the one floating above or on the other.

His thoughts were interrupted by his father's voice from the living room. The voice sounded heavy and strained, as if it was hard for his dad to get the words out.

"I know what you're saying." Despite their heaviness, the words floated up the stairs, and Cat gave up thinking of going back to his reading and listened instead. "I know you think it's important, but I'm just not prepared to put up with all the ..." His father paused. He's searching for the right word, thought Cat. "All the fuss and bother. We say *fassaria* in Greek. Airports. Five hours on a plane. And then staying there, with the way they treat you."

"It's fine," Cat's mother's voice interrupted. "You know it's difficult for them. You know they would have wanted you to marry a local girl and go back to live there."

"No, Sally. It's not fine. And it's stupidly expensive too. Tickets. Hiring a car. I'm happy to talk on the phone twice a week, but I'm not prepared to pay a fortune for a repeat of when we went last time."

"But it's been five years, Andreas. We can't keep refusing to go, and finding excuses. They must miss you terribly, and you can't keep saying you're too busy with work. Really, it's not fair of you."

Cat opened his book again. He knew that his parents weren't arguing – not like people who were angry with each other and got divorced – but it was still not nice to hear them disagreeing. He liked it when his mum suggested something and his dad agreed, or when his dad made the suggestion and his mum saw a way to make the plan even better. He tried to read again, but the words he did not like were coming up again.

"You know they never refer to you by name, don't you?" Cat's father said, and there was the sound of his mother's laughter.

"I know, Andreas. It doesn't bother me. They're never rude. They're just – I don't know – just disappointed. And the longer we stay away, the worse it is, because they think it's me who's stopping you from going. The longer we leave it, the more difficult it's going to be."

There was silence for a while. Cat knew that his dad would be tapping the arm of his chair and jiggling his foot up and down as he thought about what to say next. When the words came, Cat was surprised at their decisiveness and intensity.

"No, Sal. You're able to ignore it, but I can't. You don't get the things that go beneath the surface. I know my parents aren't bad people, but it's not worth the bother. Honestly, it upsets me, and thinking of the expense, the time, and then the treatment, it's just – it's not worth it. I know it's selfish in some ways, but we're not going. Certainly not this year, anyway."

On the page in front of Cat, where his eyes did not want to go, the disquieting words loomed. He did not wish to read them again, but something was forcing him on, and he knew that he would not resist much longer. Downstairs, his mother's voice spoke resignedly. On the page, the author had written, *Her voice was dull and slow*.

"It's your decision, Andreas. But I think you're wrong. And they would love to see Chrissie. He's their only grandchild – and they're his only grandparents. So, for his sake, too."

"Not this year, Sal."

Then there was silence. After a moment, Cat heard someone moving. There was the sense that the two unseen people in the room downstairs had moved close together. I wonder how I know that, thought Cat. How was it possible to know things like that when you could not see them? He felt glad that the voices had stopped, and that his parents were not disagreeing any longer. He looked down at the page, feeling that he had to read the words again. *Her voice was dull and slow*. He read them again. *Her voice was dull and slow*.

Now he could read on, but there was the strange feeling of disquiet. It was a sense of dread, because of what was coming, but now he had begun to read again, he would have to go on until he reached the end of the paragraph.

He frowned, he read. *He frowned.* What a strange word it was. *Frowned.* Why did it mean what it meant? He tried out a frown, but could not see a reason for the word's meaning. He heard his mother speak.

"I'll call Chrissie. It's time he got ready for bed."

Quickly, Cat prepared to read the remainder of the paragraph, and the feeling of dread settled somewhere in his chest and throat. He knew that in a few seconds his mother would come into the hall and call his name, and he would have to answer, and then he would close the book and get ready for bed, but the dreadful words would still be on the page, waiting for next time. He let his eyes travel over the lines of black print on creamy paper.

"If we stay here long," he said, *"you are going to go mad, Tenar. The anger of the Nameless Ones is heavy on your mind. And on mine. It's better now that you're here, much better. But it was a long time before you came, and I've used up most of my strength. No one can withstand the Dark Ones long alone. They are very strong."*

"Chrissie," Cat's mother's voice called. She appeared at the foot of the stairs. "Ah, there you are, darling. Stop reading now. It's time for bed."

Head still bowed over the page, Cat held up a hand, as his eyes went back over the lines again. Something was telling him to read the words a second time, and then a third, before it was safe to close the book and raise his head to look at his mother.

"Come on, Chrissie."

"There," said Cat, closing the book with a snap, at last. "Finished, mum."

"You look worn out, sweetheart," his mother said. "Come and say goodnight to your dad."

Cat's father appeared at her side as she spoke.

"No need. We'll come up to you, Cat."

His parents' voices were no longer heavy and intense. It was nice to hear them, and to watch them coming up the stairs in their reassuring, grown-up way, not racing as he would have rushed up, but with a kind of stately bustle. There was no need to think about the dreadful words in the book now, although he knew they were still there, waiting for next time. Cat stood up, and the floorboard creaked.

"What are you reading?" his father asked as he reached the top of the stairs, taking the hard-backed volume from Cat's hands. He scrutinised the cover. "*The Tombs of Atuan*? You've read that before, haven't you?"

They went into Cat's bedroom. His mother followed, a pace or two behind. It was nice when they were all three together, involved in the same thing, even if it was just getting him ready for bed.

"He's read all the *Earthsea* books two or three times, haven't you, sweetheart?" his mother said, while they began the unthinking, getting ready for bed process, each performing their own activity: Cat undressing; mum folding things; dad sitting on the edge of the bed with the novel resting on his knees, held in place by the light fingertips of one hand.

"I like them better than the *Narnia* books," Cat observed, squirming into his pyjamas. "Even though he's a wizard, Sparrowhawk seems more real than Peter or Edmund – or any of the Narnia characters." He pulled back his duvet and was about to jump into bed. "But I'm getting a bit bored of the stories now."

"Teeth," his dad said.

Reluctantly, Cat scooted across the landing to the bathroom where his toothbrush stood upright in a little glass on the window-sill behind the wash basin. His mum's and dad's brushes had their own little glasses too. He liked the way they looked: three brushes in a neat line. He turned his dad's brush a little to the left so that all three were facing the same direction. Then, he picked up his own brush, smeared a blob of toothpaste from the tube, and began his brushing routine.

Ever since his parents had made brushing teeth an independent activity, Cat had felt the need to count the strokes he applied to each quadrant of his mouth. But recently, perhaps for the last six months or so, the feeling of need had intensified, becoming increasingly pressing. And now he had started to feel a reluctance to go and brush his teeth, hoping that his parents would not notice, because of the intensity and the sense of the pressure involved in going through the process. When, just this evening at the head of the stairs while his parents were speaking in the living room, he had read again the lines about the nameless, dark forces pressing on the minds of Tenar and Ged the Sparrowhawk in his book, he had felt that a dim light had been shone into his own mind, illuminating briefly and indistinctly things about himself. He did not have a word to describe what he had felt, and he preferred not to think about it. And he had started to feel increasingly uncomfortable about reading, which had started to make him feel drained.

He had almost finished brushing. Four quadrants, each with seven teeth now, so four times seven equals twenty-eight; twenty-eight strokes per quadrant equals one hundred and twelve, the sequence repeated four times because of the number of quadrants equals four hundred and forty-eight strokes to complete the teeth-brushing routine. But when Mr Windrush at school had told them about prime numbers a few weeks ago, and his dad had expanded on the information when he had come home, he had added an extra random stroke to make four four nine. It seemed better that way. He spat the foamy spittle into the basin, rinsed his mouth and the brush, and replaced it neatly in its glass, positioning it carefully so that the bristles were facing the same way as those of his parents' brushes. As he was crossing the landing, he went back briefly to check his brush again. Then, he scooted into his room and jumped into bed.

"Lights out, or do you want to read a while longer?" his mother asked after she had kissed his forehead and settled the duvet under his chin.

"Lights out," Car answered. "I don't want to read any more tonight."

"Good boy," said his dad, planting a fleeting kiss on his hair. "*Kali nichta,* Cat."

"Good night, Chrissie," his mum said, and the light went out.

"'Night," said Cat. The door closed, and he lay in the heavy dark.

"Mum," he called. "Dad."

The door opened again, and he saw his parents' silhouettes, dark against the light coming up the stairs. The landing light had already been turned off.

"What is it, Chrissie?" his mum asked.

"Mum?" Cat said in a voice which made two syllables of the word, one high, one low. "Dad?" Again, two syllables. "I heard you talking. Downstairs. Before."

"Yes, Chrissie? What's the matter?"

"You were saying … it sounded … like there was trouble?"

"Trouble?" his dad asked. "What do you mean, Cat?"

"Like there was trouble between you. You and my grandparents. In Cyprus. You said you didn't want to go and see them."

Cat's father gave a light laugh. Cat saw his shadowy arm move to rest along his mum's shoulders, and she tilted her head to rest it against her husband's chest. Cat felt a warm feeling creep behind his eyes. It was nice to see his mum doing that.

"There's no trouble. We're just not going to go right now. It's a long way, and it's very expensive. It's hard to find the time as well. You've got school and we've got work. Maybe one summer."

"You're sure? There's no trouble?"

"We're sure, Chrissie," his mum said. "You can talk to your grandparents the next time your dad phones them."

"I can try. But it's not easy to understand what they're saying."

"I know, sweetheart. You and I will have to try harder with learning Greek."

"And you're sure there's no trouble? Would you tell me if there was?"

"There's no trouble, Cat," his dad said firmly. "Come on now. It's nearly eight and a half. Time to sleep."

"Half past eight, dad. Not eight and a half."

"Whatever," said his dad. "It's still time to sleep. Now. Close eyes and snuggle down."

"Night night, Chrissie."

"Night night, mum. *Kali nichta*, dad."

"Very good, *gataki mou*," his dad said approvingly. "Sleep."

The door began to close slowly, obscuring his parents' shapes, and the light was gradually shut out, until the room was dark once again. He heard the noises of his parents moving away. The loose floorboard made its creaky sound; then there were the sounds of feet going down the stairs. Cat lay in the dark and waited for his eyes to adjust.

Soon, he was able to make out shapes and the thin line of vague light along the bottom of the door. He wanted to believe what his parents had told him, but their conversation downstairs had sounded different from what they had just said. He thought of a word he had learned recently – rift. There was a rift. He did not like the idea of a rift. He did not like arguments and disagreements and things splitting up. He liked things to be complete.

In the warm, heavy dark, he recited silently his times tables up to twelve. Each set of numbers had a reassuring completeness to it. If he recited his tables often enough until he fell asleep, there would be no disagreement and no rift.

Eventually, exhausted, Cat fell asleep.

* * *

"'Morning, Mrs Fettes," chirped Sandra, the recently appointed secretarial assistant who Joan had been helping learn the ropes of how the offices of the aircraft factory operated. "White rabbits."

"Oh yes," replied Joan, "white rabbits, Sandra."

"I can't believe it's September already. Did you have a nice Bank Holiday? Did you go anywhere nice? We went to Brid for the day. My dad wanted to go to Hornsea because it's not as far but my mum made him go to Brid and I was glad because it's much nicer than Hornsea."

As Sandra talked, Joan was settling herself at her desk, taking the cover off her typewriter, and removing files from a desk drawer. There were a number of letters and reports for the two of them to type up, and there was filing for Sandra to make sense of, but first they had to go through the customary chatter which Sandra seemed to need to get out of the way before she could settle to the tasks of the day. Joan was happy to indulge her, since once she got going she could be efficient and precise.

"I didn't go anywhere, Sandra," she told her protégée. "I had plenty to do at home and in the garden."

"That's what my dad said," rejoined Sandra. She put on a comically deep voice in imitation of her father. "'There's so much to do at home and you all want to go gallivanting off to Bridlington, spending my hard earned.'" Sandra pulled a grumpy face. "He's such an old grump, but he had a nice time once we got there."

Joan smiled indulgently, but felt it necessary to upbraid the young woman, even though she liked her spiritedness.

"You mustn't speak disrespectfully of your father, Sandra."

"I'm sorry, Mrs Fettes," Sandra said immediately. "I didn't mean to be disrespectful." Her pretty, youthful face looked chastened, and Joan felt sorry to have dampened her enthusiasm. Although the girl could be a chatterbox, it was cheering to hear her bubbly news at the beginning of the day.

"Did you have an enjoyable time in Brid, then, Sandra?" asked Joan. "Was it busy? Was the train full?"

Sandra had been inspecting her fingernails, but could not resist looking up with what struck Joan as the beginnings of a smug little smirk.

"Oh, Mrs Fettes," she said patting the French pleat in which she had carefully styled her hair, "we didn't go on the train. My young man, Bill – I've told you about him – he borrowed his dad's motor car, and he took us – me, my mum and dad – all the way to Brid in it."

"Bill's father must be very generous and trusting."

"Bill's a very careful driver, Mrs Fettes – well, with my dad in the front seat next to him he had to be. It was a lovely day out, though. Mum and dad were ever so chuffed to be driven around like royalty."

Joan felt a pang of guilt that she had thought of Sandra's expression as smug. She was just pleased to have nice things to do with people she loved, Joan thought to herself.

"It was thoughtful of Bill to take you all out for the day," said Joan. "You're a lucky girl, Sandra, to have so many exciting things happening these days."

"I know I am, Mrs Fettes. You know what I think? I know the war was a bad thing for everyone – I was ten when it ended so I remember a lot of what it was like, but now it's been over for years, and everything seems as though it's better than ever. Bill says it's like we're living in a Golden Age. He's nearly finished his apprenticeship here. I've got this job…"

Sandra fell suddenly silent with a little hiccoughy grunt, as though stopping herself from saying too much about her good fortune.

"Yes, and if we want to keep our jobs," said Joan, lightly, "we had better get on with a little work before the end of the morning. They'll be wanting these letters for signing, and they need these reports typing up."

Joan riffled through some of the paperwork on the desk in front of her, and handed some foolscap sheets over to Sandra. The girl had proved herself to be a more than competent typist; her shorthand was reasonable and was improving; and she possessed an organised mind which understood the logical structure of things like the general filing system they used at the factory.

"Add these to your list, Sandra," Joan instructed her protégée. She had insisted that Sandra kept a list of things she had to do, and would cross each item off as soon as it had been completed. It was a system which had served her well and which had won her the good opinion of her superiors at the Blackburn Aircraft Company Limited. Her reputation for precision and reliability had been well-earned, and she could get through a remarkable amount, even though she had always only been part-time. Her confident hope was that soon Sandra, under her tutelage, would be looked on in the same way by Mr Blackburn and his associates.

Sandra quickly scribbled a number of squiggly lines and dots into a spiral-bound shorthand notebook, and the two women in the office settled themselves down to their work, feeding letterheads and sheets of carbon copy paper into their typewriters. The machines began to make their clacking and ratchetty sounds as letters and reports were produced for the next two hours.

"Right. Tea," announced Joan, extracting a newly completed missive from the roller of her typewriter. The mechanism screamed briefly as if in protest, but released its sandwich of letterhead, carbon and thin copy paper for Joan to add to the pile in her out-box. Sandra hurriedly typed a few more words on her own machine, then pushed her chair back and stood up.

"See if you can get some nice biscuits today, Sandra," Joan instructed the girl. "And don't spend too long outside the draughtsmen's offices on your way back, or the tea will be cold." She gave a gently knowing smile, which Sandra returned archly. Joan was aware that Bill, the apprentice draughtsman, careful driver and considerate prospective son-in-law, would be waiting for his fiancée to pass the Draughts Offices.

"The tea will be hot, I promise," said Sandra. "And I'll get the best biscuits they have."

With a swish of her full skirted dress and a slight wobble on heels which Joan considered a little too high, but which she had not mentioned, Sandra disappeared through the office door to make her way across the factory site to one of the three canteens which served a steadily growing work force engaged in the design, testing and construction of civilian and military aircraft. Sandra's destination was not as elegant as the Executive Dining Room, which had art-deco panelling and a view of the river from an expanse of metal-framed windows, but it was more salubrious than the workmen's canteen where the factory-men in their blue overalls sat at long, formica-topped tables. Joan and Sandra seldom took their breaks in their canteen, however. Despite the individual tables topped with linen cloths, they preferred the privacy of their own office where they could share a plate of biscuits and a pot of tea away from the pipe smoke and hearty banter of the other office workers. And Joan looked forward to her daily chats with someone who was young enough to be her daughter. While she was awaiting Sandra's return, she took her library book from her bag, sitting back in her chair to read.

The book wore a bright yellow, hardback cover, inside which a little flap of paper had been pasted for the librarian to stamp. It interested Joan to look back at the dates in their haphazard columns, and she wondered who the people were who had read the book before her. And what they had thought of it. She had often toyed with the idea of establishing some kind of reading club in the village, where everyone would read a book and then they could meet to discuss it. But she had not been able to see how it would work in practice. The village library only had one copy of each text, so it would take an age for everyone to read the book, and then the person who had read it first would probably have forgotten what it had all been about. Of course, they could all have *bought* the same book, but why buy a book when the library had such a good stock to lend out?

There were some kinds of book that Joan had no time for: soppy romances of the Mills and Boon kind, and fantasy tales about daft wizards and elves. She liked to read stories about real people, set in the real world, and was particularly keen on mysteries, especially involving clever detectives. She liked Agatha Christie, but preferred Dorothy L. Sayers. The book on her knee at that moment was one of the Lord Peter Wimsey novels. Joan thought it would be nice to talk to someone about why Peter Wimsey, who is a lord and she had never met a lord, was a more believable character than, say, Miss Marple, who was an old lady living in a village, and Joan had met plenty of them. She had, however, very recently *seen* a lord, albeit at quite a distance. At the moment, she had no one to discuss such things with, and Sandra had never expressed any interest in reading novels.

"I suppose it's something to do with how the writer fills in the background of the characters," thought Joan, recalling how, in one of the books, Lord Peter had suffered from nightmares about his experiences in the trenches during the Great War. She opened her book at the page where she had placed her bookmark the night before, and took up reading about the aristocrat's efforts at solving the mystery which was currently occupying him. It was a tale of malice, set in an Oxford college for women. Joan wondered what her own life would have been like if she had been able to go to a university, or had stayed on at school instead of going to the secretarial college.

She suddenly realised that she had not followed anything of what she had been reading, as the noise of high heels and a rattling tray of crockery announced Sandra's return. The girl's disappointed expression as she came through the door told its own tale.

"Wasn't he there, then?" asked Joan sympathetically.

"There's some kind of rush on, and they're working through their breaks." Sandra pulled a face expressing disgruntlement, as she set down her tray on Joan's desk. "What're you reading, Mrs Fettes? Is it one of your murder books?"

"It's a mystery, Sandra, but there's been no murders in it. It's one of the Lord Peter Wimsey books. You should read one. You might like them."

"I'm not a great reader, you know, Mrs Fettes. I find it lonely. I prefer talking to people than burying myself in a book. You know, and going out and meeting people."

"Well, it's like you're meeting new people by reading about the characters in books. Where else could I meet someone like Lord Peter?"

"But they're not real, are they? Not like people you meet, you know, in the real world?"

"I suppose not, Sandra, but while you're reading about them, it's as though they are real. And after you've finished the book, they kind of live on with you. In your memory."

Sandra's expressive face assumed a sceptical look of not being very convinced. She took a hefty bite out of her custard cream.

"Anyway, Mrs Fettes," she said, crumbily, "you did meet a lord – well, you saw one. Last week. We all did. Though he didn't look much like a lord to me. Very scruffy."

Joan gave a laugh as she too bit into her biscuit, and then washed it down with a sip from her tea-cup. "You're right, Sandra. We did see a lord, and he was rather scruffy, but you didn't expect him to be wearing ermine robes, did you? He was trying to walk across the river – a mile over the mud."

"No, of course not, but he just didn't look any different from anyone else. In fact, he looked a bit like my dad. And I couldn't see what the point of it was."

"He was trying to prove that the Romans, when they were here, could have invaded by crossing the river on foot. He was lucky not to sink into the sludge."

"Ooh," said Sandra with a shudder. "That would be horrible. Imagine. Sinking down into mud. Ugh."

Joan nodded in agreement. It would have been a terrible end to Lord Noel-Buxton's bold experiment. "Yes, it would be horrible, Sandra. But, do you know what I think would be worse?"

Sandra's attractively wide eyes fixed quizzically on Joan. "No? What could be worse than sinking down into that awful grey gloop, Mrs Fettes?"

"Floating off into the sky without anything to bring you back down to earth."

"You mean like going up in a balloon? Are you afraid of heights, Mrs Fettes?"

"That would give me the shivers, yes, but I was thinking more just drifting up and up without anything under your feet. Going higher and higher, and the ground and all the trees and houses getting further and further away and smaller and smaller."

"You're a very down-to-earth sort of person, Mrs Fettes," Sandra declared. "That's why you don't like it."

"I certainly prefer to have my feet firmly on the ground," agreed Joan.

"So it's funny you should be here, isn't it?"

"What do you mean, Sandra?"

"You know, working in an aircraft factory of all places. You'd feel happier on a farm!"

"Maybe that's why I like my garden so much." Joan took a final sip of her tea and replaced her cup and saucer on the tray for Sandra to clear. It was time to get back to the business of the morning, finishing the reports and letters, and taking the heavy buff folders along to the desks of the men who were their superiors. As Sandra collected the tray to place it outside their door for the cleaning ladies to pick up, Joan glanced out of the office's windows which looked out onto a central courtyard, surrounded on all sides by the factory buildings. Above the roofs, a strip of blue September sky was visible, streaked with high, vaporous cloud. A memory of shrieking gulls came into her mind, and then the thought of the moon, somewhere beyond the blue, cold and alone, surrounded by the unending blackness of space.

With a shudder, Joan reached for her shorthand pad to see what was next on today's list.

* * *

The black oblong chunk attached to the dark tunic of the uniform makes another squelchy announcement as a gnomic echo of the policeman's words. "This isn't a designated camping area. Pack up, and you'll have to be on your way." The walkie-talkie releases another incomprehensible update, but the dark figure before me, encumbered and augmented by pouches and accoutrements around his waist and across his chest, is unheeding of its messages. His shadowed eyes beneath the peak of his cap are fixed on me.

I'm aware of my voice saying something, while my own dark echo speaks in my head.

"I'm sorry," I say. "I didn't realise it wasn't allowed."

The nameless me-not-me voice tells me that I have brought this on myself by forfeiting the rituals while I have been helping Joan.

"It's a strange place to choose for a camping holiday. Are you here on your own, or are you here with some mates?"

"I'm not really here on holiday," I answer, keeping my voice level, although I can feel the sky starting to weigh down in the metallic way it has. "And there's no one with me."

101, 131, 151, 181, 191, 313, 353, 383, 727, 757, 787, 797, 919, 929, 10301

"So, where are you from? What are you doing here?" The distorted voice issues from his chest once again, a squelchy, disturbing sound from another dimension. My leg starts to do its jiggly thing.

"I used to live here," I say. "And I'm just back for a visit."

101, 101, 101

"So, you know people in the village?"

"I've been away for a couple of years, but I know some people, yeah."

There's a silence, intensified by a burst of static and the pressure of the sky.

101, 101, 101

"I'll tell you what," says the policeman, hooking his thumbs in among the paraphernalia on his belt. "I'll be back down here tomorrow. I don't expect to see your tent still here. Go and stay with someone you know."

The walkie-talkie makes a final sounding squawking noise, and he begins to move away. "Take care," he says, and I am left alone with the tent, the river and the sky, and the me-not-me voice whispering darkly in my mind.

If I had performed the rituals properly in Joan's house as I crossed thresholds and passed from room to room, my refuge by the river, sheltered from the clean freshness of the breeze would be unviolated. As penance, I remain on the path, looking down at the tent, bearing the brunt of the river's thick odour and the stinging ache of the east wind in my ears, and running long, repetitive sequences of numbers until an equilibrium will settle on me. Eventually, I think it is permissible to jump down from the path. A number of walkers, pulled along by their dogs and casting glances at me, have passed while I have been standing here. But just as I am about to leave the path, there is a shout from behind me.

"Ey, Cat. You. Whatsyername. Chris."

As I glance round, I see that it's three of the Eddie van Halens from the other day. They're coming purposely along the path, walking with a slouching swagger which manages to look both comical and threatening. Their razored cuts are being blown by the wind, which plasters the hair sleekly against their heads.

101, 131, 151, 181, 191, 313, 353, 383, 727, 757, 787, 797, 919, 929, 10301

I turn to face them.

"We saw you were talking to that copper. What was he saying?"

"Did he tell you to move your tent? I bet he did."

"I 'kin' 'ate coppers."

"No, you don't. My Uncle Dave's a copper."

"Well, except for him, I do."

It's not easy to differentiate between them: there's the dark haired one, who seems to be the leader of their group, and who asks the most questions. The other two are the mousy browns. The blond one isn't with them again. They all wear stone-washed jeans, leather jackets and high top baseball boots with studied, mid-teen nonchalance. They seem to have forgotten the animosity of our previous encounter, and once again are inexplicably interested in me and my tent.

"What's he say?" asks dark-hair Eddie. "Have you got to move?"

"I 'kin' 'ate coppers."

"He only says that 'cos they nearly put his dad away for receiving stolen goods," dark-hair tells me.

"Fuck off," says his friend with a belligerent glare. "They couldn't prove anything, dickhead."

The other mousy brown haired one chimes in.

"He got off on a technical itty."

"A what, Mikey?" Dark-hair asks with sudden amusement. His eyes gleam, and his mouth widens with the beginnings of a cruel grin. "He got off on a what?"

"A technical itty," Mikey repeats, and the other two bark with derisive laughter.

"A technicality, you twat," says dark-hair. He gives Mikey's chest a brief shove, and Mikey retaliates with a punch to the shoulder. They scuffle a little and then suddenly stop. The third one looks on without interest, pulling out his cigarettes. They remind me of three mildly aggressive puppies, almost indistinguishable, ready to fight at any moment, but immediately unresentful of each other's aggression. Mikey and dark-hair take a cigarette each. The third Eddie offers the packet to me. I shake my head, and they set about the lighting up performance.

"So, what did he say?" dark-hair asks again, exhaling a streamer of smoke from one corner of his mouth. "That copper? You got to move on, then?"

I do a quick calculation, assessing the dangers of answering or not answering, revealing or not revealing. Knowing what the policeman said can present no risk to me or to the Eddies.

"He said I can't camp here."

"Bastard," breathes the non-Mikey mousey brown one.

"Maybe he can come and put his tent up in your garden, Deez," suggests dark-hair.

Deez makes a scornful noise, and takes a deep draw on his cigarette. "You'd be lucky," he tells me. "Our garden's like a junkyard with all my dad's stuff from the workshop."

"Yeah, it's where he keeps all the stolen goods," snipes Mikey.

"Fuck off, twat-nose," says Deez.

"It's not stolen, Mikey," says dark-hair. "That's just a technical itty."

There is some more barging of each other and mocking laughter. I feel like a spectator at a badly scripted clown show. The episode comes to another sudden end. The three of them take pulls at their cigarettes and their heads are wreathed with smoke briefly until the wind clears the air around us. I'd like to get away from the burden of their company, but there's nowhere to go. I don't feel as though I can just jump down from the path and retreat into the tent, though the Eddies probably wouldn't think it rude or unusual for someone to just leave. I hang around, staring out over the brown and grey expanse of the river towards Lincolnshire in the distance. Overhead, the sky is the same colour. I realise it's getting late and I haven't eaten anything since the morning.

"Seriously, though," says dark-hair, gesturing in my direction. "You should camp out in someone's garden. You know people in the village, don't you?"

"Yeah, I know people," I say. "That's not a bad idea. I'll think about it."

"Eddie's full of good ideas," Deez announces, taking a final drag and flipping the butt away in the direction of the river. "He's a fuckin' genius."

"Are you called Eddie?" I ask, amused.

"Yeah, why?" Eddie looks at me suspiciously.

"He's not really called Eddie," Mikey pipes up. "It's just a nickname. He's really called…"

But before Eddie's true identity can be revealed, Mikey has been jumped on and a hand clamped over his mouth. There is jostling, in which Deez plays a part. Then Mikey manages to free himself and runs off some way before turning to face Eddie and Deez.

"It's not his real name," calls Mikey with a mocking lilt in his voice. "He's really called …" He turns again and runs further off, as Eddie and Deez start towards him. I watch them recede into the distance, Eddie and Deez, who are better athletes, catching up with Mikey just before they disappear around a bend in the path. I run a short sequence of primes to ensure Mikey is not too badly treated by his friends.

Then I think about getting something to eat, and returning to Joan's with a proposition for her.

*   *   *

Joan's shoes are making a curious dull, echoing sound as she walks from the foot of the stairs towards the dining room. As she passes the framed rectangle of the hall mirror, she catches sight of a fleeting movement out of the corner of her eye, but she avoids looking into the glass. She potters through the dining room doorway, gathering up a strip of paper which is lying on the sideboard. There are a few short lines of spidery writing on one side. Joan takes the paper and goes to sit in her chair by the fire. Outside the windows she can see that the daylight is starting to fade but it's not yet dark enough to put the lights on. She can still make out the words on the paper.

Check up with Dr Blaine – Monday 10 o'clock (DO NOT FORGET)

Post Letter to Muriel (forgot - on Sideboard)

Collect Pension (Book in Sideboard drawer)

Shops (see other List)

Check taps in Sink

Check taps in Bathroom

Keys (in Bag)

Hall carpet???

The coals in the grate are burning low, but there is a warm glow, illuminating Harry who is there in front of the hearth, looking into the distance from his darkly intelligent eyes. He seems to be hovering a few inches above the rug, and is shimmering gently. Joan rattles the strip of paper at him to attract his attention. It makes a quiet, rustling susurration.

"Is that a shopping list, you've got there, Joan?" Harry asks in his hushed Sean Connery voice, its sibilants blurred and its vowels musical. "I hope you haven't forgotten to put my biscuits on it? You seem to be forgetting lots of important things these days."

"Everyone forgets things," answers Joan, a little petulantly. In her day she was renowned for her memory and organisational abilities. "Don't tell me you've never forgotten anything, Harry. It's only natural. When I was at Blackburns – and when I was Convenor for the WI, mind you – I had a reputation for never forgetting a thing, or a face. You should see the diaries I kept – they're still there in one of the cupboards – full of details. They trained us to use shorthand in those days. So quick to write everything down. So you never forget anything. Or anyone. They're all still in there." Joan gestures towards the sideboard across the room. "And in here." Her finger rises and taps gently at her temple. "I remember them all. Bob – he died in the War. And Muriel and Arthur, who live in Brid. And Henry, who died at the end of the sixties. And all the rest of the family, and that Sandra who came to work at the factory. I wonder what happened to her?" Joan continues to list person after person, tapping softly at the piece of paper on her lap.

"It's all here on my lists," Joan says.

"Ah, yes," growls Harry. "Your lists."

Joan's eyes travel down the paper, squinting to make out the wavering characters in the dwindling light of the late afternoon.

"I'll read it through to you, and you can tell me if I've left anything off." She begins to read, reeling off the things she must not forget to do over the next few days.

"Biscuits," mutters Harry at one point, but Joan reads on. As she reaches the end of the list, she remembers the strange, dull echo of her shoes on the floor as she walked along the hall.

"It's very worrying what's happened to the hall carpet," she whispers. It has something to do with the young man who was at the house before. And something to do with checking the taps. That's why Joan has put the items on the list. And something to do with the old motorbike in the shed, which Bob bought just before the War started. Joan rubs the back of her hand over her eyes. Harry, shimmering in front of the fire, turns a slow somersault in the air, while someone knocks in soft volleys of raps on the front door.

EIGHT

Standing at the kerb, Joan watched the taxi-cab's hunched, black beetle-shape perform an elegant half-pirouette in the road during a break in the traffic. Then, with surprising speed, it accelerated away, taking its two black-clad passengers, Muriel and Arthur, off to catch their late morning train back to Bridlington. Joan had earlier on declined the offer of a lift to the station to catch her own train back to the village. She wanted to spend a little more time here, walking the tree-lined avenues, and maybe paying a nostalgic visit to the big municipal park, thinking about the old days when she had been a girl growing up amid the newly laid out roads and the developing clusters and lines of houses; and remembering her recently deceased brother, Henry.

Although the air in the brick-walled church had made the three mourners glad of their funereal clothing during the brief and spartan service, it was a muggily warm July day outside, and Joan was beginning to feel uncomfortably hot in the dark jacket she was wearing over her black dress. Everyone else who passed on the street was dressed for the summer weather: short sleeves and light colours, the girls in those very short skirts they had all started wearing, showing much more of their legs than Joan could ever have considered decent. She directed a sharply disapproving look at a young woman who was pushing a large Silver Cross pram along the pavement. Really, thought Joan, half her bottom was showing. It would never have been allowed when she'd been a girl. In protest, she made a little tutting noise and left her jacket on. Making her way down Laburnum Avenue, she left behind her the church where her brother's funeral service had just taken place.

It was hard to believe that well over half a century had gone by since she and Henry and the rest of the family regularly made this walk to and from St Columba's. Joan could recall looking forward to singing the hymns, but dreading the sermons of the vicar, whose name she could not for the life of her remember. Something with a P – or an S – but the name had disappeared. And later on, when she'd been old enough, taking Communion, the tasteless cloying wafer sticking to the roof of her mouth, followed by the forbidden, vinous headiness of the wine, sipped from the out-held chalice. Then, after the service, walking back along these same pavements, either to go for tea and biscuits with the rest of the congregation at the Garden Village Clubhouse, or straight home, depending on the inscrutable decision-making of parents. And sometimes, if the weather had turned out fine, Henry would take her round to East Park where they would go boating on the waters of the lake.

Funny that Henry, who had been such exciting, boyish company when they were growing up, should have become more and more reclusive as he reached manhood, never moving out of their parents' house, living with their mother after father died, and then, when their mother died at the beginning of the nineteen-fifties, living an increasingly reductive, solitary life. They had seldom communicated, at most three or four times a year. Passing the still familiar frontages of the houses, most of which had sprouted H-shaped television aerials on their roofs, Joan wondered what could have happened to her brother to make him want to restrict his life to a couple of the rooms of the family house, his job in the Accounts Office of one of the big department stores in the town, and a weekly foray to the local Bridge Club. When they had spoken or met, Joan had found little to say to him, and had also found herself missing the boy he had once been. As she arrived in front of the house, one of the few to lack a crowning H, she experienced the same sensation of loss for the boy he had been, while the words of the vicar in his very short address about someone he had never met returned to her mind: *And ye shall hear of wars and rumours of wars: see that ye be not troubled: for these things must come to pass, but the end is not yet.*

True, thought Joan, looking at the house's frontage, and reaching into her handbag for the keys which now belonged solely to her; all things must pass. Nothing lasts forever. She withdrew her hand from the bag, but left the keys in amongst her paraphernalia of purse, powder compact and lipstick, Nivea handcream, hankie, and all the other accoutrements necessary to the life of a sixty-something, respectable woman. There was no hurry; she would take a turn in the park before she went into the old house to inspect the barrenness of her brother's eremitic existence: a simple life, followed by a straightforward illness, and, according to the hospital, a swift, unfussy death.

When Joan, carrying her jacket draped over one arm, having succumbed to the sun's warmth, arrived at the park, she was struck by how unchanged the place was. Open expanses of grass, specked with daisies and fringed with trees, paths along which a few prampushers were trundling, the blue-grey waters of the lake. She hadn't set foot here in donkeys' years. Of course, the people were different: the clothes they were wearing; their hair and even their skin were different from how she recollected things had been in the past. A group of four boys and girls – young men and women really – they looked like students from the university – were sitting on the green. The boys had taken their tops off and their skins were shining, one with English pallor, the other with an olive lustre. The girls' limbs were bare. All four seemed at ease with the proximity of each other's flesh. They were laughing and talking, and throwing their heads back with wide open mouths, as though unaware of the existence of anyone else. One of the boys reached out a hand and stroked the bare arm of the girl next to him.

Joan walked on towards the boating lake, and one of the benches which faced the water. The sun glittered on the surface. Joan sat and thought about Henry and herself in one of the rowing boats. It was queer to think that he was still there in her head, as a young boy, as a grown man, and as an elderly, strange recluse; and at the same time, he was dead and in a highly polished coffin in the ground.

Someone had left a folded newspaper lying on the bench where Joan had chosen to sit. She recognised the face of the American president, self-assured, like a slightly shifty version of Dean Martin as he was speaking into a telephone receiver; and next to his picture, a snapshot of a smiling, bright-eyed young man with a microphone headset at one side of his mouth. It was one of the American astronauts who had been in the news just about constantly. Joan picked up the paper, unfolding it to reveal its banner headline: MAN WALKS ON THE MOON, and a photograph of someone in a spacesuit, looking like the Michelin Man carrying an oblong rucksack on his back. With all the bother of Henry's funeral, it had skipped Joan's mind that, while here on the surface of the Earth, she and the rest of the human race had been going about their ordinary lives, a man had been walking on the moon, millions of miles above their heads.

The thought filled her with horror. How dreadful, she thought, to be so far away, so disconnected from everything and everyone. Despite the sun's heat through the black fabric of her dress, Joan felt a cold shudder pass over her as she imagined Henry, floating off into the sky towards the men on the moon, and Bob, and her parents out there too. But all of that, an afterlife, heaven and hell, judgement and resurrection, was so far-fetched. It was all impossible to believe in, although the hymns were pretty, and the ritual beguiling. Henry, her parents, Bob, they were all gone, and would never come again, except in her memory.

Joan suddenly jerked awake, realising that she had been nodding off in the sun. She could only have dozed for a few seconds; the landscape of the park was unchanged. The sun glittered on the lake; the young people were chattering and laughing on the greensward. The boy had curled his arm around the girl's waist and she was resting her head on his naked shoulder. Joan replaced the newspaper, folded once again, on the bench, and rose to walk towards the park's exit, on her way to visit her brother's empty house which now belonged to her, the only surviving member of the Kershaw family who had once lived in Hull's Garden Village.

Although she knew a lot of folk in the village where she had lived for the past three and a half decades, only twenty minutes away down the railway line, and although Muriel and Arthur in their house in Bridlington were as close as blood relations, Joan felt an empty loneliness blooming in her like a terrible flower. She concentrated on the feel and the tapping noise of her soles on the pavement beneath her feet.

*   *   *

The streetlights are just starting to come on as I leave the riverbank path and walk past the pubs on the way to Joan's house. It's that indeterminate time of day when you're not sure if it's the end of the afternoon or the beginning of the evening. A car passes, its tail-lights flaring as it slows to take the bend, and is followed by a hunched shape on a motorbike, whose engine roars and pops. Then there is a banshee scream, and the rider accelerates away from the bend into the greyness of the evening.

101, 131, 151, 181, 191, 313, 353

There is no screech of brakes or crunching of metal.

As I walk by, the front entrance of one of the pubs opens, emitting yellow light and exuding a warm aroma of old beer and tobacco smoke, which masks vague cooking odours. I wonder if Joan will be in her kitchen at this time, and how she copes with making things to eat, given her confused state whenever I've met her. I run through how I am going to make my proposition to her, timing each suggestion to coincide with passing one of the streetlamps which line the road.

Because your garden is in such a state, I can help you get it in some kind of order.

I can keep an eye on you in case there is a problem, like with the flooding.

You need someone who can help with oddjobs and carrying shopping.

When the carpet has dried out properly I can put it back for you.

Your garden shed needs a bit of a clear out.

I need somewhere to pitch my tent, and I was thinking I could use your garden.

I reorder the suggestions into a number of different permutations, trying to decide whether to open with the main request or leave it to the end. I can hear my voice second-guessing myself all the way to Joan's house. When I arrive at her front door, most of the neighbouring houses have lights on in their windows and porches. Joan's house is in darkness, except for a faint glimmer of light from somewhere within which illuminates the pink and gold of the panel of stained glass in the front door. Other than this faint glow, there is no sign of life in the house. I wonder if Joan has gone out on some kind of errand, even though it's late and all the shops will be shutting for the day.

I rap on the door with what I hope is a friendly-sounding tattoo of knocks, not too loud but firmly audible. I run through another permutation of the suggestions and a sequence of primes. Then there is some shadowy movement in the space behind the glass. Not wanting to alarm Joan, I resist the urge to knock again, and I hear her reedy voice quavering through the glass.

"Is that you, Henry?"

"It's me, Joan," I reply. "Cat. Christopher. I know I said I'd come back tomorrow, but …" I let the sentence hang in the air, not really knowing how to continue with the door standing between us. "Can you open the door? I've got something I want to ask you."

"Who is it?" asks Joan. "I wasn't expecting anyone. I thought someone said Henry was…" She doesn't finish her sentence and the door remains closed between us. There is a long pause.

"Joan? Are you there? It's me, Christopher. I helped you with the water earlier. I want to ask you something."

There is another lengthy pause, and then the sound of the Yale lock being turned. A sliver of Joan's face appears between the jamb and the edge of the door. She peers up at me with suspiciously squinnying eyes.

"Who is it?" she repeats. "I thought it might be Henry, come from …" She tries to peer round my shoulder as though someone might be hiding behind me. Then she looks over her own shoulder, back into the carpet-less hall. The door swings a little further open, allowing the light from the streetlamps to penetrate into the gloom.

The dim light I had seen through the stained glass had come from the kitchen door at the far end of the hallway, which looks barren and temporary without its carpet. It gives off an echoey feeling and the forest-floor smell of damp wood.

"It's me, Christopher. I was here earlier when you had the flood. Remember? I cleared up the water and took your hall carpet outside to dry."

More suspicious peering, then a kind of relieved realisation filters down over Joan's features.

"So that's where it's gone," she says. "I've been racking my brains. You're that nice lad. What's your name?"

"Christopher. But people call me Cat."

"What a funny name. I've never had a cat. I had a dog."

"I know. Harry. You were looking for him at the river."

Joan looks over her shoulder again.

"I hope I'm not interrupting," I say. "If you've got guests …"

"While you're here," says Joan, "can you do something for me? Just have a look in this window and tell me if there's someone there." She stands to one side, and gestures towards the wall where a rectangular mirror in a frame hangs.

"Which window do you mean, Joan?" I ask, unsure of what she wants me to do.

"This one." She points at the mirror.

"It's not a window. It's a mirror."

The same look of relief washes over her face but is quickly replaced by an expression of worry and confusion. She looks straight into the mirror and lets out a faint breathless exclamation.

"Oh!"

Her look becomes defensive, as she turns back to me. "Of course, it is. I was reminded of my grandma looking through a window. Yes, it's the old hall mirror. It's been there for years, ever since we first moved in. Yes, the mirror. Of course."

"Joan," I interrupt. "I've got something to ask you. That's why I've come back."

"Yes? Why have you come back? Where have you been?" She glances at the mirror and then back at me.

"I've got something to ask you. A favour, really, though I want to do you a favour at the same time."

I can feel the pressure of the threshold between us: Joan on one side in her liminal space, me on the other. I do a toe-tapping routine though I'm not intending to enter the house.

"What are you doing that for?" Joan asks, pointing at my foot.

"I was thinking that it's not safe – it's not good for you to be here alone – without anyone nearby to help you, if you need anything."

"I'm not going into a home, if that's what you're getting at." Joan's voice hovers unexpectedly on belligerence.

101, 131, 151, 181, 191, 313, 353

"No. Of course, not. That's not what I mean. I was thinking about your garden – how it's all overgrown – and your shed needs tidying up – and the carpet, when it's dry."

Joan looks confused, and I can't really blame her. I do the toe-tapping again.

"I don't understand what you're saying. What's all this about?"

"I'm not explaining myself very well, Joan. I'm sorry." I take a breath. "Can I pitch a tent in your garden? And live there? Then you'll have someone nearby in case you need anything. You know, a helper. I could help you if you needed any help."

I don't think I've phrased my proposition very well, but at least I think it's now clear.

"You want to live in my garden?"

"Yes, please."

"And help?"

"Yes."

"I don't know about that. It sounds a bit strange."

"I wouldn't be any trouble, Joan. I'd just stay in the tent and fix the garden. I prefer being outside, anyway."

We stand on either side of the threshold while Joan thinks.

"Maybe I could try for a day or two, and if you didn't like me being there, I could go away?"

"You want to camp in the garden for a couple of days?"

"And if it doesn't work out, I'll leave."

"And you're going to help with the garden?"

"Yes. I'm good with my hands, and I know what I'm doing. I used to help my grandparents on the land."

Joan casts a hesitant glance over her shoulder into the semi-dark of the hallway. It's as though she's listening to someone behind her.

"Alright. We can try it for a little while. But it does seem strange."

In my head, a celebratory sequence of guitar chords resolves itself:

E F#m A B E

E F#m A B E

E F#m A B E

I play the sequence over and over all the way back to the riverbank and my tent.

* * *

"Up," said Christopher, who was also called Cat, and, here in this funny, hot place, Christophoros and *kouklos* and *moro*. There were so many names and words for so many things.

The strong, brown hands of his granddad, who was *pappou* and sometimes Thomas or *papa*, depending on who was speaking, gripped him under his arms and he was hoisted towards the brilliant blue of the sky. The sun burned in the blueness with a white hotness. Cat knew he must not look at the sun. The sun would burn his eyes. He looked at the two brown hands and their fingers which encircled his own hands. There were so many hands. Everyone had two – except the man on the aeroplane who had had one hand and a no-hand with a metal hook. Mummy had told him not to stare, but the man had waved the hook at him and smiled, and Cat had laughed. Mummy had two hands, which were soft and pink. Daddy's hands were bigger and harder and browner, but not as hard and brown as *pappou's* hands. How funny hands were with their wiggling fingers. Cat laughed about all the hands as his granddad-*pappou* settled him comfortably onto shoulders and started to walk down the hillside. Mummy and daddy were following, carrying metal buckets and big rolls of cloth and long sticks. In one of the buckets there was a smaller plastic bucket and a bright red spade for Cat. Granddad-*pappou* bounced Cat on his shoulders as they went down the hillside. They were going to do jobs. Cat liked jobs, especially if the jobs needed his red spade.

The little party arrived near the bottom of the hillside where a terrace had been carved out and a number of almond trees had been planted. The bark of the trees was rough and black; on the spindly branches among sparse, dry leaves, the almonds in their split skins waited to be harvested. Many of the nuts, in pale brown, hard casings, had already fallen to the ground, and lay in the powdery, grey earth.

"Tell your dad to put him in the shade, Andreas," said Cat's mother. "He can dig while we get on with these almond things."

Cat's father said some fast words to his own father, and Cat felt himself being lifted down. His feet in the new sandshoes he had been given for going on the aeroplane landed on the ground. He felt the soles sink gently into the soft soil.

"Dig," he said, and the bucket and his red spade appeared in his hands. He drove the plastic blade into the soil, and threw up a scattering of powder. It fell to the earth like fine, grey rain. "Dig," he repeated, running a few steps further along the terrace. Again, he plunged the spade into the ground. "More dig." He ran on. "More dig."

Then, mummy was next to him, picking him up with her soft hands under his armpits. He kicked his legs as she carried him back to where they had put the buckets and the long sticks. Cat's father and granddad-*pappou* were laying the cloths out under one of the almond trees.

"Stay here, Kitty-Cat," said Cat's mother. "Dig here in the shade while mummy and daddy help *pappou*."

While the three grown-ups did their jobs, waving the long sticks in the branches of the tree and making the almonds come showering down like bursts of hail, Cat set about digging a series of deeper and deeper holes in the soft earth under another of the trees. Occasionally, mummy or daddy would come over to inspect the holes and make approving noises. He was a very good digger. What was he going to put in the holes when he had finished? Was he too hot? He was a *very* good digger.

Once, the waving of one of the sticks sent a shower of almonds over in Cat's direction. They landed on the earth around him, but one struck him on the shoulder as he was digging. There was an unexpected, hard pain on his skin and in his bone. He felt hot tears well up in his eyes and thought about crying, but the pain went away as suddenly as it had come. He turned back to the hole he was working on, and the sticks continued their tap-tapping in the branches of the tree, and the almonds continued to fall pitter-patter onto the cloths.

When the sticks stopped waving, the grown-ups started to collect the hard-shelled almonds from where they had fallen, throwing them with a dull rattle into the metal buckets. Cat stopped digging and brought his own bucket to help collect the nuts. When he threw them into his bucket, they made a flat sound, not the rattly clang of the metal buckets. He took his bucket with the nuts over to the holes.

"Hey, Kitty-cat," called his mother's voice. "Have you finished helping already?"

Cat ignored her, and began the important job of placing a nut, and sometimes two, in each of the holes he had dug. When he reached the last hole, he looked over at the grown-ups. They were still busy picking up the almonds from the cloths. Cat reached into the pocket of his shorts. Closing his eyes, he took out the little toy he had found in one of the creaky cupboards in the room where he and mummy and daddy were sleeping in his grandparents' house. Daddy said that he had slept in that room when he was a boy like Cat, and he had shown mummy books and things which mummy had smiled over.

Still not looking, Cat carefully laid the toy into the hole and quickly covered it over with the soft grey soil. Now he would not have to worry about ever looking at its frightening eyes again. He patted down the soil firmly; then started to fill in the rest of the holes. The soil went in, covering the little nuts. They would be safe in the ground. There seemed to be more soil than he needed to fill the holes. He looked around to see if he had missed one.

Suddenly, Cat jumped and his head jerked around, as granddad-*pappou* began speaking loudly. Daddy was kneeling on the ground with his hands on the tops of his thighs. He had a strange look on his face like the time when he had once dropped Cat's porridge on the kitchen floor. Granddad-*pappou* was standing up. He had a strange look on his face too, and his voice sounded angry. Then there was a loud clang, as granddad-*pappou* kicked one of the metal buckets and all the almonds scattered onto the cloth and into the soil. Then, granddad-*pappou* turned away and went up the hillside path with stomping strides. Cat did not understand what had just happened and he felt like crying again.

"What was that about?" asked Mummy, coming over to where Cat's father was still kneeling. Daddy was shaking his head and letting out a long sigh.

"Oh, Sally." Daddy sighed again. "We were talking about the invasion."

Mummy said, "Oh dear," in a quiet voice.

"And I said the refugees will never go back unless the government is prepared to be conciliatory. And I talked about equal blame when you look back at the history."

"Oh dear," said Mummy again.

Cat did not understand the words which Daddy was using, but he understood "Oh dear". "Oh dear" was not good. He felt his eyes brimming with the hot tears. The air felt hot around him. The soil felt hot through his new sandshoes which he had been given to go on the aeroplane.

"Hot," he said miserably, and gave way to the tears.

Then, Mummy was lifting him up, and Daddy was next to them. Cat wrapped his arms tight around his mother's neck, and felt her soft skin and hair becoming wet and slippery with his tears.

"I know it's hot, Kitty-cat," she was saying, "but it's hot at home too. Remember? Everywhere is hot this year."

"Everywhere," sobbed Cat.

"It's the hottest hotness in the whole history of hotness," laughed Daddy, planting a hot wet kiss on Cat's head. Cat turned his body towards his father and put his arms out to him. Mummy let him go, and Daddy held him cradled with one arm against his chest. His other arm was around Mummy. Cat felt happy when he saw that.

"Let's go back up to the house. Try to patch things up with your hot-headed father. We all need a cool drink anyway. Don't we, Kitty-cat? Would you like a drink of water? With some ice?"

Cat nodded, and his sobbing grew less. When it was hot, ice was nice.

"Nice ice," said Cat.

Mummy and Daddy looked happy when he said that. They liked those words.

"Nice ice," he repeated, and Mummy and Daddy said "Nice ice" as well and they kept saying it as they climbed the hill towards the house where granddad-*pappou* was with his hot head. Granddad-*pappou* would have some nice ice too.

Cat was feeling happy again. The frightening toy was safely buried under the ground. Mummy would give them all a nice ice drink. They would hold the drinks in their hands and lift them up to their mouths to drink. They would say all the funny words and call each other by all the different names they had.

And they could go back later when they were cool, to collect his bucket and the red spade.

*   *   *

For some days, Harry has been constantly at Joan's heels or floating at her shoulder just out of sight, but she can sense his presence. It's possible that it's been as many as three of even four days, or perhaps it's only been a day.

"I'm not sure what day it is," Joan is telling Harry. They're standing in front of the sideboard in the dining room, looking at the cards with the names of the days of the week printed on them. "I think I've been forgetting to change the day, Harry. Can you remember what day it is, love?"

Harry is saying nothing in reply, so Joan simply straightens the pile of cards and brushes her fingertips lightly across the sideboard's surface. Her fingers leave streaky lines on the wood. She brushes some more. There seems to be some kind of powder all over the sideboard.

"I wonder where this came from," Joan says. "It's all over the sideboard." Harry is still not talking, and Joan begins to wonder what the matter is. "A lot of funny things have been happening." Still Harry does not respond. "What's the matter with you today?" asked Joan. "Cat got your tongue?"

Very slowly, Harry floats upwards from where he has been standing at Joan's feet. He comes to rest directly in front of Joan's face, staring straight into her eyes.

"Don't do that, Harry," says Joan. "It makes me feel all funny. It's not nice."

Harry stares and stares a little longer; then he is standing at the French windows a few feet away, looking out into the back garden.

"That young man is messing about in the garden again," observes Harry in a hushed voice. Joan runs her hands over the sideboard once more, and potters over to join her dog at the long window. She raps sharply on the glass. A figure turns around from the tall hedge which runs along one side of the garden. It's a young man, holding a pair of garden shears. He's surrounded by a pile of hedge clippings which cluster around his feet as though he is wading through thick, green water.

"It's only Bob, trimming the hedge," says Joan.

"It can't be Bob. He died in the War," replies Harry. His voice sounds different, more like an old lady's voice.

More like Joan's grandma's voice used to sound when she lived with them in the house in the Garden Village.

"What are you doing?" Joan says through the glass. The young man, who is not Bob, she can now see, waves and turns back to the hedge to resume his clipping. The leaves begin to fall again in a green rain, revealing brown empty spaces and thin, tangles of twigs in the interior of the hedge.

"I hope he knows what he's doing," says Harry, pressing his nose against one of the panes at the bottom of the window. "He's cut the grass as well. And he's built a little orange house."

Joan raps again on the window, and the young man turns around again.

"What are you doing in my garden?" Joan repeats through the glass. The young man drops the shears onto the pile of cuttings, and is coming towards the French windows, walking with a bouncy stride.

"He looks happy enough," comments Harry as the young man draws near. His mouth is moving, but Joan cannot hear what he is saying through the glass. She fumbles with the handle of the doors. After a couple of tries, she manages to ease the French windows open.

"Good morning, Joan," says the young man. "How are you today?"

"What are you doing in my garden?" Joan says again, batting Harry away from her shoulder. "You're distracting me. Stop it." Harry floats away back into the dining room. The young man has a confused look on his face.

"I'm clearing up your garden like we agreed, Joan. Remember? A couple of days ago? I've been digging out the weeds – cutting the grass. And I've made a start on the hedges, but it's a big job. And I've been checking that you're alright – like we said. I'm sorry if I'm distracting you. Do you want me to stop cutting the hedge?"

Joan can feel Harry's presence somewhere behind her. He is making a kind of whimpering sound.

"I'll stop if it's distracting you."

"What?" asks Joan. "Who are you? What's that orange thing on the grass? I don't know what's going on." Harry is still whimpering. Joan can feel her own throat tightening as though she might begin to weep at any moment.

"I'm Cat. Christopher. You said I could put my tent in your garden, if I did some odd jobs, and helped you. Have you changed your mind?"

"My mind? There's nothing wrong with my mind, I can tell you. I've got all my marbles, thank you very much, and I've got lists of all the things I need to remember. And the days of the week."

The young man smiles benignly and nods in a reassuring way. Joan glances back into the dining room at the sideboard where the piles of cards are stacked. "What day is it?" she asks.

"Friday," says Cat. "I'm going to go into town later this morning. Is there anything you need? Any errands?"

"Any errands? I don't know."

"Do you want me to bring you anything from town?"

"What would I want from town?"

"I don't know. We said that I'd be helping you, so I thought ... You said there was a list of things you need to do. Shall we look at the list? See if there's anything you need from town?"

"My list?" Joan looks back into the interior of the room. She can see Harry sitting patiently by the sideboard looking up at the papers and cards on its surface. "I'll just get it," Joan tells Cat.

"You'd better change the day while you remember," says Harry as Joan approaches. His Sean Connery voice is back, and he is no longer whimpering. "He said it's Friday."

Joan finds the Friday card and places it on top of the pile. Then she scans the sideboard. "Now," she says to herself. "What was I looking for?"

"You were going to get your list, Joan," Harry prompts her.

"Ah, yes." There is a slip of paper with some lines of spidery writing, and another sheet of paper which looks like a letter. Joan squints at the first few lines.

Dear Muriel, she reads. *I hope that all is well with you and Arthur, and that the weather in Bridlington is not too blustery. It's been windy here, especially down by the river, and cold, but not wet, though it has looked like rain. I've had fires on and off*

"You forgot to post it," says Harry.

"Have you found it?" says another voice. A young man is standing at the open French windows. "Is that your list?" he asks.

Harry is trotting over to the windows and sitting down in front of the young man. He gazes up at him with trusting, dark chocolate eyes, but the young man is ignoring him.

"Don't you like dogs?" asks Joan, bringing the two pieces of paper with her, as she comes to see what the young man wants. "He seems to like you." A confused expression passes over the young man's features. He holds out a hand.

"Is that your list?" he asks again. "Let's see what you've got to do. I'm going into town to visit a shop and my old school while it's still half-term. Then I can do any errands you need running." His hand is stretched out for the papers Joan is holding, gripped in tight fingers.

"Let him see the list," says Harry.

The young man gently takes the papers from Joan's hands and his eyes travel quickly down the pages.

"I'll put the hall carpet back over the weekend– it'll be dried out by then, provided that it stays fine and it doesn't rain on it. And I'll post this letter for you, Joan," he says, turning one of the sheets over. "But it doesn't seem to be finished or signed. And I'll need Muriel's address, and an envelope."

With Harry's assistance and prompting, Joan manages to track down Muriel and Arthur's address in Bridlington, and an envelope in one of the sideboard drawers. Eventually, the young man has the letter and an addressed envelope which he folds and pushes into the back pocket of his jeans.

"When I get back from town, we can look at your shopping list and go to the shops," the young man says. "You can check the taps when I'm gone, Joan. Make sure they're all turned off. And on Monday you have to go and see Dr Blaine at ten o'clock. I'll take you to the surgery if you like." He looks at the watch on his wrist. "I'd better go now, if I'm going to catch the train into town. Will you be alright?"

"She'll be fine," says Harry.

"She'll be fine," repeats Joan.

Harry and Joan watch the young man crossing the lawn to the little orange house. Behind it, weighing down the washing line, a long strip of carpet hangs. The young man brings out a strange-shaped black object through the little zippered doorway of the house; then, he fiddles around with the door, zipping and unzipping it a few times. Finally, he gives a wave and calls 'Bye' in a cheery voice as he leaves the garden carrying the object by its handle at his side. Joan waves back, and Harry calls goodbye.

"I wonder who that was," says Joan. "Was it the postman? Or the coalman? Is it his day? What day is it? I'd better check the cards." She closes the French windows and goes over to the sideboard. "It says it's Friday," she tells Harry. "But I think I've been forgetting to change the day just lately."

NINE

They say never go back. And after revisiting Music Workshop and wandering around my old school at the end of last week, I don't know what I ever thought going back was really going to achieve. I suppose there's a good reason for saying it: you're never going to find what you're looking for, even if you know what it is, because it no longer exists. That doesn't make it any easier to resist the urge, though.

I watch Joan, who's been quite on the ball this morning, disappear through the door of the doctor's surgery, and I go to perch on the low wall which surrounds the car-park. Though it's early on a Monday morning, there are already four or five cars here, all obeying the sign which asks visitors to 'Please park pretty'. All except for a mud-spattered Land Rover which has been abandoned at an inconvenient angle. Its tyres have carved up the gravel, leaving ridged tracks. Either the driver arrived in a hurry or just didn't care where the car was left. There's a sticker on the tail gate: "Farmers do it in wellies".

* * *

It feels like a good day, if a bit nippy out, and in the doctor's long thin room, where he is sitting at his desk, looking through a pile of papers which he has taken from a brown envelope, Joan is feeling well. Things seem clearer today than they have for a while. The words are falling into place quickly when she thinks of them, not drifting around or fading away like they sometimes do. The doctor, Dr Blaine, asks Joan something, and Joan knows how to answer and what to say. It feels like a good day.

"Well," says Joan, and pauses, and goes on and the words fly in like birds. "If I'm honest with you, there are good days and not so good days. I mean I have some bad days when, well, you know, everything goes on bobbins a bit. But there are good days like today, as you can see. I did have a bit of a turn recently, but no harm done. And in myself I feel fine. Well, considering, you know, that I'm eighty-six. I have a few aches and pains, but nothing you'd say Ooh that's a problem about. I eat well, and I'm quite, you know, regular. So, apart from the occasional not so good day when it all gets a bit much to be frank, I'd say I was in fairly good fettle. But you could see that from all those tests you did last time."

There is a fluttery feeling in Joan's chest, as though something is trapped in there. She takes a gulp of air, and the fluttering quietens. The doctor is looking at her and smiling. He seems like a nice man, but very young to be a doctor.

*　　*　　*

It's quite funny, in a not very funny way: "Farmers do it in wellies".

It would have been better use of my time in town on Friday if I'd gone to Milletts or one of the Department Stores to buy a pair of wellies myself for the garden, instead of traipsing up to Music Workshop and then wandering round the school like a disconnected ghost. Even though nothing happened, Friday has been playing over and over in my head all weekend, making me wonder what the point of all this is. What exactly am I hoping to achieve by coming back to where what happened happened.

101, 131, 151, 181, 151, 131,101, 101, 101, 101, 101

The mid-morning train wasn't busy, just five or six passengers to a carriage, sitting as far away from each other as possible, surrounded by shopping bags and huddled in winter coats. I sat in one of the pairs of seats on the right side of the carriage, facing forward, and watched the grey river roll past like a long swatch of dirty fabric. The huge majesty of the swooping bridge approached and disappeared; then there were docks and industrial buildings, some run-down suburbs with level crossings, and a green expanse of playing fields. The train slowed through sidings and blackened tunnels, and came to a halt under the Victorian glass and iron of the terminus. The familiarity of it all filled my stomach with a swollen, nostalgic, tightness. I made this journey each school day in my grey suit and striped tie for five years, carrying a succession of bags filled with books and sports kits. On Friday, though, all I was carrying with me was my guitar case with the Yamaha inside.

The surgery door opens. A woman, who embodies the word 'no-nonsense', emerges and pauses to allow a tall, powerfully built man, with a heavy waxed jacket draped across his shoulders, to walk past her. He's holding his arms at a strange angle, as though caught halfway through an impersonation of a duck or a chicken. His hands have been heavily bandaged. The pair walk towards the Land Rover, she with purposeful strides, he a little unsteadily but determined. They both are heading for the driver's door, but the woman gives her companion a frowning glance as if to say 'what do you think you're doing?' and he goes round to the passenger side where he waits helplessly for the door to be opened for him.

After some silent, pantomime action involving the man's seat-belt, the Land Rover performs a neat, crunching turn on the gravel and drives out of the car-park. My final glimpse of them as they leave is of the man in the passenger seat staring placidly out of the side window, his over-sized hands held before him like an agricultural Mickey Mouse, holding nothing.

I run a preventative sequence of primes and do a toe-tap routine from my seat on the wall, wondering what he could have done to himself and how he's going to manage with useless hands for however long it's going to take for them to heal.

* * *

Joan feels as though she has been talking a lot. Much more than usual, because Dr Blaine keeps asking questions. Questions about Muriel and Arthur in Bridlington. "Arthur's my Bob's brother and Muriel," Joan tells him, but she's sure she's said all this before, "well, Muriel and I have known each other since we were girls." And there are questions about if she needs any help around the house, after which words about the young man in the garden, who's called Christopher or Cat, swirl out of her like one of those big clouds of birds, a murmuration. Joan murmurs all the things that she can remember about since the young man came. And the things about the young man. It's a good day for remembering things for Joan.

"Well, I say *I* posted it," Joan tells Dr Blaine. "I wrote it and this young man, posted it. I think he and his family used to live in the village – that was before you joined this practice, so you wouldn't remember them. There was some kind of accident, and the boy went to live with his grandparents abroad somewhere. I'm not sure of the details, and you don't like to ask, do you? Not when it's something sensitive, you don't."

Dr Blaine sounds interested in the young man, and Joan tries to think of more to tell him.

*   *   *

When I arrived in front of the Music Workshop doorway at the end of a long, straight walk from the train station, nothing seemed to have changed since I last saw the place. Maybe some of the instruments on display were different, but the paintwork was still red gloss and the sign over the shop front still looked coolly primitive and amateur. With my guitar case in one hand, I pushed open the door with the other hand and toe-tapped over the threshold. And the Music Workshop guy looked with interest at the guitar I showed him after I had unlatched the case - neck latch, body latch, hinge side and handle – but it was clear that he didn't quite understand why I was there and why I was showing him an instrument he had no recollection of having sold me. Never go back, they say.

The surgery door opening again distracts me from my disappointed reminiscing about the Music Workshop guy and browsing half-heartedly through the guitars hanging on display. Someone is walking backwards out of the surgery, dragging a push-chair and encouraging a small child not to run out into the car-park. She manoeuvres the chair down a short set of steps, ignoring the ramp which runs along the side of the building. The child jumps from the top step and lands with a crunch on the gravel.

"Be careful, Darren," the woman says shrilly. "You don't want to go back in there with a broken leg, do you? Do you?" She grabs him by the arm and yanks him after her, trying to force the push-chair through the gravel. Its wheels grind down into the stones. A miserable wailing starts up from beneath the hood of the pram. The woman abandons her hold on the chair and turns to Darren, stooping so that her face is level with his.

"See? Now you've woken your sister with your daft tricks. Stop messing about and let's get home."

"But I didn't do nothing, mam," Darren complains.

"Don't argue. Now come on." His mother drags the pram backwards through the gravel, and Darren follows, scuffing his feet through the stones.

"Stop that, Darren. You'll bugger up your shoes." Darren's sister continues to wail in the push-chair, and Darren has started to sob unhappily. The threesome reaches the car-park exit, and they disappear onto the main street. Once again, the car-park is deserted except for me and the prettily parked cars.

*   *   *

"He's got a tent in the garden, and he's doing oddjobs for me," says Joan. "He's really not a bother, not like some of the youngsters you see these days. Very polite, very helpful. He's doing the garden for me, and checks I'm alright, so it's almost like I've got someone looking after me.

He came with me today. He's waiting outside in the carpark. Said he didn't want to come in. He likes being outside, he says, even though it's been getting a bit parky. He seems happy enough in his tent, I would say."

And then Dr Blaine asks Joan about how she is feeling, and Joan wants to be honest with him, because he is such a nice young man, if a little brusque sometimes, though he hasn't been today. "Well," she says. "Happy enough, you know. It doesn't do to complain, does it? Like I said, in myself I feel alright, just the usual aches, but I'm not going to go through all those tests and what have you again. When you get to my age, and when things like this DLB start, there's not much you can do, is there? Really, is there, Dr Blaine? It's been a good life. Of course, it would have been nice if Bob and I had had children, and if we'd had more time together, but you can't have everything. We wanted children, but they never came along, and then there was the War. I suppose it made us not expect too much, and to be grateful for what we'd got. People these days don't know they're born."

Joan is beginning to feel that she has been talking for a long time, and she's starting to feel tired. The words are beginning to slow, and she hopes that Dr Blaine won't ask too many more questions, about her, about the young man, about Arthur and Muriel, and her and Bob, about what the young man is doing in the garden.

"Checks if I need anything," says Joan, "like I said. And clearing up the old shed – oh, the junk there is in there. The rag-and-bone men would have a field day, though you don't see them these days, do you? I wonder what happened to them. But they never would give you a fair price. "I'll take it off your hands, Mrs Fettes," they'd say.

"But it's not worth much. I'll give you ten shillings." Well, I wasn't born yesterday. It just didn't seem right to get rid of Bob's things, though what would I do with all those tools? And a motorbike? Anyway, it's nice to know someone is out there – on hand, so to speak. In case. You know."

Joan doesn't want to keep talking, but something has been making her go on and on. Dr Blaine has been watching her and making some scribbly notes on his papers while she's been speaking. He says something about talking to this Christopher, and something about tests. When he says tests, Joan feels the fluttering in her chest begin again.

* * *

After Music Workshop I walked down a wide, tree-lined road towards the school, hidden behind railings and trees, surrounded by long terraces of elegant town-houses, most of which have been converted from private residences into flats or B and B hotels. The iron gates, bearing the school crest, stood open. A gravelled drive led under a line of mature horse-chestnuts along the side of one of the buildings. Behind the windows of one of the classrooms above my head, I used to sit with thirty other boys, reciting Latin verbs and adjectives, while Mr Hellyer, who we knew as Satan, would drill us repeatedly and discipline stupidity with swift strictness. Other rooms in various parts of the building housed similarly traditional members of the teaching staff – a dwarfish chemist with a line in sarcastic humour, a bear-like mathematician, a morose linguist – and seemingly omnipresent, the Headmaster, Mr Pole, who was strict but sympathetic.

Because it was the last day of the October half-term holiday, the school was quiet, only two or three cars in front of the main building, and a contractor's white van with an aluminium ladder fastened to its roof. As I crossed the central tarmacked space, which we used to call the quad, the electric school bell gave a hollow-sounding five second burst, but no streams of grey-suited schoolboys emerged from the doorways. After the ringing ceased, the place seemed quieter than ever. I walked through an archway, and faced the green openness of the playing fields, where rugby posts stood at the ends of pitches like enormous capital aitches on a green page. Nothing had changed, and I remembered the smell of mud and sweat, and the relief and loneliness of eventually being excused games.

A man, wearing an open-necked shirt under a v-necked argyle sweater with its sleeves rolled up, and a pair of neatly pressed jeans, had spotted me and was walking across the grass in my direction.

"Can I help you?" he asked, in a tone which implied that he did not think I should be there.

"I used to be a student here," I said. "I left a couple of years ago. I thought I'd come and have a look round. For nostalgic reasons."

"Ah, you're an old boy." His tone was friendlier. "You're welcome to have a look around, but there's hardly anyone here at the moment – just one or two of the staff – and me."

I didn't recognise him. Something about his demeanour, a kind of apologetic assertiveness, made me think he must be a teacher, but he must have joined the school after I had left.

"I thought maybe Mr Pole, the Head, might be here."

"Mr Pole left the year before last. He joined a big public school in the Midlands. I'm the Head here now."

Everything suddenly felt very distant. I had imagined that the place I knew would have continued to operate just as it had when I was there. Mr Pole had always been the Head as far as I was concerned. And he always would be when I thought about the school. But now this man, who looked too young and casual to be a Headmaster, had taken Mr Pole's place.

"What about Mr Hellyer, who teaches Latin?"

The man smiled, shaking his head. "Sorry. Mr Hellyer retired at the end of last year. We're phasing out Latin anyway, to free up space in the curriculum for other things – computers, PSE, etcetera." He continued to smile and gestured with a sweeping motion of one bare forearm. The movement took in sports fields, buildings and the whole school curriculum. "We have ambitious plans for the future of the school – get it ready for the twenty-first century. When were you here?"

"I left in 1989," I said.

"You won't see too much difference just yet. But come back in five years' time and you won't recognise the place." He glanced at his watch. "We like to welcome old boys to come and have a look around their old stomping ground, so to speak. Feel free to have a look around. Nice to meet you."

And he left me alone, staring at the rugby pitches, their tall, hieroglyphic posts and a dark line of autumnal trees in the distance. The white capital letters seemed to stand as the beginnings of sentences destined for incompleteness. If there was a message to be seen in the landscape, I could not decipher it.

    H   H   H   H   H   H

I wonder once again why it seemed so important to go back to Music Workshop;

    101

to show Tony the guitar he had once sold me;

    101

to return to the school;

    101

to come back here against the arguments and advice of my grandparents in halting English and impassioned Greek. Things change. The world moves on. Even dreadful things only seem dreadful to the world for a while. Never go back, they say, but I'm not sure where else to go.

    I think about white columns rising to a high ceiling and a sweeping flight of stairs with heavy wooden banisters; and I think of a creaking floorboard at the head of another staircase; and I think of a shrouded shape in a forgotten garden shed; and I think about something buried long ago, which had once stared at me with frightening eyes, and which now lies at the bottom of my rucksack. I wonder why all these things are crowding into my mind, and how so many things are packed into my head. And then the surgery door opens, and Joan steps gingerly down into the car-park on the arm of a man dressed identically to the new Head of the school, pressed jeans, Argyle sweater with the sleeves rolled up. A laminated ID card on a lanyard round his neck suggests he works at the surgery. He and Joan advance in my direction. I get up from my wall and go to meet them.

"This is the young man I was telling you about," says Joan.

"Hello," says the man. "It's Christopher, is it?"

"That's right," I say.

He's smiling and nodding in an approving kind of way, as though being called Christopher is somehow praiseworthy.

"And you're living in Mrs Fettes' garden?"

"That's right."

Again, this answer is rewarded with approving nodding.

"Good, good," he says. "Well, Mrs Fettes. Time to go home now. Christopher will escort you, won't you, Christopher?"

"That's right." I nod along with him. "Come on, Joan."

Joan smiles, and joins in with the nodding.

"Thank you, Dr Blaine. If I need anything, I can always ask Christopher to call you." She moves away from him, and we start to head towards the exit, but Dr Blaine calls me back.

"Oh, Christopher, one more thing." He lowers his voice. "It might be useful if you could ring me, or call in for a little chat, if you're looking after Joan, as she says you are." He proffers a business card, which I take. "Due diligence," he adds, mysteriously.

I give another nod, uncomprehendingly. "Right."

And then Joan and I are walking side by side at our painfully slow pace over the gravel. There's the noise of an engine and the mud-covered Land Rover hurtles into the car-park, crunching up the stones under its wheels. At the same time, there's the sound of a motorbike screeching to a halt on the road outside. The determined woman jumps down from the driver's side, and goes round to the passenger door. She shouts over to Dr Blaine who was on his way back to the surgery door.

"Dr Blaine. Help, please. I think he's ripped open his stitches."

The man with the Mickey Mouse hands is easing himself unsteadily out of the Land Rover. His bandages are white on the topsides, but the palms are staining blood-red. His face looks ashen, but he's wearing an embarrassed smile.

"The pigs need feeding," he says, as though this explains everything.

The three of them, Dr Blaine, the man, and the woman disappear into the surgery, leaving, in their rush, the Land Rover's doors hanging open.

"Oh, the poor man," says Joan. "Did you see his poor hands? All bloody."

I've already begun a long sequence of primes at the sight of the blood, and I don't answer her.

"You nearly fucking killed me."

An angry, leather-clad figure, carrying a black motorcycle helmet, stomps over the car-park gravel towards the Land Rover. It stops at the open driver's door and peers inside, then makes a disappointed, grunting sound, and gives the car's tyre an ineffectual kick. "Uh."

"Hey there," I say. "It's Deez, isn't it?"

The black figure turns to face Joan and me, and, yes, it's one of the Eddie van Halens from the riverbank. The heavy leathers and the helmet in his grip emphasise the youthfulness of his face. He scrunches up his features as he tries to place me.

"Oh, it's you. Cat, yeah? With the tent."

"That's right," I say, noting that I've been using this response a lot. "Yeah. Are you old enough to ride a motorbike?"

"Who is it?" asks Joan.

"Fuck off," says Deez, to me.

"What did he say?" asks Joan.

"Wasn't half-term last week? And aren't you supposed to be back at school this week?" I ask.

"Fuck off," repeats Deez, good-naturedly. "I've got a fucking cold. So I stayed at home."

"What did he say?" Joan asks again. "Is he being rude? I can't understand it when they mumble."

"No," I say. "He says he's got a cold."

"Oh, dear," says Joan. "He'd better go in. It's too nippy to be out, if he's got a cold."

"That fucking Land Rover nearly had me off my bike," says Deez.

"It was an emergency," I explain. "Somebody needed stitches."

"They'll need more than stitches if they cut me up again," says Deez with bravado, but his anger has evaporated. "Anyway, I'd better get back home before Harry notices I've taken one of the bikes out."

"You've got a lot of bikes, then?" I ask.

"My dad's a mechanic. We repair and restore old bikes. Well, Harry does most of the restorations."

"I had a dog called Harry," Joan butts in.

"That's nice," says Deez. "I'll let Harry know." He starts to put on his helmet, which is slightly too big for his adolescent skull.

"Hey, Deez," I say. "Would this Harry be interested in looking at an old bike I've found? If he's got time and if it's OK with Joan. It's in her shed." I turn my attention fully towards Joan. "Joan?" I ask. "Would it be alright if Harry comes to look at the old motorbike in your shed? Just to tell us if it still works?"

Joan gives me a confused look and there is what looks like a flicker of fear in her eyes.

"What do you mean? Harry was my dog. He didn't know anything about motorbikes. What are you talking about? It belonged to Bob, my husband."

"Yes, I know," I reassure her. "This is another Harry. He knows about old motorbikes. Would it be alright if he came to look?"

Joan still looks confused, but she answers, ""Well. I suppose it wouldn't do any harm."

Deez has flipped up his visor, and he's watching us with an amused expression.

"Do you think he'd come and have a look?"

"Tell you what," says Deez. "I'll ask. And I'll tell Harry about the dog. Harry likes dogs," he adds. "Give us a ring. The number's in the phone book. Swindlehurst's. There's only one of us." He gives a laugh. "Harry the dog. That's funny."

"What was he saying?" asks Joan, as Deez walks away with a teenage, slouching swagger.

"Nothing," I tell her. "It's time to get back."

We resume our slow progress out of the surgery car-park and towards Joan's house, and there's a noticeable difference in Joan. She'd talked more clearly on the way to the surgery, but now on the way back, the tangential vagueness is returning, and our pace slows and slows as we walk.

* * *

Every day so far this week, Joan had taken her book and a tray with tea and a couple of custard creams into the garden to have her elevenses in the shade of one of the apple trees. For company, she also had Harry, her young Border Collie, and the soporific drone of the bees in the background. It was difficult to get on with anything apart from some light dusting in the early morning. Even a walk to the shops with Harry pulling ahead on his leash made her feel worn out, and there was no sign of the heatwave, which was looking set to make 1976 a record-breakingly hot year, coming to an end any time soon. How people in those hot countries got by, Joan couldn't imagine. She'd been meaning to tidy up the rolls of chicken wire and the wooden posts from the old hen coops, but it had been far too hot even to contemplate beginning such a job. So, she was sitting under the green shadows in one of the canvas garden chairs which she had taken from the dusty recesses of the shed, dawdling over her mid-morning tea and wondering whether she would have the energy to fill a watering-can for the flowerbed at the end of the garden before the sun got to it. She gave up worrying about the lawn which is a uniform brown, a while ago. They'd imposed a hosepipe ban a couple of weeks ago, and there'd been mention on the local news of the introduction of standpipes. People had begun talking about hoarding water by filling bath-tubs. In fact, people had been talking of little else than the drought and its consequences for at least the past month.

"Ooh, Harry, it is hot," Joan commented to her dog, who had flopped down on the grass next to her chair. His tongue was lolling, as he looked up at his mistress with large, deep brown eyes. "I pity you in that big fur coat."

Overhead, there swelled the hum of an aircraft somewhere in the brilliant blue of the sky, while in the distance, on one of the roads of the village, there was the rising wail of a motorbike engine. In the silence that followed, the drowsy song of the bees reasserted itself, and Joan could feel herself beginning to doze. She set aside her teacup and picked up her book. She'd read it before, but couldn't remember what happened, though she knew she'd liked the detective. *Cover Her Face* the book's title proclaimed, and Joan found herself wondering why they did that. To preserve the dignity of the dead? To stop people from gaping? To spare people the distress of seeing the corpse? She'd never been squeamish about such things. She'd seen a number of dead bodies – her grandma, her parents, her brother, the man who'd collapsed in the butcher's right in front of her. People said the dead looked like they were sleeping, but Joan couldn't understand that. The dead looked empty, she thought; drained of everything; all thoughts, memories, personality, life. Everything gone.

Joan's head jerked up, as the book tumbled from her grip and Harry gave a half-hearted bark at the interruption of the peace. Someone was calling in the street, with drawn-out, musical theatricality.

"Any rag-bone ... rag bo-own ... any rag-a-bo-o-own?"

Joan picked up her book and the tray of tea things. She'd wash up and see what needed doing in the house. It was too hot to be out in the garden. She made her way over the parched lawn towards the back door and the dark cool of the house's interior.

"Come on, Harry," she coaxed. "Let's go in."

"Morning, my love," a rough voice called, as Joan reached the back door. A broad face under a blackened flat cap which might once have been green was peering round the edge of the garden gate. "Is it hot enough for you? Terry and me are just doing our rounds. We was wondering if …"

"I've got nothing for you, I'm afraid," Joan interrupted, but the face and cap had been followed by hefty shoulders and an expanse of torso. A pair of bright, dark eyes were flicking over the garden, taking in the trees, parched lawn, the shed, the flowerbeds and unused vegetable patch, beyond which lay the remains of the hens' run.

"Maybe Terry and me could have a quick look round for you, love. You never know what we might find – you know, something you've overlooked?"

The man, burly and tall, seeming to take up more than his share of the space around the gate, had intruded further into the garden as he spoke, and at his shoulder another, younger man was hovering. Harry was sniffing at their trousers, and the big man stooped over to ruffle his ears.

"Really," said Joan, eager for them to be gone so that she could deposit her tray and its contents in the kitchen and get out of the heat, "I've got nothing for you. Goodbye." She made the word heavy with finality.

"This drought's playing havoc with everyone's garden," said the man, ignoring Joan's words. "But I must say yours is looking better than most – except your poor grass. And that heap of old netting and wood –" He indicated the remains of the hen-run. "That's sure a bit of an eye-sore. Tell you what. Terry and me can tidy it all up for you and do the removal – and we won't charge you a penny. What d'you say, Terry?"

The younger man, who had been squatting and making a fuss of Harry, looked up sharply. He narrowed his eyes and surveyed the dismantled hen-house and chicken run, wire-netting, wooden posts and planks, at the far end of the garden. Joan's eyes followed his gaze, and it did look an eye-sore, to be sure. And certainly she had been wanting to get rid of it all for some time.

"Looks like a good hour's work, I'd say," Terry observed, with a sigh. "Not really worth our while."

The big man gave a barking laugh which Harry echoed with his own bark. A heavy arm reached round and draped itself over the young man's shoulders.

"A real businessman, this one, my love. Always thinking about profit. Me, I'm more about public service these days. Despite what Terry says, we'll be happy to clear up and take the junk away for you." His eyes dropped to the tray that Joan was still holding. "Of course, if you was to make us a brew while we're working, that would be very kind." He smiled a charming, roguish smile, while Terry muttered something about its being very hot.

"I'm sure that all that wood and wire must be worth something," said Joan. "I thought you were supposed to give me something for it?"

"Granted, it's worth something, love. But not enough to justify our costs, and I'd never hear the end of it from Terence here. You could get someone to remove it for you –

a removal firm, but you'd be paying them. Terry and me, we're doing you a favour."

Joan was fully conscious of the fact that the two roguish intruders were taking advantage of an old lady, but the wood and wire had no value for her, and the man and Terry knew that.

"Alright," she agreed. "You can clear it away, but mind you don't make a mess of the flowerbeds. And don't let Harry run out of the gate. And I might make you a cup of tea. If you do a neat job."

"You're a saint, my love. What do they call you?"

"Mrs Fettes," replied Joan. She knew better than getting on first name terms with people like Terry and his boss.

"Well, Mrs F. We'll get on with the heavy work, and you can get on with the tea. Come on, Terry."

As the two men were striding over to where the ruins of the hen-house and run lay, Joan took her tray into the kitchen and returned to the door to stand, with Harry at her side, and watch the pair who were surveying their task. They also seemed to be taking a good scan of the rest of the garden. Terry was pointing towards the shed, and Joan was visited by a memory, vivid and clearly defined in her mind, of watching two other men in a different era, standing in the garden before it had ever become a garden with trees and flowers and grass, pointing at things and making plans. The big man and Terry started to bundle up some of the chicken wire into a long roll. Terry hoiked it onto a shoulder, and Joan felt a hot prickle of sadness pass across her eyes. She pressed the heels of her hands into her eye-sockets, and a colourful blackness swirled across her vision.

"That tea," she said. "Come on, Harry."

Harry was hesitating at the threshold, obviously torn between racing over to join the men among the remains of the chicken-run and staying in the cool interior of the house with Joan. After a moment, he trotted into the kitchen and flopped onto the linoleum floor, looking up at Joan as she set about filling the kettle. She immersed herself in the enjoyable process of setting out two cups and saucers on a tray, pouring milk into a jug, and placing the sugar bowl to complete a neat square of crockery. When the kettle finally reached its rumbling climax, she let a steaming torrent drown three tea-bags in the teapot and settled it onto the tray. The tea would stay hot for a good long time in such weather, and she did not bother herself with taking out the tea-cosy. Joan pottered about in the kitchen, waiting for the tea to mash. Then she went to the door to see how the men were getting on. Although Terry's prediction had been for a good hour's work, they'd already cleared a lot of the junk and the garden was looking all the neater for it. Despite the heat and the big man's bulk, they moved quickly and with assurance, lifting and carrying, taking away the pieces which had formed the hen-house and its run of wire netting, leaving an empty space of dry, grey earth.

Once again, Joan pressed the heels of her hands against her closed eyes, feeling her eyeballs gently yield and seeing the black colours swirl under the pressure. Reluctantly, she turned away from watching the men at their work, and went to fetch the tea tray. As an afterthought, she put the half empty packet of custard creams on the tray before bearing the refreshments out into the garden.

Harry trotted behind her, his tail wagging and his tongue lolling.

"You are a queen, Mrs F.," bellowed the big man, dropping an armful of planks onto the ground with a clatter as Joan approached with her offerings. "Terry, come and take the tray from Mrs Fettes and pour us some tea."

As Terry relieved Joan of her burden and knelt by the tray which he had laid on the ground, the big man snagged the custard cream packet. With crumby enthusiasm he began to explain what the pair of them had done so far, commenting that there wasn't as much wood or netting as they had expected, praising the way that Joan had kept her garden in such good order, asking whether she had any help with it, admiring the quality of the biscuits and the china tea-cup which Terry had handed him.

"It's not often that Terry and me get to drink out of a cup and saucer," he said. "You're spoiling us, Mrs F., getting out the best china like this." He drained his hot, sweet tea in two gulps and turned the cup over in a paw-like, grimy hand, squinting at the backstamp on the bottom.

"Very nice," he breathed in a respectful whisper. "What you have in your grubby little mitt, Terence," he went on to announce, "is a lovely example of Royal Albert Crown China – second quality, admittedly." He pointed out a tiny blue cross beside the backstamp. "But still a very nice bit of crockery." He handed the cup to Terry for a refill. "You see, Mrs F., me and Terry are also by way of being antique dealers – nothing big, you know, but we keep an eye out for opportunities. If you wanted to clear out any old stuff you've had hanging around, we'd give you a fair price for it."

"Like you're doing for the chicken wire and the wood, you mean?" asked Joan, starting to wonder whether she had been entirely wise to allow the charming, rakish fellow and his companion to come onto her property.

"Now, now," said the big man with a twinkle. "That's a different matter completely, Mrs F. We're doing you a favour, clearing away old junk of no value." Terry handed him his second cup of tea into which he spooned three heaps of sugar. "As far as any antiques or vintage items are concerned, we'd give you a very fair price, wouldn't we, Terry?"

"I couldn't help noticing some nicely crafted tools and gardening equipment that you've got as I went past," commented Terry airily, indicating the little shed, whose door was standing open. Joan felt certain she had closed it when she had taken the canvas chair into the garden earlier on.

"Now, that's the sort of thing that can fetch a very good price at auction, especially if there are collectors in. We'd set a reserve price, of course."

"I told you, Mr … What is your name?" asked Joan, starting to feel her misgiving beginning to change into an angry, rising frustration.

"Robinson."

"But everyone calls him Robbo," chipped in Terry.

"I told you, Mr Robinson. I don't have anything for you. I need everything I have in the house – and in the shed."

"What about that old motorbike you've got covered up in there?" asked Terry. "I'm sure you haven't got any need of that, have you?"

"Vintage motor-cycles – especially in good working condition – are always worth something. There's a good market among collectors," said Robbo. "We could take it off your hands, clear up a bit of space for you. How much would you say it's worth, Terry?"

Terry rubbed a pensive chin and made a pursing shape with his mouth.

"Oh, I don't know. Fifty? Sixty? Maybe as much as seventy-five?"

"Do you hear that, Mrs F.? Seventy-five pounds for an old bike that's just rotting away. It's lucky Terry and me came today, don't you think?"

"No, Mr Robinson," said Joan with the stern composure she had developed with various trainee secretaries during her years at the aircraft factory. "I don't have anything for you, except the old hen-run, which you are welcome to finish loading onto your cart. I'll take the tea things back to the house, thank you, Terry."

Joan held out her arms to receive the tray which Terry hastened to pick up from the ground.

"It's your loss," said Robbo with a rueful shake of his broad head. "It's a shame to hoard stuff away till it loses all its value and falls to bits."

"I don't intend to let anything 'fall to bits'," rejoined Joan with haughty superciliousness. She was feeling pleased to see that Terry looked cowed by her manner, although Robbo remained as cheerfully ebullient as ever. "All the equipment in the shed belonged to my husband, and it will never lose its value as far as I'm concerned."

Robbo assumed a look which could have passed for abashed.

"You're right, Mrs F.," he said in a treacly voice. "It's important to hold on to some of your heirlooms, to pass on to the next generation. As part of their ... oh, what's the word, Terry?"

"Inheritance?" suggested his companion.

"Heritage," Robbo corrected him. "Part of their heritage. And a lot of your stuff has historical value, I'd say. Walking into to your shed is like going back in time."

"I'm sure I never asked, or gave you permission to go poking around in my shed," said Joan, feeling angry once again. "Now, I'll thank you to take the rest of the junk, and be on your way. It's too hot to be outside. And please do not set foot in the shed again."

Joan left the two men and headed back to the house with Harry following at her heels. When she entered the cool of the kitchen, she let out a long sigh as she placed the tray on the draining board.

"We must make sure that shed stays locked," she told Harry. Then she leant against the sink, looking down at the knuckles which were gripping the edge of the porcelain. "When did my hands get so wrinkly?" she asked Harry. "What a pity. It was nice to see two men working in the garden again."

She emptied the remains of the tea into the sink. The three tea-bags landed with a plop next to the plug-hole and an orangey-brown stain began to spread out around the soggy little sachets. From outside, she could hear Robbo and Terry removing the rest of the junk, and finally there was a shouted farewell and the sound of the garden gate closing. She picked up one of the Royal Albert tea-cups in a hand whose skin was ridged with papery creases, turning the porcelain this way and that to inspect its roses and geometrical gilding.

"I do have some lovely things," she told Harry, who had gone to lie on the cool lino again. She could sense the presence, in cupboards and in drawers, in suitcases and trunks, on shelves and on surfaces, of all the possessions she had accumulated over the seventy-one years of her life so far. The ornaments and jewellery, crockery and silverware, implements and appliances, clothes and shoes and bags, hundreds and hundreds of things which all defined who she was and who she had been.

"I wonder what will happen to it all," she mused, fishing the tea-bags from the sink and preparing to wash up the cups and saucers. "In the end."

TEN

Although the sky gleamed with a clear, blue brilliance and the sun had been climbing steadily above the hills on the eastern horizon, it was a cold morning on the lower terraces. Cat and his grandfather were glad of the thick work gloves they had donned, since the cold air of the night had not yet disappeared and would make handling tools difficult for another couple of hours. They had carried the heavy petrol-driven chain-saw and a variety of hand-saws and digging implements down the hillside and were preparing to fell two blackened, skeletal almond trees which, according to the old man, had not given any fruit for the past couple of years. The empty branches had once sported pinkly white blossom at the end of every winter and had then carried velvet green cases containing sweet, white-centred nuts, but now they looked lifeless. The only evidence that these had been fruit-bearing trees was a few hardened shells clinging to emaciated twigs. *Karrettes*, grandfather called them, inedible, diseased casings, which would eventually destroy the tree. *Athasha'* was the name of the tree, and the almonds were called *atha'sha*, though in Greece they were called *amygdala*. Cat had learned many words for things around the countryside, although his Greek was still not good in general. They were going to cut down the *dendra* with the chainsaw and remove the smaller branches with the *svana*. Then, they would burn any useless wood before planting two new trees in the holes which Cat was about to dig with the *tsappa*.

His grandfather was filling the chainsaw with petrol and oil, adjusting the tension on the vicious-looking chain and surveying the two ancient trees. Meanwhile, Cat began to open up the first of two holes, driving the *tsappa* into the soft earth and scooping out a satisfying cubic foot of soil. Grandfather had told him to dig good, deep, wide holes for the new trees. They would add *kopri* at the bottom of the holes to provide nutrients and the saplings would thrive, even after Cat had left, since he was determined about his plan for going back after his eighteenth birthday next September. Grandfather-*pappou* and *yiayia* could not hide their sadness about this whenever it was mentioned.

Cat scooped more earth from the hole, widening and deepening it, as a pile of excavated soil grew into a mound. He stood back, looking on with satisfaction at his handiwork, and then set about digging the second hole. Grandfather-*pappou* was still fiddling around with the chainsaw.

"*Maskaraliki*," he said as he twiddled the tensioning screw. "Stupid thing."

Once again, Cat drove his digging tool into the soil and lifted a hunk of earth.

"Dig," he said to himself and scooped again. "More dig."

Among the grey-brown of the loosened soil, something artificially green showed, not a piece of rock or stone or vegetation. Cat reached into the hole and picked out the green thing.

"I remember this," he said.

In his hand he held a plastic toy spaceman, an oriental-looking rounded helmet moulded tightly to his head and a strange, heavy weapon in his hands. The spaceman's boots were improbably flat and wide with thin flashing around the edges where the plastic had seeped from the mould during the figure's making. It was as though the surface of the worlds on which the spaceman walked had adhered itself to his boots to be taken with him wherever he travelled. Cat turned the toy around in his fingers. There was no indication of who or what the figure was supposed to represent.

"I remember this," Cat repeated.

He turned the toy the right way up and looked at the crudely formed features under the rounded helmet. In an attempt to give the face, which was not quite human but not obviously alien, more definition, someone had gouged into the eye-sockets with something sharp. The spaceman stared up at Cat with vacant, angry eyeholes.

"I was so frightened of this," Cat whispered to himself.

A hollow sequence of mechanical coughs introduced an exuberant roar from the chainsaw as grandfather-*pappou* pulled the rip-cord, and the machine came to life. It sat on the ground at the old man's feet, grumbling angrily like an especially bad-tempered pet dog. Cat pushed the toy soldier into his trouser pocket and quickly finished digging the second hole.

"*Bravo*, Christophore," said his grandfather, lifting the heavy chainsaw as Cat joined him at the foot of the first tree they were going to fell. "These *athasha'* were good trees. Plenty of *atha'sha* every summer. But now they are very old trees. *Mavra dje kataxera.* Black and dead." He gunned the trigger of the chainsaw which roared ebulliently and puffed out a cloud of grey-blue smoke into the cold air. So we *kofkoume.*" He gunned the machine again.

"And then we plant new trees," said Cat. "*Yia to mellon.*"

His grandfather gave a laugh. "You learn, Christophore. *Matheneis. Bravo.* For the future." He revved the chainsaw in celebration, but then his face fell. "But soon in the future you will…" A tilt of his head signified Cat's going away. "You will not see the new *athasha'* grow *dje anthisoun.*" He made an upwards lifting gesture with the heavy machine which somehow managed to convey the idea of young trees establishing themselves and bursting into airy clusters of pinkish blossom. Then he turned towards the trunk of the doomed tree and set the blade of his saw against the blackened bark. Cat moved to stand out of the line of the tree's falling. The engine roared and screamed as the chain bit easily into the wood. In a matter of seconds the tree began to topple, and then fell with a dull crash to the ground.

Cat picked up one of the smaller, hand-held saws and began to remove the thinner, useless wood, dragging the bone-like branches away to the edge of the terrace where later they would be burned. His grandfather dabbed the blade of the big saw into the thicker branches, dismantling the tree into parts for Cat to haul away. They worked silently, immersed in the physical exertion, not needing to communicate more than could be said by the movement of labouring muscles and limbs. In less than an hour, the first tree was finished and they set about the second, a smaller companion to the first and quicker to remove. Eventually, there were only two stumps left where the almond trees had stood, a pile of thin branches destined for incineration, and a stack of long logs to be chopped into shorter lengths to burn in next year's winter. There were also the two holes Cat had dug, ready to receive the new trees, which stood in plastic containers at the side of the steep path.

The sun had climbed higher in the sky, and the air was less chilly, though by no means warm. Cat and his grandfather had removed their sweaters, though, heated by the physical labour.

"*Nero*," said grandfather-*pappou*. "I will bring for us to drink and for the new trees."

Cat watched him trudge up the path towards the house, carrying the heavy chainsaw in one hand and the petrol canister in the other. The old man's body moved with an unhurried, lugubrious determination, one dogged step after another, the weight of the burdens drawing his shoulders down, as up he went towards the house at the top of the hill. Cat reached into his trouser pocket and drew out the plastic toy spaceman with its scratched-out eye-sockets. He went to sit on one of the logs, and turned the little figure around in his hands, his lips moving as he recited a long sequence of numbers quietly to himself. As the sequence came to an end, a question rose in his mind, like a slow fish from the depths of the sea.

What did all these things signify? he wondered. Why did some things seem so important? The trees which became logs, the saplings which became trees, an ancient talisman of fear which then was revealed to be a child's toy, disfigured by some long-forgotten, meaningless act. The spaceman had belonged to his father when he had been a boy. Cat recited more numbers as he felt the surrounding air beginning to press in on him, and he returned the toy to his pocket. Perhaps there was no meaning to any of it. Everything was either transient or defective. All was disconnected randomness, like a dismembered tree, awaiting the consuming extinction of the fire.

After some time, he heard his grandfather returning down the steep path, carrying two metal buckets whose handles made a squeaking noise as he walked. A canvas bag was slung over his shoulder. He descended with the same stolid gait, but this time resisting the pull of the path which threatened to send him hurtling downwards rather than battling against it to ascend.

"*Nero* for trees," his grandfather announced, setting the two buckets down as he reached the terrace. "*Nero* for men," he continued, handing the canvas bag to Cat. It contained two glass bottles of water, and two packets, wrapped in kitchen paper.

"*Halloumi*," said Cat's grandfather, and the two munched on bread filled with the white cheese and tomato slices, sluicing the food down with water from the bottles.

"*Tora*, we plant new trees," his grandfather announced when they had finished their snack. They poured some of the water from the buckets into the bottom of the holes and freed the saplings from their plastic containers, loosening the pot-bound roots and surrounding the little trees with fresh earth. They patted down the new soil around the slender trunks and poured the remaining water into the reservoirs they formed with a low wall of earth around each tree. *Leganes*, grandfather-*pappou* called them, but Cat did not have an English word for the enclosed space filled with muddy water.

"*Leganes*," he repeated.

They had put on their sweaters again, since without the exertion of chopping wood they could feel the chill of the air, although there was no breeze.

"Good for fire," said grandfather. "No *aera* – no wind. We can burn the wood and we do not worry about *kapsalisma*."

"What does *kapsalisma* mean?" asked Cat.

As he set a match to a clump of dried grass which he then thrust among the twigs and branches of the almond trees, grandfather-*pappou* explained how farmers would burn off dry grass and weeds or stubble from their fields, and how if they were not careful a fire could get out of hand. The process of burning was called *kapsalisma*, and the aftermath of a wildfire on the parched landscape could be disastrous, reducing acres of land, trees and buildings, to blackened scrub.

"So, we take care, Christophore," said Cat's grandfather as the flames took hold. Gouts of grey smoke from the burning grass gave way to sparks and light flames. Very quickly, the branches began to sizzle and hiss, and then there was a roaring conflagration which consumed the wood and twigs of the old almond trees. Cat and his grandfather stood back and watched the shimmering heat, mesmerised by the fascinating process of fire devouring wood. When the yellow flames began to subside and the thin twigs had collapsed into ash, the thicker branches were left burning with hot redness. Once again, Cat removed his sweater, feeling the heat on his face and torso.

"*Eyinin kotshinos fothkia,*" laughed Cat's grandfather. "Why are you so angry, Christophore?"

Cat looked uncomprehendingly at the old man. "I'm not angry, *pappou,*" he said.

"It is a saying in Cypriot," said his grandfather. "He is red fire. Your *fatsa* is ..." He widened his eyes and waggled the fingers of both hands about his cheeks. "*Kotshinos fothkia,*" he laughed again.

"No, I'm not angry, *pappou,*" said Cat, but he did not know how to explain, either in Greek or in English, how he did feel. Perhaps it was never possible to explain to another person, or even to yourself, what you were feeling. He felt happy to be helping his *pappou,* exhilarated by the fire and the work, cold at his back and hot where he faced the flames, weighted down by a feeling he could not name but which was mixed up with books in the library they had visited a few months ago, the toy in his pocket, and the dreadful thing which was impossible to think about. He reached into the pocket of his trousers and drew out the toy, feeling the imperfection of the plastic flashing against the skin of his thumb and looking down into the ruined eye-holes.

"Look what I found when I was digging," he said.

* * *

When Joan opens the door at the rear of the house, cold October evening air seeps into her kitchen. There are people standing outside in the dark. In the sky, far above the trees and the rooftops of the surrounding houses, the clouds are glowing, outlined with yellow ghostliness, backlit by an unseen moon.

"Who is it?" asks Joan, trying to make out the faces in the dark. She can feel Harry's presence somewhere close at her shoulder.

"Hello, Joan," says the voice of one of the figures in the dark. "This is Harry."

Up in the sky the clouds are moving, driven by a wind high above the ground. The moon appears briefly and is hidden again.

"But I don't see how it can be," says Joan. Harry is flickering on the edge of her sight. The sky is stretching higher and the clouds are massing like towering fortifications, huge castles in the night. Joan feels Harry passing the side of her head like a gust of chill air. "Harry is …" She is about to note how Harry is right there at her side and cannot be standing out in the cold, but then off he goes, floating towards the huge clouds in the vast sky.

"Be careful of Harry," gasps Joan, gesturing with weak hands at the floating dog. "Oh dear," she says.

The figures move in quickly towards her.

*   *   *

Somewhere behind a wall of enormous evening clouds, the moon is shining. I watch the shapes change as the wind moves things around high above me. It's as though an unseen team of stage-hands is repositioning the scenery between the acts of some drama played out in the sky. I imagine the ruined towers of a medieval castle, and now the dizzying heights of a soaring cliff-face.

It's chilly out in the open at the end of Joan's street, which seems to funnel icy air along its length. Behind the hedges which enclose her garden there is shelter, but I've agreed to wait in the road for the arrival of Deez and Harry, who is coming to have a look at the Ariel motorbike in the shed after work. Every time I unfasten the weighty padlock, which itself is a reminder of another era, heavy iron and brass with a little sliding cover over the keyhole, it is like unlocking a portal into the past. Implements and tools, crafted to last for decades, stand against the walls or lie in their nested cases. Tins and boxes line the shelves from which I've removed most of the dust. And shrouded in its sacking against the back wall, the old bike is waiting. I'm not sure why I'm so keen to see if the machine can be made to work again. I've never been particularly interested in motorbikes or cars.

101, 131, 151, 181, 191, 313, 353, 383, 727, 757, 787, 797, 919, 929, 10301

But there is a kind of compelling beauty about the Ariel Red Hunter which makes me lift the sacking and admire the chrome and steel of its construction whenever I set foot in the shed. I perform a complicated ritual involving a backward sequence of primes and stepping on and off the kerb to silence the me-not-me worries in my head which tell me that Harry will not come or will pronounce the engine a heap of junk fit only for the scrap-yard.

From the top of the street where it joins the main road there is the sound of a motorcycle engine complaining about its rider slowing to take the turn, and then an exuberant howl as it accelerates towards where I'm standing. A powerful-looking black and silver machine comes to a halt in front of me, with a hunched, black, leather-clad shape crouched over its handle bars. The shape separates itself into two helmeted figures who straighten, raising their heads in unison. The rear-most figure jumps from the bike rather clumsily, avoiding a large box strapped to a luggage rack at the back. The foremost rider kills the engine and heaves the bike up onto its stand. After the noise of the engine, the silence of the evening in the quiet cul-de-sac seems deeper than ever. In the windows of one of the houses, a curtain twitches. Joan's neighbours don't like to be disturbed.

Deez, who was riding pillion, is pulling off his helmet, revealing his adolescent face and Eddie van Halen haircut.

"Cat," he says in greeting, with a laconic nod.

"Hi, Deez," I answer. "This Harry?"

Deez gives a grin and unzips his leather jacket to extract his cigarettes and lighter from an inside pocket. "Yeah, this is Harry."

The other figure, who is slighter and shorter than Deez, is also unzipping a leather jacket and removing a helmet.

"Harry the Dog," laughs Deez, placing a cigarette between his lips.

"Fuck you, Desmond," says Harry, and takes a swipe at Deez's face, knocking his cigarette from his mouth. "What are you staring at?"

I'm staring at Harry, who is not what I have been expecting. Instead of some big-bellied motor mechanic with a beard and maybe a pony-tail, Harry is a girl, or rather a young woman with very short, cropped hair which makes her look younger. Under her jacket she's wearing a dark sweatshirt with a psychedelic cow's head in a swirling vortex and COOL AS FUCK printed across the chest.

"Are you looking at my tits?" she asks belligerently.

Deez has retrieved his cigarette from the gutter and is lighting it.

"He'd need a fucking microscope."

Harry takes another swipe, but Deez pulls his head back and her fingers find only air.

"Fuck you, Desmond," she says again.

"I was reading your tee-shirt," I tell her guiltily. She glances down at her chest.

"Inspiral Carpets," she says. "I hate their music, but I wear this because of …" A gesture across her front conveys a desire for aggressive confrontation with the rest of the world.

"Except you're not," snipes Deez, pointing at the wording with his cigarette.

"Fuck you, Desmond." Harry doesn't seem to have much else to say to Deez, but despite the insults, there doesn't seem to be any real animosity between them.

"So Deez is short for Desmond?" I ask.

"Desmond was our grandad's name, so he got that," says Harry.

"Better than Harriet." Deez squeezes sneering contempt for Harry's full name into his voice.

"So you're brother and sister?"

"My lovely little sis," says Deez oilily.

"Eight years older than you, you dickhead," says Harry.

"Eight inches shorter," Deez comes back at her.

"So where's this bike Deez says you've got?" asks Harry, bringing this round of sparring to an end.

"It's in the shed in Joan's garden," I tell her. "We'd better let her know you're here before we look at it, though. She's an old lady and is a bit … you know. If she hears people in the garden she might get a bit …" The gaps I've left haven't stopped Harry from understanding and she gives a business-like nod.

"OK." She shrugs the leather jacket closed, obscuring the logo which now reads L AS F. "You stay here, Deezmond, and finish your fag. If the old dear sees your spots she might have a stroke. Cat and me'll go and see this Joan."

We leave Deez standing by the bike like a resentful squire guarding his master's steed. Harry walks with an assured stride beside me down the side of Joan's house towards the gate into the back garden. Her Doc Marten boots make a wheezy, creaking sound as we go.

"Fucking boot," she says in her belligerent way. "I must've trod on a fucking nail."

The garden is dark as we go through the gate, the trees and hedges casting enormous shadows over everything. The moon is still obscured behind the towering walls of cloud. There's a dim glow in the window of the kitchen door from inside Joan's house, but the kitchen itself is in darkness. Somewhere in the shadows of the garden stands my tent and elsewhere there is the shed, but nothing can be made out in the blackness.

"It's dark as fuck here," says Harry unnecessarily, as I knock on Joan's back door. "I hope there's a light in this shed, or we won't be able to see a fucking thing."

A light flicks on in the kitchen, making the square window in the door stand out with sudden brilliance. For some reason, this makes Harry and me both take a step backwards. Then the door opens a little way and Joan's face appears, cropped between the jamb and the edge of the door. She peers squintingly into the darkness of the garden.

"Who is it?" she asks in her unsure, reedy voice.

"Hello, Joan," I say in a reassuringly chipper tone. "This is Harry."

As if according to a cue in a lighting script, the moon appears from behind the tall clouds and illuminates Harry's head and features. The severely cropped, dark blonde hair is obviously a calculated distraction from a softly pretty face. So is the way she holds her mouth, tightening her lips into a straight, unimpressed line. Then the moon is hidden again.

"But I don't see how it can be," says Joan in confusion. She gives a twitchy glance over one shoulder. "Harry is ..."

I look over at Harry who is watching Joan with an expression of incomprehension drawing her eyebrows in towards the bridge of her nose. The flustered figure in front of us keeps transferring her glance from her side to the dark of the garden beyond us. Suddenly, she raises her arms in a kind of weak supplication to the sky, and she gazes wide-eyed towards the high clouds, backlit by the hidden moon, craning her neck as though following the trajectory of some rising object.

"Be careful of Harry," she says in a breathless voice. And then she loses her balance and begins to stagger backwards into the kitchen.

"Oh dear," she gasps, her arms flailing. Harry and I both dart forward to catch hold of her before she falls to the floor.

"Fuck me, she's heavier than she looks," grunts Harry as we catch hold of Joan, Harry on one side and I on the other.

"We'll take her through into her back room," I say. "She's got a chair by the fire."

Carefully, we lead Joan, who is staggering between us, out of her kitchen and into the dining room where there is a small fire burning in the grate and her chair beside it. The air is fragrant with a sooty, old-fashioned smell, like something preserved for long ages. We settle her into the seat and stand back, unsure of what to do next.

"What was she looking at in the sky?" Harry wonders aloud. "And what did she mean be careful of me? I don't need fucking looking after."

"Harry's her dog – or was her dog," I say. "I think she thinks he's still alive, but I think he died some time ago. Like I said, she's a bit ..."

"Doolally?" suggests Harry unsympathetically, turning away from Joan, who is still looking around herself in some confusion, to inspect the room's furnishings. "It's like a fucking museum exhibition in here," she says. "*How We Used to Live in the 1950s.*" She sniffs the air, and pulls a face. "Coal fires," she says. "Fucking hell."

Joan's eyes settle on Harry, who has started looking over the objects set out on the long sideboard at one side of the room. She stoops to peer at a black and white photograph, her boots and leather jacket incongruous against the décor of Joan's post-war, middle-class home.

"What have you done to your hair, Sandra?" Joan asks, scrutinising Harry. "It doesn't suit a pretty girl like you, short like that."

"What the fuck's she on about now?" whispers Harry. "Who's Sandra?"

"Joan?" I say, squatting in front of the chair. "If you're alright, we're going out to look at the old motor-bike in the shed. Are you OK? You almost had a fall in the kitchen just now."

Joan does not answer my questions, though, and starts to talk about things that I can't follow, using names she hasn't mentioned before. She looks comfortable enough, and doesn't seem to be bothered by the turn she had in the kitchen.

"I've got the key," I tell her. "We won't be long." I stand up and leave her mumbling to herself. "Come on, Harry. I'll show you the bike."

Harry doesn't wait for me to lead the way out of the dining room and through the kitchen. I follow her diminutive figure, broad-shouldered in the leathers, moving with confident strides but one boot making its squeaky wheeze on each step. It spoils her cool a little.

"Fucking boot," I hear her mutter to herself as we go out into the dark.

"I've got a torch in my tent," I say.

"Don't bother," Harry says. "I'll tell Deez to bring the Yamaha into the garden. We can use it. More powerful," she adds.

I'm confused for a moment until I realise she's talking about her bike and its headlamp. "I thought you meant a guitar," I say.

"Hunh?" she grunts, and strides away, ignoring my stupid comment.

There's enough light in the garden, once your eyes have adjusted, to see the way to the shed. I fumble with the old padlock and pull the door open, my nose itching from the salty earthiness of the air inside. From the direction of the gate comes the sound of two voices, one giving instructions, the other complaining, though I can't make out the words. A white beam of light reaches into the garden like an outstretched arm feeling its way through the dark.

"Over here," I call, and the beam sweeps into my direction illuminating the shed and me standing by the open door.

"Come on, Deez. Get a fucking move on," says Harry's voice.

"This grass is too fucking long," complains Deez's voice. "It's not easy to push the bike through it, you know."

Although I have cut most of the lawn, there are still areas where it's a bit overgrown. I can hear Deez grunting as he forces the tyres through the grassy patches. Eventually, the Yamaha is in position with its headlight shining into the interior of the shed. Harry pushes past me through the doorway and pulls aside part of the sacking which shrouds the shape against the back wall.

"Fuck me," she breathes. "This is a beauty."

ELEVEN

Arthur had stayed at the window hatch of the little kiosk to collect three trays of fish and chips, haddock for him and cod for Muriel and Joan, who had wandered away to look over the sea-wall at a panorama of white-topped waves. A clear, blue August sky soared overhead and the promenade undulated with people enjoying a day of sunshine. There were families, laden with multi-coloured bags, and groups of boys with their tee-shirts off, their Yorkshire skins white in the sun, pushing each other boisterously as they strutted along. Teenage girls wearing bikini tops and very short shorts were parading themselves, while a pair of aloof-looking young women, dressed in layers of tulle and lace above heavy-looking leather boots in imitation of singers seen on Top of the Pops, progressed through the crowd like queens of disdain. Their hair, braided and long, entwined with bright, polka-dotted ribbons, cascaded about their shoulders. They glanced superciliously with heavily made-up eyes at the two old ladies looking out to sea. One of them muttered something to the other, and Joan heard the friend answer, "I hope you'd shoot me."

"It's shocking what people wear in public these days," noted Muriel, making a disapproving tutting sound.

"It all started in the nineteen-sixties," Joan said. "And it's been getting worse ever since. Our parents would never have let us go out like that."

"It would be nice to be young again, though," mused Muriel.

"I can't see *you* wearing *that*," commented Joan as a couple passed by, the young man in shorts and what Joan thought of as sandshoes, and his companion wearing a skirt which barely concealed her buttocks and a shirt knotted beneath bulging, bra-less breasts.

"Oh my goodness," laughed Muriel, mildly scandalized. "Poor Arthur would have a fit."

Arthur was coming towards them, carrying the three portions of food. The long hunks of battered fish sported little wooden forks which stuck up from them like wide, flattened flagpoles marking the brows of low, golden hills.

"Here you are, ladies," Arthur announced gallantly. "Salt and vinegar for you, Joan. Just vinegar for you, love."

The two women took the polystyrene trays from him, each slipping her handbag up into the crook of her elbow.

"Blood pressure," said Muriel cryptically, but Joan understood what she meant.

"It's terrible, isn't it?"

Their mutually sympathetic smiles acknowledged an entire world of medications, diagnoses and aches and pains. In unison, the three old people set about forking mouthfuls of the battered fish between their lips, resting the flimsy trays on top of the sea wall and staring out at the huge water as they chewed their food. From over their heads streamed the querulous, high-pitched shouting of the gulls which were wheeling low in the sky.

"Fish and chips in Bridlington always reminds me of Bob," said Joan through her mouthful of fish. "It's funny how a taste makes you remember things."

"Like in that book you were reading," Muriel said to Arthur. "For your Book Club. He's gone all intellectual, you know," she added to Joan.

"Oh, I never finished it," Arthur said, his mouth stuffed with half-chewed chip. "I couldn't get on with it. No plot. I liked it when we were reading things like John Le Carre, but that French thing left me cold."

"*Remembering the Past Times* or something, it was called. He read me a bit of it. It sounded quite nice."

"Too descriptive for me," Arthur concluded.

"Well, fish and chips in Brid always reminds me of Bob. When we stayed on our honeymoon at that big hotel. We should walk up there when we've finished eating." Joan crinkled up her nose and squinted her eyes as she tried to summon up the name of the hotel where she and Bob had stayed on their honeymoon in nineteen twenty-three over sixty years ago.

"We can't do that, dear," Muriel told her. "It burned down in the seventies. Don't you remember? We've often talked about it. The Alexandra. Such a sad thing."

Joan stared blindly out at the waves, tasting the tang of vinegar over the gentle, bready oiliness of the batter on her fish, and feeling an overwhelming sensation of welling pressure in her throat and behind her eyes.

"Oh. Yes. Of course," said Joan. "The Alexandra. I mean we should walk up there, you know, to where it was, for the exercise. It burned down. Yes." The gulls overhead continued their chorus of raucous shouting, punctuating Joan's speech. "How sad."

Muriel speared another chunk of fish, looking at her friend who was prodding at her own portion with the little wooden fork. Arthur gazed out to sea, munching busily, lost in his own thoughts.

"How have you been since you saw the doctor, dear?" asked Muriel quietly. "I didn't ask before, because …" She popped her morsel of cod into her mouth. "You know, with the …" She pointed her empty fork at her temple in a vague spiralling gesture.

"Oh, my goodness. I feel fine," said Joan quickly, but then her voice dropped as she continued hesitatingly. "At least, most of the time, I do. Then sometimes – not often, mind – it's like there's a sudden gap. Well, not so much a gap – more like a blank space like where words on a page have been rubbed out." She pushed her chips around on the tray a little as she thought. "I don't know how to describe it, really. A gap, a space? It's like there's something there, but hidden, covered over and I can't get to it, but I know it's there – or it was there." She looked helplessly at Muriel. "I'm not making much sense, am I?"

"We all forget things, dear," Muriel reassured her.

"No. It's more than forgetting. It's all there, but gone, at the same time."

"I'm sure that Dr Blaine will be able to help," said Muriel in a gently sympathetic tone. "Our young woman is ever so helpful. And so kind. She's been very good with me and my blood pressure. Of course, Arthur's as fit as a fiddle. Except for his knees."

"Nothing wrong with my knees," Arthur chimed in.

"It's so strange," mused Joan, ignoring Muriel and Arthur's medical conditions, "to think that soon it will *all* be gone. No matter what you think you remember. In the end, nothing is left."

Muriel stabbed vigorously at her tray, sandwiching a white flake of fish between two flat chips. "Oh, Joan. Don't go getting all melancholy on us. It's a lovely day. Let's enjoy our fish." She took the forkful between her lips; then spiked some more flakes and batter. "Best fish in Yorkshire," she declared.

"I'm sorry, dear," said Joan. "I suppose I'm missing Harry, and it is worrying …" She breaks off, as tears welled into her eyes. "Oh, look at me. How silly." She fumbled in her handbag for her hanky, leaving the half-finished tray of food on the sea-wall, and dabbed at her eyes. Muriel compressed her lips in a compassionate half-smile.

"There, dear, there," she breathed, with phatic sympathy.

"I don't know what's wrong with me," said Joan lightly. "Have you ever known me to be weeping like this? I didn't weep when Henry died. I didn't even cry for Bob – except that once, and not in public anyway. But, look at me." She dabbed again and blew her nose softly into the lacy square of fabric.

"There, dear," said Muriel again.

"You know," said Arthur, turning his gaze away from the sea and the wide, gentle arc of horizon, "we *should* take a walk along to where the Alexandra used to be. It's a lovely day and the walk will do us good. You two always enjoyed a nice walk."

"Watch out for your chips, grandma."

One of the polka-dot ribboned girls was coming back along the promenade, holding the hand of a tall, gawky young man, wearing a tee-shirt with the wildly bearded face of Karl Marx glaring out from the front. She was pointing a ringed finger past Joan's shoulder at the sea-wall where one of the gulls had landed and was in the process of making off with Joan's half-devoured piece of cod. There was a flurry of arms as Arthur, Muriel, Joan and the Karl Marx boy all windmilled to scare the bird away. The gull flapped its wings and rose majestically into the sky, holding the battered fish in its gaudy, yellow beak.

"Fucking sea gull," barked the boy.

"Mind your language, young man. There are ladies present," said Arthur sternly.

"Oh dear. It's all gone," said Joan.

"Sorry, granddad," laughed the boy, as he and the girl bounced on past.

"You watch your cheek," said Arthur, but the pair were already yards away in a flouncing swirl of fabric and hair, and had not heard him.

"Never mind, dear," said Arthur, patting Joan's arm. "I'll get you another piece of cod." He made a move to return to the kiosk on the other side of the promenade, but Joan held him back with a tug on the sleeve of his jacket.

"Don't bother yourself, Arthur," she said. "I've had enough. If you and Muriel are ready, we can take that walk."

The three of them - Arthur striding ahead as though to demonstrate the health of his knees despite his eighty-plus years, and Joan and Muriel following in his wake, falling gradually further and further behind – progressed along the promenade, passing groups of holiday-makers seated on the benches facing the sea, and encountering other couples and families approaching from the opposite direction. The air was filled with the noise of people being alive, while all around but ignored there was the constant complaining of the gulls. Eventually, Joan and Muriel caught up with Arthur who had settled himself on an empty bench, waiting for them and massaging a knee beneath a slow hand. He was gazing out at the wide vista of the waves while at his back white, many-windowed buildings rose up like man-made cliffs.

"That's where the Alexandra used to be," Arthur observed, indicating with a thumb over his shoulder. "It's all flats these days."

Muriel and Joan took a seat next to him. "Such a shame it's gone," said Muriel. "It was a lovely old building. So elegant."

"Have you got my book, love?" asked Arthur and Muriel rummaged in her handbag, withdrawing a slim, paperback volume which she handed to her husband.

"It's for my book club," Arthur told Joan, whose eyes were still fixed on the frontage of the block of flats behind their bench. "I've got to get through it by next week. It's not as bad as that French thing, but it's a bit of a grind."

Joan brought her gaze back from the building in the background to glance at the orange and white book in Arthur's liver-spotted hands. A leather bookmark protruded from between the last few pages. On the cover, *The Great Gatsby* was announced in the stylised Art-deco print of the title.

"You're almost at the end," commented Joan.

"It'll still take him a while," said Muriel. "He only manages about half a page before he nods off."

"That's only if I lie down after my dinner," said Arthur defensively. "I'll finish this this afternoon while you two chat." He opened the book at his marked page and began to read. Joan and Muriel stared out at the sea and the beach, watching the groups of people in their clusters on the sands.

"It *is* a lovely day," observed Muriel once again.

From down on the beach, above all the other sounds of the sea-side, even the cries of the gulls, a child's wailing cry rose up, like the howl of a small animal in cruel torment.

"It's not here," wailed the voice. "Where's it gone?" The final word was broken into at least four sobbing syllables. Joan's eyes and Muriel's eyes were drawn to a small child in a pair of colourful swimming trunks, standing on a patch of the sand. He or she – Joan found it impossible to guess the child's gender, although the bright hair was long – was casting frantic glances all around, arms held wide apart. "It's not here, mummy," the child repeated in a gasping wail. "It's gone."

"Stop your mithering, Jaydon," said a shrill voice, cutting through the child's distressed sobs. "You can build another one today." Joan and Muriel watched a young woman catching the child by the arm and dragging the resisting figure away.

"What kind of a name is Jaydon?" asked Muriel. "Boy or girl?"

"I don't know," Joan answered. "All the names are different nowadays. You don't find the old names any more. You know, names like Henry or Arthur. How many Muriels are there these days? I don't know. It's like everything's ..."

Joan knew what she wanted to say, but could not find the nice combination of words which would bring together the change in naming fashions, the destruction and redevelopment of the fin-de-siecle hotel which had once stood behind them, the transient distress of a child whose sandcastle had been washed away by the tide. But the words would not order themselves for her to express her thought. "It's not like it used to be," she concluded, lamely.

"It would be nice to be young again," Muriel repeated. The two women stared out at the white-topped waves and two tiny, triangular sails which were inching their way across the far distance. Joan thought of all the people who had disappeared from her life, taking their names with them, each leaving their own empty space which no-one had come to fill.

"That was quite good, in the end," announced Arthur, closing his book with a satisfied snap.

"Oh, you've finished your book, love," said Muriel. "Well done."

Arthur smiled a guilty, schoolboyish smile. "Well," he admitted sheepishly. "I cheated a bit. I skipped the last chapter or so and just read the last page. But you'll like this. Listen." He opened the book again and flicked to the final page, giving a brief, introductory cough as he began to read aloud.

"'*And so we beat on, boats against the current, borne back ceaselessly into the past.*' Isn't that good? I think I might go back and read the last chapters anyway." He placed the book on his knees, folding his hands over the cover, obscuring the elegant, spoiled faces which were gazing up at him from the illustration. Joan looked at him, an old man with a half-read book in his clasp, and then at Muriel, whose hands were resting on the bag on her knee, and then at her own hands which had been scored and lined with age.

"Hmm," nodded Muriel appreciatively. "Lovely." She gathered up her handbag, and Arthur gave her his book to place inside it. "I don't know about you, Joan, but I'm ready for a cup of tea back at home."

"Alright, dear," said Joan, feeling somehow adrift after Arthur's reading. "Perhaps it is time we were getting back."

* * *

There must have been a noise somewhere in the house – perhaps the central heating had come on, making the radiators do their tick-tick-ticking sound. Or perhaps there had been a cat yowling in the garden, or someone outside on the road beyond the trees, shouting in the night. Or maybe Cat had had a dream, one of those horrid dreams where your legs won't work properly although you are trying to run as fast as you can. Whatever it had been, Cat was now awake, staring straight upwards, feeling the dark pressing down on him like a heavy blanket.

He knew that all around him, hidden in the blackness, were his things: his clothes for the morning, folded on the chair; his toys in their boxes neatly stacked against the wall; his books lined up on their shelf beside his bed. When his eyes grew accustomed to the darkness, he would be able to make out the shapes of all the things in his room. Already he could see the strip of light along the bottom of the door from the dim bulb his parents left burning on the landing throughout the night. But during the time it took his eyes to adjust, it was easy to imagine that he was buried in the earth and the thick darkness was like soil pressing down on him. Cat recited his times tables as quickly as he could, not allowing himself to breathe until he had finished each of the sets of twelve numbers.

When he reached the end of the twelve times table – one hundred and forty-four, one gross, a heavy, unpleasant number, Cat thought – he allowed his eyes to drift around the room, identifying all his possessions by their shadowy shapes. It was as though he was a boy-pharaoh, entombed in his dark burial chamber, like Mrs Hawthornwhite had told them in their History lessons last year. He would have all his belongings to take with him to the afterlife, everything he needed and which was proper for a young king.

Cat began to recite the tables again, like a magic spell, he thought, but he did not think that magic could be real. Or like a prayer, but again how could that be real? Praying for dead people to go to heaven? Where they would be alive again? How would that work? He did not like to think about being dead and buried – or even worse, being alive and buried, trapped in a tomb, or a dark, underground labyrinth with no way out. And his mum and dad up above ground, searching for him, worrying about where he had disappeared to, arguing about rifts and divisions and invasions. Perhaps they would take him to see his Cypriot grandparents, and there would be another war while they were there and there would be explosions and he would fall through a rift in the ground to be lost and trapped in a foreign place like the wizard in the book he had been reading.

There, on the nightstand by his bed, was the shape of the book, *The Tombs of Atuan*, the second in the Earthsea trilogy. Cat tried not to think of the words he had been reading, but they were there in his head, whispered to him by his own voice: words about the Nameless Ones in the underground labyrinth, exerting the weight of their powers on your mind until you went mad.

Cat took a deep breath and tried to recite all his times tables before he had to take another, but his chest began to ache and burn, and he found himself gasping before he had even got to the end of the threes. He sat up and swung his legs out from under his covers, tapping his toes on the bedroom carpet in a hastily improvised ritual. If he tapped properly, the voice in his head – and the Nameless Ones in the book – would let him stand up.

Cat stood up, and reached for the hard-backed volume on the nightstand. Carrying it before him like an offering to some dark god, he pattered barefoot across the floor to stand before the door. Hesitating, he tracked three stutter steps backwards and then approached the door again. He felt very tired, and the book weighed heavy in his hands, although it was not a thick volume. He supposed it was because he had not slept well and it was still the middle of the night. Cautiously, fearful of waking his parents, he turned the handle and pulled the door gently open. The dim luminescence of the landing light seeped into his room, bringing the shadowy shapes of his belongings into their true forms: his pile of clothes, his toys, his books. Gingerly and stutteringly, Cat tiptoed across the landing to the head of the stairs where he stopped and listened. All was silent, except for the distant hum of the refrigerator downstairs in the kitchen. All the doors on the landing, except for his bedroom door, were closed. He lowered himself to his knees and pulled aside the strip of carpet which ran the length of the landing. There was just enough room to insert his hand under the carpet and to reach the loose floorboard which creaked whenever someone walked over it. With his fingertips he prised the board up and reached his hand a little way beneath the floor, taking care not to reach too far in case he touched any of the other things he had hidden in the empty space previously. There were things down there which he did not like to think about, and now *The Tombs of Atuan* with its distressing words would join them. Carefully, he took the book, avoiding looking at its cover, and slid it under the carpet and into the cavity. It made a flat sound as it dropped into the dark hole. Cat settled the floorboard into place and smoothed the carpet back into position. Standing up, he pressed his foot tentatively onto the board which creaked gently with each step. Now the passage with the Nameless Ones and their threatening power was safely buried away under the floor. Every time he heard the floorboard creak in future, there would be the reassurance that the threat had been contained. For good measure, he recited silently as many prime numbers he could think of, stepping on the board and making it creak with each number.

"Cat? Are you OK?"

His father was standing in the doorway of his parents' bedroom, watching him. Cat turned around, guiltily in confusion.

"Daddy," he said tremulously. "I had a nightmare ... I got up."

"Hey hey hey, there, there," said his father in a softly reassuring voice, coming towards him and taking him into his arms. "That's not like you. You never have nightmares. Come on. Let's get you back to bed."

His father hoisted him up, even though he really was too old to be carried, and they went back into Cat's bedroom. His father put him down next to his bed and waited while Cat bundled himself under the covers. Then his father knelt down at the side of the bed and placed a hand on his forehead.

"You don't feel hot," he said. "You're fine. Go back to sleep. Do you want me to stay?"

Cat wanted to say yes, and feel his father's reassuring presence as he lay in the darkness. But he was nine years old, and he did not need to worry about the words in the book anymore.

"No, dad. I'm OK now," he said bravely. "Just a dream." He gave a theatrical yawn, and turned onto his side. His father pressed his lips softly against Cat's hair.

"OK. *Kali nichta, gataki mou*," he whispered.

The door closed. Cat lay in the blanket-like dark once again, waiting for sleep to come.

*   *   *

"Well, you've got to admit it's a bit fucking weird, though," says Harry, who is kneeling with her back towards me. The bottoms of a brand new pair of boots are facing up at me, declaring that Dr Martens has installed an air-cushioned sole on each of them. The treads are chunky, inlaid with dagger-headed crosses, which give the impression of a spiky defiance. It's hard to imagine Harry wearing any other kind of footwear. She's taken off her leather jacket, since it's been mild for November the past few days, and the sleeves of an AC/DC sweatshirt are pushed up to her elbows as she manipulates a socket wrench somewhere in the innards of the Red Hunter's engine. This is the second Saturday she's spent with me in Joan's back garden with the motorbike on a square of tarpaulin, unscrewing things and turning nuts with a variety of professional-looking tools, squirting fragrant, oily liquid from a can with a long straw protruding from its nozzle. As she works, she likes to talk.

"Living in a fucking tent in an old lady's garden. No wonder people talk about you. Deez and his mates have got lots of stories about you, you know? Living down on the riverbank and doing weird animal sacrifices in the night. They're full of shite, as you've probably realised. But you are a bit of a weirdo, Cat, to be honest."

She applies more force to a nut which is reluctant to move, and the muscles in her forearm make ridges under her pale skin, which is downed with light, golden hair. I enjoy watching the cool confidence she has with the metal.

"Fuckity fuck fuck fuck," Harry breathes suddenly as the nut yields and her knuckles scrape against the engine block. She drops the wrench and sucks on her skinned flesh.

"Are you OK?" I ask, picking up the wrench. It seems the most helpful thing to do.

"Fucking bastard nut fucker," says Harry, pushing herself up from the ground and stretching her back. She presses her knuckles into her sweatshirt and the fabric tautens across her chest. *AC/DC Who Made Who*, says the lettering which surrounds a tiny, lightning struck, schoolboy figure hunched over an electric guitar. I make sure not to look too long at Angus Young and his Gibson SG, posing over Harry's breasts. "Pass me a can," she says, pointing at her toolbag with her good hand.

In the bag there are four gleaming Carlsberg Special Brew cans, cinched together by a thin plastic collar. I ease one of the cans free from the plastic and hand it to Harry to take. She licks her knuckles once more and then pops open the can. An effervescence of froth wells up through the gap around the ring-pull and she slurps it away.

"Have one, if you like," she offers.

"Nah, I'm OK," I say. Beer is not really my thing. I've never liked the dry bitterness of it. I put the remaining three cans back into the bag, setting them in and removing them in three juddery movements until they can be safely left inside. Harry takes a deep swallow of her Special Brew.

"And you do those weird things as well," she comments, tapping her knuckles with the tip of her tongue. The skin has been lightly grazed away and pink, raw flesh is peeking through.

"What do you mean?" I ask.

She waves her can in the direction of the toolbag on the ground. "Weird stuff like what you did with the cans. It doesn't bother me. I don't care what you do. But Deez and his mates can be..." She takes another swig of her beer. "Little bastards. Always on the lookout for something to take the piss out of people for."

I give a nod, remembering the banter between the three lads, and Eddie chasing his tormentor along the riverside path, desperate to stop the revelation of his real name.

"Yeah. I've seen them with each other. By the way, do you know what Eddie's real name is? You know the one whose nickname is Eddie, though they all look like Eddie van Halen."

Harry gives a snorty kind of a laugh.

"It's funny, but it's also a bit sad," she says. "Eddie was a really weird kid when him and Deez were at Primary

School. Really weird. Obsessed with …" She snorts again. "… toilets – how they flushed – what colour they were. Fucking nutcase. He used to go up to other kids at school, and fucking interrogate them about their toilets at home. Deez and Mikey and all the other kids took the piss out of him, of course." She takes another gulp from her can. "And not just because of the toilet thing. What his mum and dad were thinking I've got no idea, but his name…" Harry has started to snort uncontrollably, and is having difficulty getting the words out. "His real name is Tobias Weasel. The kids used to call him the Toilet Weasel." Her face crumples up as she surrenders herself to gasping paroxysms. Eventually, she calms herself with a couple of pulls at the can.

"It's bad enough being called Weasel, but *Tobias*? What the fuck? Anyway, when they all got a bit older, Eddie got into listening to stuff like Whitesnake, van Halen, AC/DC, and he was suddenly the kid people like my dickhead brother wanted to hang out with. Doesn't stop them remembering the Toilet Weasel stuff, though. Kids are bastards, aren't they?" She lifts her can to her lips again, and stares blindly into the ring-pull aperture. "So what is it with all your weird shit, Cat?"

Part of me wants to try to explain the compulsions and obsessions, the overwhelming need to perform the rituals and do things which other people see as weird. I open my mouth to speak, but then shut it again.

"It's OK," says Harry, tossing her empty can at the toolbag. "You don't have to tell me. Everyone's got weird stuff going on as far as I can tell. I mean, look at that poor old sod." She points towards the house where Joan is standing at the dining room French windows, gazing into the garden. Harry waves, and after a pause Joan waves back. "I don't think she knows what we're doing in her garden, you know."

"She's OK sometimes," I say, relieved not to be talking about myself. "But she's got some form of dementia. You know, when you start forgetting everything. Where you are. Who you are even."

Harry retrieves the socket wrench she had been using, and kneels beside the bike again. The soles of her boots gleam up at me, glowing with newness. She fits the wrench to the nut again, turning it carefully.

"You know, Cat, the good thing about these old bikes is they were a simple push rod single. You don't need any special tools, or much expertise – not like that fucking Yamaha of mine. Joan's kept this covered, and it's dry. Admittedly, it looks a bit worn, and the seat leather's knackered, but once we've done the carb and cleaned it up, it should be fine." She continues to fiddle around inside the engine block. I consider asking what a push rod single is, but she continues talking.

"It's a shame people aren't as simple," she goes on. "You can't just change the plugs and check the points, and polish them up. Once they're fucked, they're fucked."

"People get better," I observe.

"Not if their minds go," Harry says with an air of finality. Then she drops the wrench with a soft thud onto the tarpaulin and turns herself round into a cross-legged sitting position, pulling her Doc Martens in between her thighs. "Give us another can," she orders, reaching for her leather jacket and draping it over her shoulders. I pass her a second can of Special Brew and sit down opposite her while she performs the ring-pulling and slurping process.

"Once the mind goes," Harry says authoritatively, wiping her mouth with the back of her hand, "you're screwed. Like you said, she's started forgetting everything. As though little bits of who she is have gone missing, like lost pieces out of a jigsaw puzzle." She nods in satisfaction at her image. "And there's no way of finding them again."

I can't think of anything to say to that. Harry's voice is unusually sad, without its accustomed angry energy. We both sit staring at the tarpaulin while she sips her beer. I open my mouth to speak again; close it immediately; then, words come out unexpectedly.

"I came back here because there were bits *I* was missing. From myself, I mean."

Harry looks across at me, uncomprehending.

"What?"

"I had this feeling. When I was away. That there were missing things that I had to find. And I went into an old library with a massive staircase going up, and tall columns reaching to the ceiling. And before that I'd found something that I'd buried under the ground a long time ago – when I was a little boy. And there are other things I've buried – or hidden. So I came back."

Harry is watching me with a frown creasing her forehead, and the can at a forgotten angle in her hand.

"I didn't understand a fucking word of that," she says.

"I know it sounds mad," I tell her. "But I had this feeling that I had to come back here and look for some things I used to have. Which would help somehow. I'm not sure how," I finish feebly.

"You mean, like buried treasure?" Harry asks. "Valuable stuff?"

"No, not really. Not at all. In fact, stuff I was frightened of when I was little. I hid it away so I didn't have to look at it, but now I want to look at it again."

"You're right," says Harry. "It does sound mad." She swigs her beer. "Fucking bonkers if you ask me. But I'll tell you something. Because you've told me this." She pauses, inspecting the golden can in her hand. "When I was younger – fourteen or fifteen – they sent me to see someone – anger issues, they said – like I said, everyone's got weird stuff going on. Anyway, she got me to talk about stuff I'd hidden away – anger at my mum and dad for having Deez, that kind of thing. And digging it all up and looking at it again helped a lot. I'm not nearly as angry now as I used to be. It was as though I'd managed to remember all the parts of a story that had been bugging me – all the words and sentences and people in it and I could understand it all – and then I could feel more peaceful." She chugs back the rest of the beer and gives a short laugh. "Though you wouldn't know it to look at me." She hurls the empty can at its companion, lying next to the toolbag, and gets to her feet.

"There's a saying in Greek Cypriot," I say. "*Eyinin kotshinos fothkia* – if someone is so angry they are red fire – that sounds like you, Harry."

"You speak Greek?"

"Not really," I admit. "I lived with my Cypriot grandparents when I went away, and I learned some. Not as much as I should have, though."

"So, why did you go away?"

101

"I'm sorry, Harry. I don't like talking about some stuff. Remembering things."

101 101 101

"Yeah. I know… But it's important to remember things – even the bad things, though there's nothing you can do about them. Like a wound." She licks her knuckles with her pink tongue. "You can't make it unhappen. You just look at it, lick it a bit, and get on," she continues, retrieving the wrench and turning back to face the bike again. "Tell you what, though. I bet if you were Eddie, you'd be grateful not to remember all the Toilet Weasel stuff. Poor bastard."

She settles herself back to work on the engine, the dark amber of the soles of her boots once more facing up at me with their uncompromising treads. A movement over at the house catches my eye, and I raise my hand in response to Joan who is waving again.

*   *   *

The windows are between Joan and the garden, a glass wall which stops things from going out and coming in. Except the light, of course, and Harry, who floats in and out, but he's not here just now. There are those other people, though, outside in the garden, messing around with the whatchamacallit. Joan's sure they're not doing any harm, but you never know if you've done the right thing, do you? Giving them the keys from the tin with all Bob's things in it. He left so many things, keys, his comb, the tools in the shed, the whatsit on wheels.

And there are so many things that happen. Joan thinks how hard it is to keep up with it all. All the comings and goings. People delivering things, and taking things away. Coming and going all the time. The light comes in through the glass. The smoke from the fire goes out up the black hole. The chimney. Joan remembers the sooty smell of the chimney when the sweep used to come with his flat, round brush on long poles. A black, cold and dusty smell. You can't see a smell, but it's real enough. Really there, even though you can't see it. The smell of your house, though you don't notice it when you live somewhere, not unless you've been away. Joan thinks that she hasn't been away for a long time. She tries to remember the last time she did go away. To Bridlington? With Muriel and Arthur? She wonders whether that really happened.

Some things are real, and some aren't. Joan remembers that she used to like a good book, a thriller or a mystery. But how do you know what's real and what's made up when they write it in a book? And they have that voice telling the story that seems to know everything.

When Joan was a girl, they used to make her go to the church. She remembers the stories the man at the church used to tell. About heaven and hell. And how if you were bad you'd go to hell. Hull, Hell and Halifax, they used to say. "From Hull, Hell and Halifax, good lord defend us." It was in a song, Joan thinks, and she hums part of a jaunty tune, stumblingly.

She can't believe that all that stuff can be real, though. Burning in hell because you'd been bad? Surely that's all just made up. Outside the windows, in the garden, the two people are sitting, talking to each other. Joan wonders what they can be saying. Or maybe they're not talking, just sitting in silence, saying nothing.

Some of it must be real. Some things really happened. Joan knows that. There are photographs. Like the photograph of her and Bob at their wedding. And that picture of the man on the moon. Joan wonders if they had really sent a man up there. She knows that she had really married Bob, but what if she hadn't? What if she was remembering something that had never really happened? What if the not real things seemed just as real as the real things? Where did that leave you?

"Up in the air, that's where," says Joan to the air in her house. "Not burning down in hell. But just as bad."

Outside, one of the figures has started to do something to the engine of the motorbike. Bob's motorbike. Joan knew that she knew the word for it.

"I hope you know what you're doing," Joan says to the people beyond the glass, and waves a hand to attract their attention. Then, a thought floats into her mind like a speck of soot from the fire that burns in the grate, as one of the people waves back: nobody knows everything.

TWELVE

Anyone observing the figure which stood beneath the bare branches of the big trees in front of the house would have commented on the nervous tension it radiated. Although it was not an especially cold day for the time of year, the figure's shoulders in a heavy khaki jacket were hunched up and its hands were thrust deep into the pockets of a pair of denim jeans. The right hand was still, but the left was fiddling with something in its pocket, the tremulous motion making the stiff fabric undulate as though a small, frightened animal were hiding inside.

But no-one in the house was at a window, looking out, to see the young man who was gazing over the garden gate at the dark front door. The curtains on the ground floor had all been drawn against the fading afternoon light, but there was a glow behind the heavy material which indicated that there were people at home. Two diminutive bicycles, one lying on its side, the other upright, supported by stabiliser wheels, had been abandoned at the edge of the path leading up to the door. The young man withdrew his hands from his pockets, ran them through the wiry curls of his hair, and approached the gate. It made a low squeal as he pushed it open, and then swung closed behind him. After three paces, he made a brief, halting pause, performing a stuttery dance step which he repeated after two more paces and then again after another two. An observer would have commented on these strange, unbidden actions, but there was no-one watching.

Reaching the door at the end of the concrete path, the young man rapped three times, and waited, his lips moving slightly, as though he were reciting a private mantra. There was the snicking sound of a lock turning and then the door opened, allowing yellow light to spill over the paintwork and out onto the path. In the lamplight, the paint glowed with a deep midnight blueness.

"Hello?" said the middle-aged man who was standing in the gap between the door and its frame. "Can I help you?" As he spoke, he raised two thick, bristly black eyebrows in emphasis.

The young man hesitated. "Er. Hi. My name's Christopher. Christopher Thomas. People call me Cat. My initials, you know. I – er – I used to live here. In this house."

"Oh, yes?" said the man, opening the door a little wider and revealing a hallway with a staircase leading up to the upstairs landing.

"Er. Yes. I was – I was wondering if … You're going to think this is weird."

The man raised his eyebrows a fraction higher. "Oh yes? Try me." He leaned a shoulder against the jamb of the door. Cat noticed that his v-necked sweater and slacks matched exactly the fawn fitted carpet which ran along the hall and up the stairs.

"You've changed the carpet," Cat observed. "And the walls used to be a brighter white – not so beige."

The man gave a laugh. "Is that what you've come round for? To assess our decorating? That is a bit weird, I grant you." The eyebrows made an impatient, twitchy movement.

"No. Sorry. That's not the reason. Obviously." Cat spoke apologetically, and pushed his hands deep into his jeans pockets in confusion. "You see, I used to have this thing about hiding things when I was younger. Things I was scared of. Like this." He pulled a little plastic figure from his pocket and held it up for the man to look at.

"A spaceman toy?" The man's eyebrows did a little jump as he spoke. "What was so scary about it?" he asked with an amused lilt in his voice.

"I don't know really," Cat answered. "I was very little, and I buried it in Cyprus. But I dug it up last year, by accident, and it didn't seem scary any more. Then I came back to England."

The man's eyebrows did their impatient twitch again. "I see," he said. "So, how can I help you, Cat? That was your name, yes?" The eyebrows rose again.

"Yes. You see. The thing is. There was a loose floorboard at the top of the stairs. When we lived here. Does it still creak when you reach the top of the stairs?

The man said "Ha" in a tone which told of annoyance and inconvenience. "I had quite a bit of trouble with the floors upstairs," he said. "We had to replace quite a few of the boards before we could lay the new carpets."

"Did you find anything?" asked Cat. "You know, under the floor, when you took up the old boards?" As though to prompt the man's memory, Cat waved the plastic spaceman briefly in front of him.

"As a matter of fact," said the man, turning his head to the interior of the house. "Jackie," he called, raising his voice. "Jackie. Come here a minute, will you, sweetheart?"

He turned his face back towards Cat. "Jackie's my wife," he said, as they waited for Jackie to appear.

"What is it, Simon?" called an impatient female voice. "I'm watching *Countdown*. Who's at the door?"

"Someone who says he lived here before we moved in. He wants to ask us something."

The voice said something which could have been 'oh for goodness sake', and a dark blue woman came into the hall. She stood at her husband's shoulder, peering out of the doorway at Cat, still holding up the spaceman figure for scrutiny.

"Yes?" said Jackie. Her voice did not require the assistance of twitching eyebrows to communicate impatience.

"Er. Hello. I used to live here," said Cat.

"Simon said. What do you want?"

Her husband interrupted before Cat could speak. "Do you remember when we laid the new carpets, Jackie? There were some things under the floor? What happened to them?"

"Things? Oh yes," said Jackie, making a scrunchy, thinking expression and fingering the string of pearls she wore over her navy polo-neck. "There was a collection of junk under one of the floorboards at the top of the stairs. Little toys and stuff."

Cat waved his spaceman as a visual prompt.

"Do you remember what you did with it all?"

"Did with it?" asked Jackie. "We chucked it, of course."

Cat's face fell and he pushed his hands back into his jeans pockets in a gesture of disappointment. "Oh."

From the front room, the television played a jaunty sequence of descending electronic notes. Jackie glanced over her shoulder in irritation.

"Except there was a nice book. I think you kept that, Simon?"

"Did I? If I did, it'll be on one of the shelves."

"There was a book," Cat said enthusiastically. "A green book. *The Tombs of Atuan*. By Ursula Le Guin. A hardback. If you've still got it, I wonder if I could have it back?"

Jackie looked dubiously at her husband, and then at Cat.

"Well, I don't know," said Simon, his eyebrows performing a short routine expressing thoughtfulness. "I suppose it does belong to you. I'll see if I can find it." He went down the hall and into one of the rooms. Jackie fingered her pearls. There was an awkward silence, broken by a child's voice from somewhere inside the house.

"Mum-mee! When's tea ready?"

"So. You used to live here," Jackie said, after a moment, and ignoring the calling voice.

"Yes."

"Hmm."

There was another silence. Jackie glanced over her shoulder to see if Simon was on his way back.

"And you used to hide things under the floor?"

"Yes. When I was little."

"Hmm. Why?"

"Found it," announced Simon, coming back down the hall and holding out in front of him a hardbacked volume with a line drawn illustration in dark and light green on the cover. "*The Tombs of Atuan*," he read. "It's a nice looking book." He rejoined his wife and held the book out to Cat. "I thought maybe the girls might like to read it when they're older, but since you've come back …"

"It's the second book in the Earthsea trilogy," said Cat. "They'd have to read the first one first." He was about to say more about the three books and the tales of the wandering mage, Sparrowhawk whose true name was Ged, but Jackie interrupted.

"Why did you put the book under the floor anyway?" she asked. Simon also seemed to be interested since his eyebrows rose expectantly.

"There were bits in it," said Cat, looking down at the book in his hands, turning it over to the back cover where there was an illustration of a broken amulet on a loop of chain, white against a deep blue background. "Bits that I was afraid to read."

"Is it a horror story, then? I'm glad you didn't give it to the girls," said Jackie to her husband.

"No, it's not horror," said Cat. "But it made me afraid." He flicked through the pages, turning and turning until he came to a place close to the end. "Look," he said, handing the open book back to Simon, and pointing out a passage, Simon and Jackie bowed their heads over the page to read.

"It doesn't sound very scary," said Simon after a while. He closed the book and returned it to Cat.

"It's not," said Cat. "That's the point. Like the spaceman." He patted the pocket of his jeans. "Thank you for giving it back to me."

"You're – you're welcome," said Jackie haltingly. "Well, Simon and I have got to give the girls their tea, so …" She did some more pearl-fiddling, then reached for the door, pushing it closed a little way.

"Right," said Cat. "I'd better go. Thank you again. Thanks." He turned from the door, which Jackie continued to push further closed.

"Goodbye," said Cat over his shoulder.

"Goodbye," echoed Simon and Jackie in unison.

"Weird," said Simon's voice, just before the door clicked shut.

Cat continued down the path, pausing at steps three, five and seven, before he reached the gate. He made his way through the village, which at this time of day was unusually busy, a line of cars waiting at a crossroads for the lights to change and a number of hurrying pedestrians making their way home. The faces behind the windscreens stared straight ahead, expressionless, as Cat passed. He thought of the words in the book, words which had seemed so frightening to a small boy.

"Just words," he said aloud. "Just words in a made-up story."

He hurried on, indistinguishable from the other pedestrians, and after a while turned off the main road onto a long, straight avenue of pebble-dashed bungalows, leading down to a cul-de-sac of larger, two-storey properties. At the end of the road lived the old lady in whose garden he had been living for the past few weeks since he had come back to the village.

Under a streetlamp in front of one of the last houses on the road, a rather run-down semi-detached suburban villa with Art Deco stained glass in the front door, a dark, helmeted figure was sitting astride a large, powerful motorbike. Its paintwork gleamed blackly, highlighted with gold from the sodium light overhead. The dark figure swung itself out of the bike's saddle and removed its helmet, revealing short, spiked hair and a grimly pretty, girlish face.

"Hi, Harry," said Cat. "What are you doing here?"

"Waiting for you, dickhead. What do you think?" said the girl called Harry. "I thought I'd come and see how you got on. Did they tell you to fuck off?" She hung her helmet by its strap from one of the bike's handlebars and left it swinging gently. Cat put out a hand to arrest its movement.

"No," he said. "They were ... They'd kept the book, but they'd thrown away the rest of the stuff. Look." He held up his copy of *The Tombs of Atuan*.

"And they didn't think it was completely fucking weird?"

"Not at all," said Cat. "Well. Maybe a bit." He smiled an embarrassed smile. "Well. Maybe a lot."

Harry gave a laugh. "I fucking told you."

"But I've got the book, and I've read the words. Listen." He opened the book at the page that he had shown to Simon and Jackie on the front step of their house, which had once been his house, and began to read aloud. "'I've used up most of my strength. No one can withstand the Dark Ones long alone'."

"And that's what you were scared of? Fucking hell." Harry laughed again, somehow managing to sound sympathetic rather than derisive.

"I know," said Cat. "It seems stupid now. I think it's impossible to understand something like that from the outside. Unless you're in it, living it, you don't get it. Even I can't really understand it now. But your mind can convince itself of anything. And find meanings where there are none."

"I like you Cat," said Harry, smiling a rare smile which disclosed a row of neat, small teeth. "You're so fucking deep. Let's have a look at the book, then." She held out a gloved arm for Cat to hand over the volume. "Yep," she said, turning it over and scrutinising the cover, both back and front. "It's just a fucking book." She gave it back to him. "Now, what do you want to do?"

"What do you mean?" asked Cat.

"It's simple enough," said Harry. "What do you want to do? We can go for a pint at the Station, if you like."

"I've never been to a pub just for a drink." Cat hesitated, doing a brief stepping on and off the kerb routine. "If we go, I'd better just check that Joan is OK. You know. See if she's had something to eat. It's what I usually do, you know."

"Yeah. I know. You're a nice bloke, Cat. Weird as fuck, but nice." In a swift movement, Harry lifted her face and placed a fleeting kiss on Cat's cheek with dry lips. Then she snatched her helmet from the handlebars of the Yamaha and thrust it onto her head. "Come on," she said, her voice muffled by the visor. "I'll take you on the back of the bike."

"But I haven't got a helmet," protested Cat.

Harry swung a leg over the saddle and kicked the machine into life. It made an impatient roar as she flexed her wrist on the throttle.

"What about Joan?" asked Cat over the noise of the engine, which suddenly died. Harry sat back in the saddle, and made a pantomime of looking at her wrist.

"You've got three minutes," she said. "Then I'm off and you'll have to walk."

"But I haven't got a helmet."

"Don't be a twat. It's not far."

"But ..."

"Three minutes. Starting now."

Flustered by the memory of Harry's kiss against his cheek and the prospect of riding on the back of her motorbike without a helmet, Cat hurried round the side of the house into the evening shadows. Very soon, he reappeared, out of breath, no longer carrying *The Tombs of Atuan*.

"She OK?" asked Harry, laconically.

"She's fine," Cat started to say. "She'd managed to make herself ..." But the noise of the motorbike starting up again drowned out his words, as Harry stamped down on the kick-starter, and, unable to think because of the engine's voice and the sound of his own blood pulsing in his veins, Cat threw a leg over the bike's long saddle.

"Put your arms round me," Harry commanded.

No sooner had Cat felt a slim waist through the hard leather of the jacket and had placed his palms flat against her taut abdomen, than Harry gunned the engine, released the clutch, and the Yamaha accelerated with shocking speed to the top of the road. Almost immediately, they were on the main street, rounding a sharp bend, and passing between rows of parked cars which flashed by along one of the narrower village streets. Then, the bike slowed, and Harry allowed it to roll gently to a halt on the forecourt of a large, white-painted building. A sign above the entrance depicted a steam train puffing clouds of pale grey smoke into an unreally blue sky. Gold lettering announced The Station Inn.

Unsteadily, Cat dismounted, and sat down suddenly at one of the picnic tables which stood in front of the pub. The ride had seemed to take no time at all, and had simultaneously gone on for long ages. He held his hands out shakily in front of his face.

"My legs are all wobbly," he said in a squeaking voice, as Harry deposited her helmet on the bench opposite him. Light from wall-mounted lamps spilled over the tables, which were all vacant. A beery, smokey smell reached them from the open front door, accompanied by the subdued hum of voices and an undertone of unidentifiable music.

"I'll get the drinks," said Harry, ignoring him. "If you're not cold, we'll sit out here. They're wankers in this pub, so I prefer to stay outside. Even if it's a bit chilly." She disappeared through the pub's entrance.

Gradually, Cat's pulse returned to normal as he sat on the hard bench. He felt confused and exhilarated, and could not make his thoughts travel in a straight line. He kept thinking of a rushing cold wind and the sensation of paper-soft lips pressing against his cheek.

"Fucking wankers," said Harry, emerging from the pub, carrying a tray with three glasses arranged on it, two pints of chestnut-coloured beer, topped with a thick white collar of foam, and a smaller glass of colourless, fizzy liquid. "I got you a pint of bitter, but if you don't like it, there's a lemonade as well. And I'll drink yours." She set the tray down on the table, and slid onto the bench opposite Cat.

"If they're wankers, why do you come here?" asked Cat, lifting the pint glass to his mouth and taking a tentative sip.

"The beer's drinkable. Not like the piss they serve at the Ferry down the road. But you have to put up with dickhead comments about lovely ladies and shite. That's why I prefer cans at home." Harry lifted the glass to her mouth and took an experimental draught. "If you prefer the lemonade, it's OK," she said.

"No," said Cat, wiping his mouth on the sleeve of his khaki jacket. "I don't mind it. It's not as bad as I remember." He took another mouthful.

"Have your legs stopped wobbling?" Harry asked, and he smiled at her, nodding.

There was a silence, while they drank some more of their beer.

"You were going to tell me what Joan had managed to make for herself," said Harry.

*   *   *

The couple next door, having inherited the house from the young woman's Auntie Rose, were often concerned, when they thought about the future – a growing family, moving back to the town, maybe one day emigrating even – that the state of the adjoining semi might adversely affect the value of their own property. Auntie Rose's generosity in remembering her great-niece had been a great windfall, of course, and had meant that they could use their money for other things than buying somewhere to live – renovating the old 1930s house, IVF treatments, and then after sometime, joyfully, decorating the big back bedroom as a nursery and getting a bigger car. But the house next door with its overgrown garden and dilapidated appearance remained a concern. And, frankly, the old lady who lived there was a worry. Not a problem, exactly – in fact you would hardly know she was there most of the time, but she sometimes said strange things if you were out with the pram in the street. And recently there'd been some funny goings-on in her garden. From the nursery window, looking out over the high privet hedge into her garden, you could see that someone had put up a little orange tent and was living in it. And whoever it was, together with a friend, had been messing about with an old motorbike at the weekends, taking it to bits on a square of tarpaulin on the lawn. Admittedly, the garden had also been tidied up a bit, with a selection of antique garden tools which now leaned along the wall outside the back door like an off-duty platoon of stick-thin, elderly soldiers. And the hedge had been cut, and some of the trees had been pruned, but it was a worry living next door to such a funny old woman. If you put a glass to the wall, you could often hear her talking away to herself. It certainly wasn't the television. Neil and Judy, the young couple, didn't think the old lady even had a telly, although there was one of those very old-fashioned H-shaped aerials on the roof, like they used to have in the nineteen-sixties.

As Neil, having finished putting the baby to bed, was taking the glass from his wife and was pressing it gently to the magnolia wall which their dining room shared with next door, Joan Fettes, who had once been Joan Kershaw, was sitting in a chair next to the coal fire in her dining room with a tray resting on her knees. An empty bowl with the orangey-red remains of a tin of tomato soup smearing its inside, stood on the tray next to a side-plate dotted with the black and brown crumbs from a slice of toasted bread.

"Well," said Joan, conversationally, placing her soup spoon in the bowl with a tinkle of metal on porcelain, "if that was my dinner, I've had it."

With some difficulty, because her joints were not as supple as they had once been, she shuffled herself forward to the edge of her chair and levered herself upright. The tray and its contents made a worrying rattle, and the bowl slid perilously towards the edge as Joan performed this manoeuvre.

"I'll leave these on the thingummy, and take them out when I make my tea," she announced, moving with cautious steps across the room and depositing her burden beside a cut-glass bowl and a black-and-white photograph taken in the nineteen-twenties when she had been no more than a girl, dressed in her bridal white, standing next to her young husband.

"We were a handsome couple, weren't we?" Joan commented, speaking to the empty room, although, for her, a black and white Border Collie was sitting on the hearth rug by the fire. "Of course," she went on, "we knew how to dress in those days. You wouldn't have caught Bob going about in the scruffy things they wear nowadays. That young man who was here before – he always looks like he's just come in from the fields." She assumed a listening expression, since the Border Collie was saying something to her, and she nodded in agreement. "It *is* nice of him," she said, tapping at the glass in the picture frame with a forefinger. "Him and her." She tapped again, as to attract the attention of the two figures behind the glass. Turning away from the little window into the past, she focused her gaze on the black and white dog by the fire. He was her old Border Collie, Harry, but there was something odd about him. It looked like he was *flickering,* as though a wind was blowing across her vision, one of those bitter, strong winds which came in off the wide, flat mirror near the path. Joan sat herself down in her chair. She didn't mean mirror, she thought. It was something else. But the strong, flickering wind seemed to have blown that word away.

"I don't know, Harry," Joan said, raising her voice to stop the dog flickering. "I don't know where they've all gone." She found herself thinking about a long list of words she had made and put somewhere, a list of things she had to remember. Like a shopping list or a list of tasks which had to be done.

"There was that Sandra," she told her dog. "It seems like only yesterday since she was here." More names began to float into her mind, bobbing like buoys on water, accompanied by faces and clothes. "There were so many," Joan said, but the dog, whose name was Harry, after the Harrison shipping line, was not listening. He sat on the rug in the firelight, flickering. "I said there were so many," Joan repeated more loudly. "So many people, like them in the little window over there." She pointed towards the picture frame with the diminutive bride and groom. "That was me and that was him. I was Joan." She smiled at Harry the dog, who was finally paying attention to what she was saying.

"You're a good boy," she said fondly. "We'll mend the fire, and sit for a while. Then we'll see about making something for our dinner."

Joan busied herself with heaping hunks of coal from the scuttle into the grate. A dusty, fiery smell rose up as the iron of the shovel clanked and scraped. A flurry of sparks shot up from the black pile and disappeared into the chimney, like golden stars into the depths of space.

"There," said Joan, sitting back in her chair, folding her hands contentedly in her lap. After the noise of the fire irons, the room was very quiet, apart from the whispery crackle of the coals burning in the hearth. Neither Judy nor Neil, on the other side of the party wall, paid heed to the silence that had fallen in the dining room of the house next door. Some time ago they had put down their glass and had gone to sit in front of their television to eat their dinner.

"Mad old bat," Neil had said, and Judy had laughed.

*   *   *

"The weird thing is," said Cat, swirling his glass so that the creamy white lacing was washed into the beer's dark amber body, "the weird thing is that sometimes she seems with it. You know understanding things and managing everything. Like tonight. She'd heated a tin of soup, and made some toast, and had it all ready for herself on a tray. Then another time, she'll be going on about her dog and talking nonsense, though it seems to make sense to her."

Across the picnic table in the orange light of the pub's outdoor lamps, in the cold evening air, the girl compressed her lips into a sympathetic smile, scrunching up her nose and making two v-shapes appear across its bridge. "Yeah," she agreed. "It is weird." They both raised their glasses to their lips, but Harry returned hers to the table-top without drinking. Her strong, small fingers encircled the glass, tilting it back and forth in a contemplative, repetitive motion.

"I know I asked you this before," she said, "and I'm not being funny. Just interested." She relinquished her hold on the glass and settled her chin onto the heels of her palms, her elbows resting on the table with the pint between them. "What is it with all the weird shit you do? You know. Living in a tent. Counting. Stepping to and fro. Honest, I'm just interested. I'm interested in who you are, Cat."

The young man opposite her lowered his glass to the table, tapping its bottom in three broken movements against the wood. It made an almost inaudible tip-tip-tip sound. Above and around his head, he could feel the beginnings of a terrible pressure, like a storm brewing in the atmosphere. Across the table, Harry's eyes, darkened by the shadows cast by the lamps, were fixed on his face. She gave him her straight-mouthed smile and her eyes crinkled at the corners.

"I don't know what I can tell you," Cat said in a low voice. If there had been drinkers at the other tables they would not have been able to make out the words. Harry leaned in a little closer. "I do stuff which other people think is weird. And I know it looks weird. It is weird. But there's this voice, my voice, telling me to do it. Except there aren't any words – well, there are, kind of – but not so as you could write them down or repeat them. It's more a feeling – like a compulsion. That I've got to do certain things – counting prime numbers is one. Tapping and stepping's another, especially going through doors. And checking things – checking doors are closed, that kind of thing. It can get very tiring."

Without lifting her chin from her hands, Harry nodded. She had not moved her eyes from his face all the time he had been speaking.

"You see, if I don't do these things, I feel that something bad will happen. To me. To other people," Cat continued.

"Like what?"

"Oh, tons of things. An endless list. A car might drive off the road and knock down someone with a pram. Someone might get pulled into the river and drown in the mud. There might be a war. Or you might just miss your train or your bus. I know it's not real, but it is real to me."

Harry gazed at him, unspeaking.

"It's who I am. I've always been like this, I think."

"And living in the tent?"

"Like I said, doorways are difficult. The tent only has a flap."

Harry gave a snort of laughter.

"What?" Cat asked, with the thought that she was laughing at him.

"It just sounds funny. Flap. It's a funny word."

"Is it? I suppose it is. But all words are funny when you think about them. Flap, flap, flap. Door, door, door. Door. They kind of lose their meaning when you say them over and over."

Cat lifted his glass to his mouth again, taking a gulp of his beer. Harry sipped at the layer of froth near the top of her glass.

"You're not drinking your beer," observed Cat. "You normally knock back your cans. Don't you like this beer?"

"I'm driving," said Harry, tapping her helmet with the palm of her hand.

"It doesn't usually stop you."

"I don't usually have you on the back of the bike. I kind of feel responsible." She pushed her pint away from her and reached for the glass of lemonade, which had been standing disregarded on the tray, like a forgotten guest at a party. Her eyes fixed again on Cat's face.

"You think about things a lot, don't you?" she said. "Maybe too much. You shouldn't think so much."

Cat contemplated his hands which were flat on the table in front of him. He made no comment, but drummed his fingers gently on the wood. Harry reached across and placed her own hands on top of his, quelling the movement.

"And what about what happened to your parents?" she asked softly.

"Hello, lovebirds," interrupted a boisterous voice from behind Cat's shoulder. One of the barstaff, a tattooed young man in a black polo shirt with *The Station*, embroidered on its breast pocket, had just come out of the pub's entrance, lighting a cigarette and making a show of looking for empty glasses to collect.

"Fuck off, dickshit," said Harry, drawing her hands away.

"You must have the foulest mouth in East Yorkshire, Harriet," said the barman, emphasising the three syllables of the name with relish. "And that's against some fucking tough competition. It must be like kissing a – kissing a dustbin, kissing you." He took a deep drag on his cigarette and exhaled a satisfied cloud of bluish smoke into the evening air.

"Don't worry, Tommo," Harry replied, not looking at his hovering figure. "I'd make sure I'd drunk a pint of bleach if I was going to have to kiss you. Oh, but then I'd be fucking dead, wouldn't I?" She reached for her helmet, as Tommo cast around for a suitably stinging comeback. "Are you ready to go?" she asked Cat.

Harry stood up, leaving her beer, still over half-full, and the lemonade barely touched. Cat pushed his own beer away, and stood as well, shuffling sideways to extricate himself from the picnic table and its bench. He felt disappointed and relieved at the same time, half glad to have been saved from Harry's probing, and half dismayed, like a dental patient finding their appointment has been cancelled.

"Are you not finishing your drinks, then?" Tommo asked. Receiving no reply, he placed his cigarette between his lips and arranged the half-full glasses on the tray. Neither Harry nor Cat heard the impotent insult he muttered under his breath as they walked towards the Yamaha.

"Do you want to drive back?" Harry asked, offering Cat her helmet, when they reached the bike.

"I don't know how to," Cat replied. "I've never driven a motor-bike. Or a car for that matter."

"I'd better teach you, if you're going to ride the Ariel." She swung herself into the saddle. "I'll show you where everything is, and then I'll explain what I'm doing as we ride back."

"But..." Cat began, protesting.

"You start the engine like this," said Harry, turning the ignition key and stamping down on the kickstarter. The Yamaha gave its customary, enthusiastic roar.

"This is the throttle – the clutch – brake – and you change gear with your foot – one down and four up." Harry's ankle in its boot flexed as she demonstrated the gear pedal.

"What about reverse?" Cat asked.

Harry laughed. "Not on a motorbike, dickhead. We only go forwards."

*   *   *

Judy had, as usual, fallen asleep in front of the television with her head in Neil's lap, trapping him. He sat at his end of the settee, absently stroking her hair and watching some characters he did not care about, yelling at each other in Southern accents. Judy's hair was soft under his fingers, and he twiddled with it, while one of the actors on the screen shouted in a voice which elongated all his vowels and strangled his tees. Neil found himself thinking of a boy he had known in his first year at college and how things would have been so different, as his eyes began to close.

In the house next door, a few feet from the drowsing young couple, their neighbour, Joan Fettes, had also been dozing in her chair. Or perhaps she had not been asleep. Sometimes it seemed as though there were gaps in time, and she could not remember what she had been doing. She must have had her dinner, because the tray with things on it was sitting on the long box-like thing at the side of the room. There were words for all those things, but somehow they were missing. Joan looked down at her hands resting in her lap, and wondered at how misshapen and discoloured they had become. She searched her memory for the name of the white stuff she had used to massage into her skin. It had come in a round, blue tin with its name on the lid. Blue with white letters, but what the letters said she could not recall. It was as though they had been erased from her mind's picture of the tin.

From the fireplace, there came a sudden, muffled crash as some of the coal collapsed in the grate. Joan must have mended the fire, she thought, as the flames roused themselves and a shower of sparks flew up. Then there was smoke curling upwards, and in the swirls, with the sparks, there were faces. Joan recognised some of the faces. There was her brother, Henry, when he was a little boy sitting opposite her in a boat on a lake; and there was a man on the pier at Bridlington, smiling and taking a penny from her. Then, in the smoke, her mother and father's faces rose up, and her friend, Muriel, showing her some flimsy material, itself smoke-like. And two young men, no more than boys, wearing some kind of uniform with caps, like sailors'. And all of them were smiling.

Another flurry of sparks shot upwards and disappeared into the chimney, like golden snuff snorted into a filthy nostril.

"What a horrid idea," said Joan.

*   *   *

The big motorbike, carrying its rider and an unhelmeted passenger on the back, travelled with unexpected sedateness down the length of the street, its exhaust bubbling quietly, passing the silent bungalows with their softly lit, curtained windows. It came to rest beneath a streetlamp in front of one of the larger, semi-detached houses in the cul-de-sac at the end of the road. Its helmeted rider gunned the engine once noisily before killing it with the turn of the ignition key. A few seconds later, a curtain twitched in the house next door, and the pale face of a man, like an angry ghost behind the glass, looked out momentarily and then disappeared behind the material. The helmetless passenger released his hold on the waist of the figure before him, and swung his leg over the saddle. The rider sat back, straddling the bike and removing her helmet. She set it between her thighs and rested her leather-jacketed forearms on its crown.

"Well?" asked Harry.

"I'll never remember it all," said Cat. "I'd have to practise."

"Of course. I'll take you out for a run at the weekend. Then you can ask Joan if you can take the Red Hunter out, when it's finished. She won't say no. I doubt she'll know what you're asking her. And anyway, she owes you for all the work you've done in her garden."

"I'm not sure about that, Harry. I think I owe her for letting me stay in her garden." Absently, Cat laid a hand on the Yamaha's handlebar, caressing the smooth metal of the polished grip with which Harry had customised her bike's steering. "I mean," he went on, "I've had somewhere safe to pitch the tent and keep all my stuff."

"All your stuff? What've you got in that tent? You can't have much in there. It's not the fucking Tardis."

Cat smiled at the sudden thought of himself as a Time Lord like Doctor Who.

"It's true. There's not much, but it's important to me. In fact, apart from clothes and things, all I've really got is the tent and the Yamaha."

Harry's face became a mask of confused incomprehension.

"My guitar. You're not the only one to own a Yamaha. It's the one thing I wanted to keep when I went away." He tap-tapped along the metal of the handlebar until Harry's gloved hand stilled the movement and held his fingers against the smoothness.

"Maybe one day you'll play me something?" she suggested. "And tell me why you went away." She squeezed his fingers briefly. "If you want to."

"I've never really played for other people," said Cat, hesistatingly. "It's always been a kind of private thing. But sure."

"I'll tell you what," said Harry. "I'll bring some cans round one night and we can have a bit of a party in your tent. Just you and me." She withdrew her hand and lifted her helmet ready to return it to her head. "I'd better go. I've got a busy fucking morning tomorrow. I'm glad you got your book back. At least you've got two possessions now."

"Three," Cat corrected her. "I've got my spaceman too." He pulled the little plastic figure from his jeans pocket and held it up for Harry to see.

"You are a fucking nutter," said Harry fondly, lowering the helmet over her head and kicking the Yamaha into life once again. "Bye," she said, her voice muffled by the visor. With sudden aggression, she swung the bike round and roared away, hunched tautly over the body of the machine. Momentarily shocked, Cat stepped backwards, and a sequence of palindromic prime numbers ran through his head.

"See you," he said aloud, unaware of an angrily twitched curtain in the window of the house behind him.

When he had fumbled his way back to his tent through the darkness of the garden, taking care not to send the garden tools, which stood against the back wall, crashing as he stepped cautiously past; and had crawled through the flap, smiling to himself as he thought of the sound of the word, Cat removed his trainers and the khaki jacket. He wasn't hungry, but he did feel tired, so he slid, still dressed, into the cocoon-like sleeping bag. He lay in the dark, with the taste of beer in his mouth and the memory of the touch of Harry's lips on his cheek and the pressure of her hands on his. He played some chord sequences in his head, imagining cadences and progressions, thinking of what Harry might like to hear. Feeling peaceful, he fell asleep.

Cat did not usually dream, or at least his mind did not usually allow him to remember what he had dreamed. But he had had *this* dream before, or part of it. And when he opened his eyes, he thought that he must still be in his dream. He was back in the mountain village in Cyprus, and his grandmother, his *yiayia*, had been offering him something to eat, holding out a plate to him. And Joan was there, too, standing next to her, holding out an empty bowl, smeared with the remnants of a tin of soup. Then they had stepped aside, saying *Look* and *Koita* simultaneously, and he had seen a car, parked beneath the citrus trees in the garden, its windscreen shattered and two figures in the front seats slumped, their faces streaked with red. From one of the back windows a face stared out directly into Cat's eyes, smiling with a straight-lipped smile. Then a hand was raised in front of the face, and a pink tongue, like a cat's, flicked out to lick skinned knuckles. And somewhere on the hillside his grandfather must have been burning almond branches, for he could smell the smoke, and from somewhere he heard his *pappou* saying "*Kotshinos fothkia!*" and laughing.

So, when Cat opened his eyes in the dark of the tent, and smelled the tobacco-ey tang of burning, he thought that he was still dreaming, one of those weird dreams when you awoke, only to find you were still in the dream. He gave a cough, and realised that he must really be awake and that something was on fire. He squirmed out of his cocoon and crawled to the flap of the tent.

"Fuck," said Cat, who did not usually swear.

Behind the glass of the French windows of Joan's dining room, flames were licking up the fabric of the curtains, flickering and sending dancing shapes into the shadows of the garden. Smoke had begun to seep out from the gap at the bottom and from where the two doors met in the middle. Cat grabbed his trainers and stuffed his feet clumsily into them, not bothering with laces; then, he scrambled out and ran across the grass to the back door.

"Joan," he shouted through the glass in the little window in the wood panel, as he rattled the handle, trying to push the locked door open . "Fuck," he said again, and tried to drive his elbow through the glass. A pain, both sharp and dead at the same time, shot up into his shoulder, but the glass remained intact.

"Think," he muttered to himself. "Think, think, think."

Without seeming to think at all, he suddenly snatched up one of the garden implements leaning against the back wall, a garden spade with a solid wooden shaft and a handle like a polished isosceles triangle. Holding the spade by the shaft, Cat thrust the handle through the window in the door, splintering the glass and knocking the remaining shards through with repeated stabs. He reached an arm inside, feeling around for the key in the lock. There was no key; Joan must have taken it with her when she had locked the door.

"Fuck," said Cat, picking up his spade again and running around the side of the house to the front door. He repeated the glass-shattering process, destroying the gold and pink Art Deco roses in the stained glass, which creased inwards, held together by the leading. The ugly noise of breaking glass under the repeated thrusts of the spade handle sounded loud in his ears. He reached through the gaping hole he had created and unlatched the Yale, pushing the door open into the hallway. Smoke was roiling along the length of the ceiling like a grey-brown storm cloud in a time-lapse film, although there were no flames to be seen.

"What's going on?" said a voice from the next door front garden. A man in his late twenties was standing on the front porch, dressed in a baggy sweatshirt and a pair of tracksuit bottoms. The letters UCL were emblazoned boldly across his chest in block capitals. Cat recognised his pale features as the ghost from behind the glass of the front room window.

"Joan's house is on fire," said Cat, and the man said, "Fuck."

"I'll call the Fire Brigade," he went on, after a moment's hesitation, and disappeared into the house.

Cat ran across the threshold into Joan's hall and down to the dining room. The door stood ajar and the room seemed full of flames and smoke. Cat covered his mouth and nose with his hand.

"Joan!" he shouted indistinctly, stepping into the room, but immediately he had to jump back as he felt the heat on his face. Briefly, he had glimpsed Joan's chair by the fire. It had been empty, but engulfed by smoke and flame.

"Joan!" he called again. "Where are you?" Coughing and gasping between his fingers, he darted into the kitchen, where the lists and labels decorated walls and appliances. The kippery smell of smoke was strong in the air and the noise of the flames was growing louder, crackling and roaring as the fire ate through the dining room. The kitchen, too, was empty. Cat retreated down the hall and pushed open the door of the front room. The smoke had not penetrated here yet, although its stench was strong in the air. Cat took a gasp of air deep into his lungs.

"Joan?" he said as he entered and surveyed the empty space, its seldom used furniture shadowy in the gloom.

"Hello?" said a choking, weak voice from behind him in the hall.

Cat swung round. Peering down at him from between the banisters, halfway up the stairs, was the face of a frightened old woman. She gave a wheezing cough and gasped desperately to catch her breath.

"Joan," called Cat, stepping back into the hallway. The choking smoke above was coiling thickly through the banisters of the staircase, snaking onto the upper floor. "Stay there," he said, coughing as the fumes seized his throat. He pulled his tee-shirt and sweater up over his mouth and nose, but it was still impossible to breathe. He clamped his throat shut, and raced to the staircase. Joan was huddled half-way up the stairs, her legs in their thick, old-lady stockings protruding immodestly from her rucked up dress. Feeling light-headed and with his lungs beginning to ache, Cat leapt up the stairs and tried to slide his arms under her body. She was clutching something tightly to her, which made it difficult to get an arm to drape around his neck so that he could begin to lift her. As the smoke began to roil around them, he pulled roughly at her arms and a picture frame tumbled past him and down the stairs.

"Oh," gasped Joan. "They're gone. Save them." Then she was seized by a fit of breathless coughing.

Cat's chest felt as though it would collapse inwards as he heaved the old lady's body up and stumbled backwards down the stairs. There was a crunching, splintering sensation under his foot as one of his trainers smashed the glass of the picture frame which Joan had dropped. He felt his eyes stinging unbearably.

Then, he was outside in the open, sucking in huge gouts of cold, clean air, and coughing. Someone was in front of him, taking the weight from his arms, and he heard a man's voice telling him that a fire engine was on its way. He bent forwards with his hands on his knees, coughing and gulping and coughing again. After the coughing subsided, he looked up and saw through stinging eyes, the ghostly UCL man from next door, holding Joan in his arms like an ancient bride about to be carried across the threshold. She was staring with strange eyes at the house's open front door from which smoke was curling.

"I left them in there," she said in a weakly rasping voice. "The little people in the window. They were looking through the little window."

"It's alright, Mrs Fettes," said the UCL man. "The firemen are coming."

"But Bob and Joan will burn," sobbed Joan, raspily. "They were in the window."

"Is there someone still in there?" asked UCL.

"It's her picture she means," said Cat, coughing again. Then he turned to go back to the house.

"You can't go back in there, you fool," said UCL, but Cat was already at the front door, burying his face in his sweater, and darting in towards the stairs where the shattered frame and its black and white photograph of the two young, antique people lay. Above the noise of the flames which were starting to lash from the dining room doorway, he heard a distant siren becoming louder. Picking up the frame, he ran across the threshold through the front garden and out onto the street, where the UCL man was squatting next to Joan whom he had placed in an ungainly sitting position at the foot of a streetlamp. A disoriented looking woman clutching a baby tight to her body was standing a few feet away, repeating a dull mantra under her breath.

"Neil, oh my god, Neil, oh my god," she said again and again.

Other figures were starting to emerge from the surrounding houses, drawn by the commotion and the wail of the great, box-like fire-engine which was pulling to a halt as helmeted firefighters leapt from it, the fluorescent strips on their uniforms glowing and flaring in the flashing blue emergency lights.

"That was a bloody stupid thing to do," said UCL Neil. "Was there anyone else in there?"

Cat shook his head, feeling something behind his eyes move with a sickly jolt, like a fatty egg-yolk, slipping in the bottom of a bowl. His stomach heaved and he tasted acrid vomit rise into his mouth.

"No," he said, wiping the wetness away with his sleeve. "It was her picture she meant. It's her and her husband, Bob, when they got married." He placed the broken frame on top of Joan's outstretched legs. The two images behind the shattered glass looked out, unsmiling and inscrutable. "Here you are, Joan," said Cat. "I saved your picture."

Joan's eyes flickered open and her fingers found the splintered glass.

"Careful not to cut yourself."

She squinnied at the black and white photograph before her.

"They're no more than children," she said. "And so small. They would have been so frightened. So many dreadful things. And so much time. Perhaps it was for the best." A bout of coughing took hold of her.

"What's she on about?" asked UCL Neil.

"It's alright, Joan," said Cat, ignoring him. "The ambulance is here."

More blue flashing lights were approaching, accompanied by a different wail which rose in tone as the white vehicle drew near. Joan tapped her fingers fondly on the faces of the two in the picture.

"This one and this one," she said. "They went up and disappeared into the blackness. Like they didn't weigh a thing." She coughed and gasped for air. "Take Harry out for a walk for me."

Then, capable, heavily uniformed bodies were all around them, and there was the sound of clanking machinery and gushing water.

THIRTEEN

Harry says it's OK, and the uncle of Mikey, one of the Eddie van Halens, who's a copper, said he'd make sure that blind eyes were turned, if necessary. In fact, according to Harry, I shouldn't even give it a second fucking thought. But that's Harry.

So now, I sit with the hard, cracked leather of the Red Hunter's saddle under me, sensing the weight of the iron and chrome and rubber as I balance the motorbike, waiting to kick it into life. Harry's rudimentary and off-hand approach to teaching, since we sneaked the bike out of the shed behind Joan's ruined house and drove it away, has given me enough confidence to go for my first solo ride on the long, straight country road outside Harry's dad's workshop, where the Ariel now lives. It's strange to grip the handlebars, which a young man named Bob had gripped when the bike was his, over half a century ago. And strange, too, to think that the memory and shared experiences of that young man and the young woman he had married are gone forever now that Joan is dead.

I kick the starter once, twice, and the Red Hunter's 350 cc engine coughs and shudders. The upswept exhaust pipe releases a belch of fumey soot, and settles into a deep-throated bubbling. I think of Joan's gasping breathing as the paramedics loaded her prone figure into the ambulance, fitting an oxygen mask over her ashen face, and talking of smoke inhalation in coolly urgent voices. I give the throttle an experimental twist and the engine makes an impatient grumbling snarl, much deeper and more visceral than the histrionic screams of Harry's Yamaha. She tells me that this is because of the OHV and the large bore, down-draught Amal carburettor, and slowly I'm starting to understand what she's talking about.

She also tells me that it's not what happens that matters so much as how you think about what happens. And you shouldn't think too much. And when Harry says something with that angry, straight-lipped look in her face, you don't feel like arguing with her. Thinking about things too much, and giving things too much meaning, has always been part of my problem.

Another twist of the throttle makes the needles in the pressure gauge and the speedometer, mounted on the scarlet fuel tank in front of me, twitch and tremble, as the engine races beneath me. I can feel its reined power in my flesh and bones and muscles, its need to move, and what's more, to move fast. And when I think about it, everything does move so quickly; everything goes by so fast, although it seems to take such a long time while it's happening. Joan's life and all the things that must have happened to her, and her husband, Bob's life, and the lives of all the people they knew and met – I think I know what she meant when she said they had disappeared into the blackness. In the end, people are as weightless as ghosts.

I engage the clutch, push my foot down once on the gears, and let the clutch out. The Ariel bounces forwards and the engine stalls, while my pulse races and I feel my heart thumping in my chest. I hear Harry's voice in my head: "Fucking idiot. Let it out gently." I get ready to start the bike again, and with a kick it roars awake, settling down again into an expectant thrumming.

Clutch in.

Gear.

Gently out.

And the Red Hunter rolls dutifully forwards. I travel ten yards and brake to a halt, engaging the clutch and balancing the bike between trembling legs. I feel an enormous sense of accomplishment, and power, and relief, the kind of feeling you get when you play a song through, or when you solve a puzzling problem. Or, really, when you get to the end of anything that feels as though it means something or is important. It's the feeling I had when I took Joan from her smoke-filled house: relief, as though something had been resolved, though Harry says some things can never be properly resolved. You just have to accept them for what they are. Give it a lick, and get on. And again, you don't argue with Harry and her angry opinions. *Kotshinos fothkia*, I tell her, and for some reason the sounds of the words make her laugh.

In the days since the fire at Joan's house, Harry has been telling me a lot of things, and laughing at a lot of things I tell her. Like, for instance, she tells me to change gear when the speedo's needle reaches a certain point, and I explain that it would be more comfortable for me if the dial had only prime numbers. "Dickhead," Harry said, as she laughed. "How would that work?" And, of course, she's right, but I've explained how some numbers feel more *safe* than others – palindromic numbers like this year's date, one nine nine one, and how it factorises to two palindromic primes, eleven and one hundred and eighty-one, which are also dihedral primes, the same up and down and back and forth. And sometimes Harry nods in understanding.

I engage the clutch once more, and go into first – one down on the foot pedal. Release the clutch, throttle, and the bike moves forwards. Clutch again, two up, and the speedometer begins to climb as I go up through the gears. Out of the corners of my eyes, I see the trees and hedges begin to flash past, and with them, newly remembered and understood images from my hesitating talks with Harry.

10 – a boy is walking towards a car, and sliding into the back seat behind his parents in the front.

20 – the boy is reaching forwards, pulling his father's arm and the car is veering, while voices shout.

30 – there is an impact and a dreadful rending of metal and glass.

40 – there is the realisation that he has caused a dreadful thing to happen.

50 – the trees and the hedges continue flashing by, and the numbers are only numbers on the speedo. The clean East Yorkshire air batters at my face.

I slow the Red Hunter, and bring it to a halt at the side of the road. Above the trees, the clouds are brightly grey, shrouding a weak December sun, and moving with almost imperceptible slowness across the sky. Soon it will be the end of the year, and Harry's right: some things cannot be resolved, even after years and years. They simply are. They can't be made to unhappen; but they can't be kept either, framed or shrouded, unchanging. I think of Mr Hellyer, Mr Pole, Tony from Music Workshop, my Cypriot grandparents and Uncle Pambos on their sun-scorched terraces, even Dr Angela and her pale rooms – we blow across each other's skies like seabirds fighting a winter's wind. Or pass through each other's lives like trains through night-time stations. We tell each other things, and all the thousands and thousands of words we speak disappear, weightless, into the blackness. But I know that I would rather have Harry's voice in my head telling me these things, than any other voice. And I know also, when I turn the Ariel around and head back to where I've pitched my tent and keep my things, in a space among the old engines and bike parts especially cleared on Harry's orders by Deez and his mates, that she will find plenty of opportunity to tell me I'm a dickhead or a fucking nutter. But that's Harry. And that's me.

And I know they say never go back, searching for things that are past, but there's something in my head telling me they're wrong.

Acknowledgements

For their assistance in researching and writing *The Quiet Voices*, I'd like to express my grateful thanks to the following people, who have been without exception kind, helpful, and encouraging:

Tony Trotman-Beasty of Music Workshop in Hull, which sadly is no longer trading, though Tony and his band are still gigging.

J.W. Houlton for building the website of the History of the Garden Village Area, which provided huge amounts of detail (http://www.houlton1.karoo.net/GardenVillage.htm).

Alison Suckling, Administrative Assistant for Member Services of Douglas Borough Council in the Isle of Man, for providing information about the boating pool in which Joan and Bob paddle like daft youngsters.

Michael Waller of Britannia Motorcycles in the USA for his detailed knowledge of the inner workings of the Ariel Red Hunter motorbike.

Dave Griffith-Jones, the vicar St Columba's Church in the Garden Village, Kingston-upon-Hull, for his help in explaining what might happen after a funeral service like that of Joan's brother, Henry. Apparently, given the close ties of the community around St Columba's, such a poorly attended funeral would be very unlikely.

The Hull Trinity House School for pictures of the uniform worn by Trinity House boys, like Bob and Arthur, in the past.

The staff of the Limassol Municipal University Library for allowing me to wander around and take pictures of their magnificent building.

Alicia Rouverol for suggesting substantial alterations to the book's structure and title.

Christodoulos Damianou for letting me help him collect almonds, prune trees with dangerous chain saws, and make enormous bonfires on the family land in Sanida, Cyprus.

My wife, Aegli, for listening to me read the drafts aloud, and correcting my Greek.

Glossary of Cypriot Greek

Cypriot/Greek	English
ela (έλα)	come
mana mou (μάνα μου)	Literally, my mother, but used as an endearment to anyone
Na se voithiso? (Να σε βοηθήσω;)	Shall I help you?
Then milai ellinika (Δεν μιλάει ελληνικά)	He doesn't speak Greek
Ma prepei na mathei (Μα πρέπει να μάθει)	But he has to learn
yiayia (γιαγιά)	grandma
pappou (παππού)	grandpa
kyria (κυρία)	lady, madam, Mrs
kyrios (κύριος)	gentleman, sir, Mr
Panayia mou! (Παναγία μου!)	Mother Mary!
efharistoume (ευχαριστούμε)	thank you, we thank you
re (ρε)	man, mate, you
'Po'tha, re goumbare! ('Πο 'δα, ρε κουμπάρε!)	Over here, mate!
Pos paei to moro mas? (Πώς πάει το μωρό μας;)	How's our lad doing then?
sto vouno (στο βουνό)	on the mountain
diplo-cambino (διπλοκάμπινο)	double-cabin pick-up truck
horio (χωριό)	village
droshia (δροσιά)	cool
siopi (σιωπή)	be quiet
ziziri (ζίζιροι)	cicadas
fae kati (φάε κάτι)	have something to eat
signomi (συγγνώμη)	I'm sorry
Etsi, bravo (Έτσι, μπράβο!)	That's the way, well done
proyevma (πρόγευμα)	breakfast

Kali sas imera (Καλή σας ημέρα)	Good morning to you
doro (δώρο)	gift, present
apotheki (αποθήκη)	storeroom, shed
Englezos (Εγγλέζος)	Englishman
stratiotis (στρατιώτης)	soldier
monos sou (μόνος σου)	by yourself
ΕΞΟΔΟΣ, exodos	Way Out
entaxi (εντάξει)	OK
vivliothiki (βιβλιοθήκη)	library
paedi mou (παιδί μου)	my child
meli tis vivliothikis (μέλοι της βιβλιοθήκης)	library members
den katalaveno (δεν καταλαβαίνω)	I don't understand
Kitaxe, oute ego den katalaveno ti thelo na sou po (Κοίταξε, ούτε εγώ δεν καταλαβαίνω τι θέλω να σου πω)	Look, even I don't understand what I want to say
Kali nichta (Καληνύχτα)	Good night
gataki mou (γατάκι μου)	my little cat
kouklos (κούκλος)	beautiful boy
papa (παπά)	father, dad
karrettes (καρρέττες)	dead husks of almonds
athasha' (αθασιά)	almond tree
atha'sha (αθάσια)	almond nuts
amygdala (αμύγδαλα)	almond nuts
dendra (δένδρα)	trees
svana (σβανά)	handsaw
tsappa (τσάππα)	digging tool, mattock
kopri (κόπρι)	dung, fertilizer
maskaraliki (μασκαραλίκι)	thingummajig, stupid thing
mavra dje kataxera (μαύρα τζαι κατάξερα)	black and dried out

kofkoume (κόφκουμε)	we cut
yia to mellon (για το μέλλον)	for the future
dje anthisoun (τζαι ανθίσουν)	and they flower
nero (νερό)	water
tora (τωρά)	now
leganes (λεκάνες)	reservoirs
aera (αέρα)	breeze, wind, air
eyinin kotshinos fothkia (εγίνην κότσινος φωθκιά)	*Literally,* he became red fire, *in the sense of* he is very angry
fatsa (φάτσα)	face

Printed in Great Britain
by Amazon